"The glove com
my other pistol in there!"

"What?" Mad Dog hollered as the safety glass continued to rain down on him.

"My pistol!"

Mad Dog's brain wasn't working, at least for a few seconds, then it kicked in like a lawn-mower engine after a few pulls on the cord. He fumbled in the dark, his hand finding the weapon.

Gunfire pinged and ricocheted off the car, and one of the tires suddenly blew out.

Yury reached under his seat, produced another gun, tugged open his door, then burst from the vehicle, screaming something at their assailants, unseen in the rising smoke of the collision.

"Kat, get down!"

"No shit," she groaned. "I already am. The colonel set us up!"

"Or Bibby!"

Two more rounds cut into the car, and Mad Dog wasn't sure if he'd been hit.

Another pair of shots thundered.

Yury let out a bloodcurdling cry.

And that was it.

Mad Dog became a being of pure action and reaction, a being of pure instinct, became a guy half his age wearing a United States Marine Corps uniform. He ran into the light. Literally. Squinted, turned, saw a man to his left, fired!

Then, a flinch later, he dropped to his knees, rolled as two rounds came in from somewhere above.

By P.W. Storm

The Mercenaries
Blood Diamonds
Thunderkill
Mad Dogs and Englishmen

Force 5 Recon
Deployment: Pakistan
Deployment: North Korea
Deployment: Philippines

THE
MERCENARIES

MAD DOGS AND ENGLISHMEN

P.W. STORM

HARPER

An Imprint of HarperCollinsPublishers

This is a work of fiction. Names, characters, places, and incidents are products of the author's imagination or are used fictitiously and are not to be construed as real. Any resemblance to actual events, locales, organizations, or persons, living or dead, is entirely coincidental.

HARPER

An Imprint of HarperCollins*Publishers*
10 East 53rd Street
New York, New York 10022-5299

Copyright © 2008 by Peter Telep
ISBN: 978-0-06-085809-4

First Harper paperback printing: April 2008

Printed in the United States of America

Visit Harper paperbacks on the World Wide Web at
www.harpercollins.com

10 9 8 7 6 5 4 3 2 1

For all the volunteers of Operation Shoebox

Acknowledgments

....

I owe a special thank you to my editor, Mr. Will Hinton at HarperCollins, for taking on this series and trusting in its vision.

Vietnam veteran and Chief Warrant Officer James Ide, a fellow Floridian with twenty-one years of active naval service, brought his considerable experience and expertise to this series. Jim helped me brainstorm and refine ideas and build a working outline. Then he read and responded to every page of the manuscript, going so far as to draw diagrams to clarify issues and write certain scenes, drawing from his considerable naval background. What you read here is the product of our collaboration, and I'm eternally grateful for his efforts.

Troy L. Wagner, TMC (SS), EOD, USN, is a retired Chief Torpedoman, a submariner, and a specialist in Explosive Ordnance Disposal who, along with Will Reeves, helped me figure out how to gain access to an armored Mercedes. If it absolutely, positively must be blown up overnight, Troy is your man.

Major William R. Reeves, U.S. Army, helped me throughout the writing of this series and fielded my many questions. He's a continued source of inspiration, and I'm honored to know him.

Many other retired military personnel were willing to speak to me about their work "in the private sector," though understandably, they requested that their names not be listed here. I still would like to acknowledge them, and they all know who they are . . . though you never will.

Lastly, I'd like to acknowledge the work of everyone volunteering at Operation Shoebox (www.operationshoebox.com) for their unceasing support of our troops in the field. "Shoeboxers" send everything under the sun to our fine men and women serving their country, and these volunteers are a testament to the great American spirit.

"Only mad dogs and Englishmen go out in the midday sun."

—Noel Coward

THE
MERCENARIES

MAD DOGS AND ENGLISHMEN

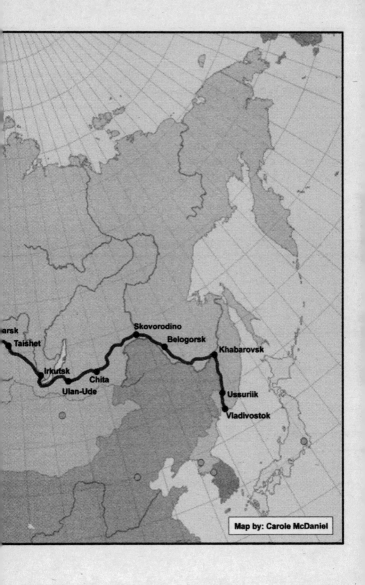

arsk
Taishet
Irkutsk
Ulan-Ude
Chita
Skovorodino
Belogorsk
Khabarovsk
Ussuriik
Vladivostok

Map by: Carole McDaniel

Prologue

....

Kazachay Lane
Zam District
Moscow
0745 Hours Local Time

The four men inside the armored Mercedes G500 were exactly forty-one seconds behind schedule, but the delay was of no concern to them.

Their tardiness did, however, make Erik Gorlach, who sat in the passenger's seat of the parked shipping van, clench his fists and repeatedly check his watch.

"Of course they're late," said Leonid Mykola, who was at the wheel and grinning with irony. "Maybe they were tipped off."

Gorlach ignored the man and spoke into his walkie-talkie, reminding the six others he had positioned between the parked cars to wait for his signal. As he finished, he glanced back through the van's tinted rear windows.

The black Mercedes rumbled toward them from about fifty meters away, slowing as the driver navigated around several potholes, scars of the country's rough winters.

The vehicle was an SUV off-road model, capable of handling much worse than broken asphalt, but the men inside were quite civilized and would bristle if the driver failed to provide them with the smoothest possible ride.

This was the fifth time Gorlach had observed these men; thankfully the last. Weeks of arguing, waiting, and planning had come down to this moment.

The driver of the Mercedes would neither notice the two chunks of asphalt placed in the middle of the road nor spot the Ballistic Disc 260 mounted near the rear bumper of an old sedan parked along the lane about twenty meters ahead. The chunks of asphalt marked the trigger line for Gorlach.

One of his men in the street reported in. Gorlach acknowledged the call, told him to wait.

"Here they come," said Mykola.

Gorlach gave his keen-eyed accomplice a dirty look. "Thank you."

Mykola swallowed. "Svetlanov told me he'll kill us if we fail. Did he tell you the same?"

"Shut up. If we fail, I will kill him." Gorlach dialed a number on his cell phone, his thumb poised over the Send button. He raised a pair of binoculars to his eyes and squinted as the Mercedes reached the chunks of rock.

Four pedestrians walked briskly down the sidewalk, probably on their way to work. They were in for a shock.

His mouth going dry, his breath held, Gorlach slammed his thumb down on the Send button.

The reaction was not instantaneous. It took several heartbeats for the signal to finally reach the ballistic disc.

Six-point-nine kilograms of explosive that had been cast into the 260's aluminum lining and capped with a steel disc exploded with a breath-robbing bang and a huge fireball that illuminated the early morning street.

In that same nanosecond, a steel slug embedded in the disc leapt forward at high velocity and struck the armored car's engine compartment with over 8,000 kilojoules of energy, more than enough to penetrate all forms of protection, pierce the engine itself, and render the vehicle immobile. Gorlach wasn't sure if the slug would pass through the entire car, but it was a risk he was willing to take.

"Let's go!" he cried, stuffing a small hatchet into his waistband.

He and Mykola donned their gas masks and hopped from the van, jogging down the lane and passing through the toxic smoke created by the disc. The air was growing thicker, hotter, and for a moment the entire street lay under a gray blanket, then suddenly reappeared.

The Mercedes sat dead in the middle of the lane, fumes pouring from its front grill and shattered radiator. Two men still moved about in the backseat, one on his cell phone. The driver and passenger up front were slumped forward, onto the dashboard. Gorlach figured the disc's steel slug had struck the compartment's armored plating, releasing metal fragments that instantly killed the two men.

A glance to the right gave him some relief. His man Bratus had already shouldered the RPG, taken aim, and now squeezed his trigger.

A flash of orange light and a familiar whoosh sent Gorlach ducking for cover.

The specially made RPG round's spiked tip issued a solid thump as it penetrated the vehicle's bulletproof windshield. A sensor went off, and a canister inside the round released a stream of liquid tear gas. The high-tech poison dart had performed beautifully.

Gorlach and his men had debated the kind of gas they should use, but the more powerful substances would require biohazard suits, and Gorlach wanted all of his people, especially those placed along the street, to be part of the operation. Biohazard suits were anything but discreet.

As the tear gas continued to flow, two of his men set up the charges for the hood, then gave the signal to stand back.

Twin booms resounded as the hood blew off. Before the smoke began to clear, his computer man got to work, attaching a portable car brain to the vehicle's computer in order to trick it into opening the doors. They had practiced this on the exact same vehicle a half-dozen times and routinely gained access within seconds. Gorlach waited, swung around as two of the pedestrians gaped and staggered away, all of it unfolding in broad daylight before their eyes.

"Hurry!" he shouted, his voice muffled behind the gas mask.

"There is a problem!" cried the computer man. "The disc caused too much damage! I have to run a bypass."

"Mykola?" Gorlach called. "Get us into this car!"

Gorlach's right-hand man, toting a sledgehammer for insurance, climbed onto the roof and began swinging at the windshield, where the glass had been compromised by the RPG round. Mykola took several massive swings, the windshield splintering but remaining intact. Gorlach began screaming at his men, glancing around the street, his pulse ticking off the seconds.

Then they heard the door lock click, and his computer man raised a thumb. "We're in!"

Gorlach rushed to the passenger's side rear door, wrenched it open, and found a middle-aged, balding man coughing and rubbing his eyes. He was the courier from Lazare International, his left hand cuffed to a black carrying case about the size of a paperback book. The case's lid contained a small lock.

"Mykola, get down and get the van!" Gorlach hollered, then he dragged the courier out of the Mercedes and slammed him onto the cold road as gunfire sounded behind them.

Gorlach used one hand to pin the courier's forearm to the street, while he clutched the hatchet in his other. He sucked in a deep breath, bared his teeth, then reared back.

It took a pair of concerted blows to sever the man's wrist. The courier was so overcome by tear gas that he barely struggled, though he wailed against the pain, unable to see the blood jetting from his stump.

Even as Gorlach freed the carrying case and tossed the severed hand aside, one of his men pointed a pistol at the courier's head and, *bang,* the man went silent. The other security man in the backseat had already been executed.

Mykola came roaring up in the van, and Gorlach scrambled inside, along with several of the others. They took off down the lane, leaving the still-smoking Mercedes behind them.

His breath ragged, Gorlach handed off the carrying case to another of his men, an expert at picking locks. Within a minute he had the case open, then returned it.

Inside, nestled in black velvet, sat twenty-five matched, twenty-five-carat, round, D-flawless Siberian diamonds.

The stones made everyone gasp.

Almazy Rossii-Sakha (ALROSA), the state-owned diamond producer in Russia, was second only to De Beers in world diamond production. Lazare Kaplan International was the largest diamond cutter in the United States, and the ALROSA-LKI contract allowed LKI to

select up to $100 million or more of ALROSA rough
each year to be cut and polished in Moscow and then
exported abroad. The LKI cutting and polishing facility
for exceptionally large rough was located in Moscow,
and Gorlach and his men had been charged by their boss
to intercept one such shipment of polished gems.

As a former mercenary and now a member of a Russian crime syndicate, Gorlach had been up to the challenge. At just thirty, he had already traveled the world
and stolen over $20 million worth of diamonds. He
would retire by forty, a very rich man. The mafia owed
him that now.

Barely able to breathe, he slammed the case shut,
clutched it to his chest, then threw back his head on the
seat and sighed. "Mykola, you dumb piece of shit, we
did it . . ."

"And now we rush back to Svetlanov, before anything
else happens, and he pays us our fee."

"Fuck Svetlanov. Maybe we'll keep the diamonds.
Maybe we'll move them ourselves."

The men in the back fell silent. Gorlach had no intention of stealing the diamonds. In fact, he was fiercely
loyal to Vladimir Svetlanov's son Sergei. But it was wise
to pretend he hated Svetlanov in order to weed out those
whose loyalty was beginning to wane.

"If Svetlanov doesn't get the diamonds," Mykola said,
"he will get us."

"You're a coward, Mykola. You're afraid to make a
really big score."

"I'm not. I don't let my ego get in the way. Listen to
me. Svetlanov knows what he's doing. Only he knows
how to turn those rocks into cash—"

"No, he's a punk whose father runs this operation. But
we are the New Russians. We are the ones who see the
future. Not some old man."

"Give Svetlanov a chance. He's young. He's one of us. He doesn't listen to his father. He's going to be more aggressive. And I believe him when he says he rewards loyalty more than anyone in all of Moscow."

Gorlach turned around and faced the rest of the men. "Do you believe that?"

None of them answered.

He raised his voice. *"Do You?"*

Zakarova Party
Southern End of Lake Baikal
Near Irkutsk, Russia
1310 Hours Local Time

The vodka wasn't helping. Nonetheless, Major Viktor Zakarova took another swig as he and the other seven men traveled in two trucks toward the lodge, following a tortuous path through the mountains.

Lake Baikal, the oldest, deepest, and largest freshwater lake on earth, glistened in the moonlight and swept out into the jagged silhouettes of the hills beyond.

Zakarova found himself staring absently at the placid waters, wishing his life were much simpler, that he wasn't a military man, that he was a fisherman who brought in great catches and told wonderful tales. What a different life that would be. Instead, he had spent the last thirty years with the army, only to be driven to a place he had never wanted to go. Then. And now. He took another sip.

Soon he dozed off. He wasn't sure how long he'd been asleep when the truck suddenly ground to a halt, the brakes hissing and squeaking. They had reached the lodge.

All eight men hopped out of the trucks, their breaths hanging in the air, their noses already growing red. But the mountain air was fresh, and Zakarova hoped that at least two of them were noticing how good it was, how the little things in life could be a great joy—

Because when he raised his hand in the air, three of his men turned on the two, brandishing their silenced pistols, and *thump, thump,* the two toppled like trees.

Quick and clean. The others dragged the bodies into the dark lodge. Zakarova followed and switched on the lights.

The two dead, both lieutenants, had been part of the original operation and were threatening the others, demanding greater cuts when the time came and arguing that they would go to the authorities.

Fools. Their threats now meant that the remaining six would share greater pieces of the pie, once it arrived fresh and steaming from the oven.

But Zakarova regretted killing them. While they had not been close friends, they all shared an amazing and terrible secret that affected each man in his own way. Some had chosen the path of greed.

Was he really a man without conscience? Zakarova wondered. He wasn't sure yet. But if he went through with it, he would have his proof, and then . . . God help his soul.

Zakarova had been one of many missile specialists assigned to Major General Fedor Nikitchenko and stationed near Irkutsk. About eighteen months ago, a lightning strike at their complex's artillery ammo stock sparked a huge fire that destroyed a vehicle park, a barracks, a dining room, and the unit's stockpile. Thankfully, no casualties were registered, but nearby residents in the villages of Nagorny and Zarechnoye, as well as children and personnel of the Solnnechny Summer Health Care Camp, had been forced to evacuate.

The fire had burned for days, and Zakarova and his men were sent to help fight it. During the chaos, he and his men had pulled "to safety" five tactical nuclear warheads, each designed for the Iskander SS-26 missile, code-named "Stone" by the United States and NATO. In the meantime, a half-dozen other warheads were destroyed in the fire. But like all warheads, they had been designed to produce only H.E. explosions, with no nuclear yield.

Zakarova had deemed the fire a perfect opportunity to gain control of some very valuable assets. Moreover, because of the threat of radiation, the entire facility had been quarantined, severely limiting the number of personnel present. Taking possession of those saved warheads had been remarkably simple. The destruction of the others allowed him to report that all of them were lost. Postincident inspections had been perfunctory at best.

Consequently, the warheads, each weighing nearly 480 kilograms, were taken off the base in the middle of the night on heavy trucks and driven to the mountains. At the time, only eight men had known of their existence.

Of course, with typical Russian efficiency and gross negligence, the entire complex site and ammo depot had simply been plowed under and fenced off to keep out the summer health-care camp children.

Now, he and his group would begin the arduous task of retrieving two of those five warheads. It was time to cash in some of their assets.

Once Zakarova was satisfied that the bodies of the two men were sufficiently prepared for disposal in the lake, he drifted outside.

His most trusted man, a senior lieutenant named Ekk, came out of the hunting lodge rubbing his cold hands. Though barely thirty, Ekk was a capable officer, and Zakarova treated him like the son he'd never had. All girls in his family: three daughters, two grown, the other killed in a terrible car accident that left his wife in a deep depression, and she had finally taken her own life. Oh, how a boy might have changed everything.

"Sir, we should wait a few days until we are sure. It would be a shame to load them for nothing."

"Yes, but I'd rather be early, in case there are any unforeseen problems."

"You mean with the Brit?"

"I mean with everything."

"All right, we'll get to work." Ekk neared him, pursed his lips, tugged down his rabbit fur *ushanka* to better cover his ears. "But Major, you don't look well."

"It's been a long time since I ordered a man's death. And not one this evening, but two."

"It was their responsibility. Not yours."

"There is no honor among thieves."

"And who do we blame for that? The politicians, the greatest thieves of all, who've left us starving. You can only beat a man down for so long before he dies or fights back."

Zakarova sighed. "You're too young to remember the days when we trained because we loved our country, the days when we crossed the bridge into Afghanistan and fought with honor."

"I know how that story ends, and I'm glad I wasn't there. I don't want to remember."

Zakarova shook his head. "Old Russia will return!"

"We all have our dreams." Ekk shrugged and tipped his head toward the truck with the crane mounted on its flatbed, the outriggers already extended, feet planted firmly on the snow to provide the vehicle with more stability. "Shall we get to work?"

They crossed to the rear of the lodge, where two of the men were already sliding aside big panel doors, like those on a barn. A second door built into the lodge's ceiling was drawn open by a man who stood on the roof. Opening these doors allowed the crane operator to swing the boom over the gap. Below, another series of panels built into the wooden floor had been removed, revealing all five of the nuclear warheads, dark brown cylinders resembling the front third of the missiles. They lay in sharp and surreal juxtaposition to the rustic furniture and art adorning the lodge's walls.

The weapons had first been buried, and then Zakarova decided to build a hunting lodge over them, one that only he and others used to both check on their assets and enjoy a little rest and recreation. They fished for taimen, grayling, pike, burbot, and Baikai omul, which was unique and inhabited only that area. They hunted lynx, as evidenced by the many hides inside the lodge. They were in tune with the tundra, outdoorsmen first, soldiers second, men who slept above more explosive power than they could ever imagine.

Zakarova watched as two metal belts were attached to the warhead, then secured to the cables. His pulse mounted as the crane's hydraulics whined and the bomb slowly rose from its eighteen-month-long slumber, floating precariously over the others. Ekk and the outspoken, hard-faced Parshin guided the crane operator, their hands pressed firmly on the weapon, while two others worked guiding cables to swing and turn the warhead as it slid through the gap.

The second truck's driver backed into place, and the crane operator swung the warhead around, lowering it down toward the flatbed, where a pair of rectangular storage crates labeled AGRICULTURAL MACHINERY had been placed atop a wooden pallet.

Suddenly, the operator lost control of the main cable, and the warhead plummeted the last meter, slamming into the crate. Nearly all of the men acted out of reflex, dropping to their hands and knees, but Zakarova knew better. He was more concerned about damage to the crate than to the weapon. It would take a lot more than a drop like that to compromise the warhead.

He strode over to the truck, climbed up and onto the flatbed, then examined the heavy straw lining and wood. Everything was intact. "No more mistakes!" he cried to the operator, who complained that he hadn't practiced the maneuver in over a year.

While Ekk and Parshin began sealing the first crate, the crane operator moved to pick up the second warhead, which was loaded without incident.

While the others celebrated inside with vodka and cigars, Zakarova stood out near the trucks, staring at the stars and stroking his gray moustache. The others . . . they didn't care what happened to the weapons once they were gone, so long as they received their payment. For them, this was a cold, hard business transaction.

Ekk came out, glass in hand, just as Zakarova's satellite phone began to ring. He recognized the number and answered with a curt statement of fact: "You said you would call two hours ago."

"I was delayed."

"And now you interrupt me."

It was the Brit, wanting him to make sure he had the bank access codes for the wire transfer. Zakarova withdrew the codes from his pocket, read them off, then scheduled their meeting in Irkutsk, at the train station.

"You must promise to speak with me first," said the Brit.

"We will. Good-bye."

As Zakarova thumbed off the phone, Ekk said, "I still don't believe he's working alone."

"You need to trust me on this. He operates alone. And I would rather hunt lynx than hunt him. He's too easy. There's no sport there."

"Who do you think he's in bed with? The Koreans? The Iranians? Surely not the United States . . . "

"We still don't know. But if his money is good, then it doesn't matter."

"Are you trying to convince yourself? Because you don't sound very convincing."

"It's just . . . the warheads can never be used."

"They are political weapons, first and foremost."

"Yes, but not all believe that."

"So . . . you won't sell them to him?"

"Of course not."

"Have you heard from our contact in Petersburg?"

"He confirmed our own check. The Brit is in fact Mr. Alastair Bibby, a mercenary currently employed with the International Philippine Group. He has thirty million dollars with which to buy our candy."

Ekk grinned darkly. "Eating too many sweets is always bad for your health."

Zakarova mustered a weak smile, then started back for the lodge.

"Major?"

He turned, lifted his brows at the young officer.

"You're right. Those warheads can never be used."

"Yes, Lieutenant. And in the old days, we would all understand that. But not anymore. Not anymore . . . "

Chapter 1

Freedom Star Aviation
Near Sacramento, California
0905 Hours Local Time

After spending a restful week of wine tasting in Napa Valley, Michael "Mad Dog" Hertzog was ready for some work. All those years spent in the Marine Corps had taken their toll: He wasn't able to play for much longer than a week at a time. He just got antsy, didn't know what to do with himself, and felt as though his life were slipping away because he wasn't *doing* something productive.

His recent bout with colon cancer, now in remission, had made him even more restless. Though only in his forties, his life clock ticked louder now, and retirement, it seemed, would be a living hell.

Thank God for Kat, who had talked him out of closing up shop. They would continue working as mercs and see what happened. More important, she was now teaching him how to relax. Ms. Katharina Kugelkerl had reminded him that he was on vacation, that he should slow down, that they both needed time to mend their hearts and minds. The gunshot wound she'd sustained back in Uzbekistan was healing nicely, although her shoulder was still very sore.

The men he had lost during that same job still whispered in his ears, and they weren't going away. Part of him didn't want them to; he deserved to be miserable. He had hauled them across the globe, not realizing they were set up by the Russians to take the fall for the president of Uzbekistan's assassination.

Mad Dog thought they were doing the CIA a favor, thought they were helping out the American military, thought they would kill a terrorist, collect their money, and go home. He had never been more wrong about anything in his life, and now he saw that he had to pay for his sins with ulcers, alcoholism, and insomnia, something . . .

Yet every time he looked at Kat, he knew he should forgive himself. She made him feel grateful to be alive.

A glance in her direction confirmed that. She had pulled her beautiful blond locks into a bun and wrestled herself into an eye-catching pair of jeans and tight blouse. With her Chanel sunglasses impaling her thick hair, she squinted and did another walk around the helicopter, an MD520N with NOTAR (no tail rotor) technology identical to the one they'd lost back in Uzbekistan.

They were standing on the tarmac in the cool morning air, waiting for the assistant sales manager to come out and take them into his office to close the deal. They would have the chopper shipped back to the Philippines and use it as part of a new training contract they'd signed with the Philippine army.

The job was aboveboard and involved teaching commandoes a few of the more unconventional skills he and his mercs had picked up over the years.

Of course, Kat had talked him into the deal, and it was a small one, to be sure, but it was a start. Tommy Wolfgang and the still recuperating Billy Pope were back home, already coordinating with the C.O.'s, Pope doing his part from a wheelchair, God bless him.

Mr. Bibby had returned to England to spend a few weeks with his friends from MI6, but just before he left, he shook Mad Dog's hand and said, "Mr. Hertzog, working for you has been quite interesting. I won't soon forget Angola, Uzbekistan, and all the other shitholes we've visited over the years. I trust you won't, either."

"No, I won't."

The Brit had nodded and climbed into the taxi, bound for the airport.

"He's always been an odd bird," Kat had said. "Sounded like he was saying good-bye for good."

"Who knows, maybe he was. After what we've just been through, I wouldn't blame him. He's threatened to quit before."

"But he always comes back, huh?"

"Glutton for punishment, maybe. I think he just takes pity on me, and he gets off on being the brains behind this operation."

"He's a smart man. But he does have one fatal flaw."

"Oh, yeah? What's that?"

"He keeps too many secrets. And when there's a lot to hide, you become too occupied keeping inventory because there's a lot to risk."

Mad Dog shuddered off the memory and drifted behind Kat. He wrapped his arms around her torso and let his cheek brush against hers. She smelled like that jasmine bath soap, intoxicating. "You like your new toy?"

"Yeah, but I wish he'd shave."

He chuckled. "Is that all I am?"

"Of course not. Otherwise I'd replace you with a zucchini." She pulled out of his grip, gestured to the chopper. "So, what do you think?" She tugged open the pilot's door. "Is this a bargain, or is this a bargain?"

"We should've gone to Wal-Mart. I saw in the ad that they got Chinese-made helicopters at half price. This week only."

"Yeah, but they get you on the weapons package. It's way overpriced. And you know, beggars can't be choosers."

"Yeah, now we're beggars." Mad Dog glanced up, spotted the pudgy sales guy tottering toward them. "Well, let's go spend some money."

They turned back toward the salesman, whose expression had grown very long. "Mr. Hertzog, I'm afraid we have a problem."

Mad Dog looked at Kat, who frowned.

Yaroslavsky Railway Station
Trans-Siberian Express
Moscow
2010 Hours Local Time

Every other day the Rossiya—Russia—Train Number 2 left Yaroslavsky Station in Moscow on its seven day journey east to Vladivostok. The ride covered 9,258 kilometers, or over six thousand miles, and was one of the longest and most famous train excursions in the world. The train had second-class four-berth compartments and first-class two-berth compartments, a restaurant car, and several cargo carriages.

Sergei Svetlanov, twenty-nine, as "new" a Russian as they came, would never travel with the peasants and tourists jammed into a *kupe,* and risk having one of his silk suits soiled, let alone his reputation. That would be barbaric, to say the least.

And so he had booked first-class compartments for himself and Hannah, and for the rest of his men. They would ride to Vladivostok in style, with both beds in their compartments on the lower level. They had lots of leg and storage room, and the compartment even had windows with fancy curtains. Sure, the toilets and washrooms were positioned at the end of the narrow corridor, so you had to go for a little walk, but an occasional stretch was always welcome. There were nine compartments in their carriage, and Svetlanov and his people occupied all of them.

After a long delay due to a mechanical problem, they finally left the station, and the first provodnik was coming around, asking for their tickets and the small bedding fee to obtain the two sheets, a pillowcase, and a towel in sealed packs. These attendants, who worked in shifts, resided in a small room at the front end of the carriage, near the toilets and hot water boiler. They prepared cups of chai for four rubles and got off at every station to remind passengers in Russian and in hand signals not to stay on the platform too long. They were grossly underpaid, and Svetlanov had decided early on that he would inspire their loyalty.

"Your tickets, sir?" asked the young man, who eyed him suspiciously.

Svetlanov handed over the tickets, while behind him, Hannah leaned back in the armchair, typing on her laptop.

"These look fine, sir."

Svetlanov cocked a brow at the man. "What's your name?"

"Alek."

"Well, Alek, as you've seen on our tickets, I am Mr. Svetlanov. And this is my lovely friend Hannah Lamoureux. We're going to a wedding in Vladivostok, traveling with a group of friends on board this carriage."

"Yes, sir, I assumed you were all together. And if there is anything we can do—"

Svetlanov pushed a bill into the attendant's hand. "I think this should cover the bedding fee. The rest is yours."

Alek unfolded the bank note: five hundred rubles. He gasped. "Sir?"

"Just see to it that we're well attended and undisturbed, and there'll be several more of those waiting for you when we leave."

"Yes, sir!"

Alek moved on to the next compartment, and Svetlanov slid the door closed. He smoothed back his hair, which he kept plastered to his head with a heavy dose of hair spray, then moved to Hannah and tore the computer from her grip, tossing it onto the bed.

"Hey! You bloody fool! I was in the middle of—"

"Kissing me," he finished. He drew her up from the chair, slammed her into his chest, pressing her breasts tightly to him, then gave her a long, hard kiss that tingled his groin.

When he pulled back, her rage had already subsided. She eyed him salaciously. "If you weren't so good, I would leave you tomorrow, you know that, don't you?"

"You whore. Don't speak to me that way!" He grinned and wheeled her around, began spanking her ass.

They hadn't been on the train an hour and already they were ready for sex. He'd told her that spending long days on board the train would finally allow them to talk, the way she had wanted, and fuck, the way he had wanted.

She was an exchange student, just twenty-two, born in France and raised in England, and they had met at the Sixteen Tons Club, a famous night spot in Moscow whose ground floor was designed as a traditional English pub, consequently attracting many students from the UK who sought a little taste of home.

She winced as he spanked her, the diamond in her nostril flashing, her long, dark brown hair whipping in his face. She was an incredible-looking woman, perfect on his arm, but more than that, she was still naive, didn't ask the hard questions, simply accepted that his family had made a fortune and that he was an international businessman on a brief holiday to attend a wedding before heading off to a convention in Japan.

She knew nothing of the diamonds he had hidden inside the two bars of soap in his luggage, and that, of course, was the way he preferred it.

With a giggle, she twisted out of his grip and spun around, then suddenly ripped off her blouse, undid her bra, and exposed her firm breasts. She smiled, pinched one nipple, then extended her tongue.

The door slid open then and Gorlach appeared, with Mykola at his shoulder.

"Oh, sorry!" cried Gorlach, whose jaw fell open, his gaze locked on Hannah's breasts.

Svetlanov's eyes bulged. "Get out!"

Gorlach slid the door shut.

"I forgot to lock it," grunted Svetlanov.

Hannah wriggled her carefully tweezed brows. "So what? It's not like they haven't seen a woman before."

"Don't get too close to the wolves. They bite."

"So do I," she gasped. "Now, on your knees!"

"You're supposed to be a little innocent exchange student," he said, lowering himself to the floor.

"I said, get down!" With that, she raised her foot, brought her heel down on his back and drove him onto his chest, flat on the compartment's floor. "Now, baby, tell me what you want."

Chills spread across Svetlanov's shoulders. He was not used to being controlled. "I want you."

"Well, you can't have me, bitch."

"My God, Hannah, what would your father think of his little girl?"

"He wouldn't care." She kicked off her heel and shoved her foot in his face. "Suck on my toes!"

Svetlanov pushed her foot away and slowly rose to face her. "Hannah? What's the matter with you?"

She swallowed. "I don't know. But I like it. Don't you?"

"No." He closed his eyes. "I just want to make love to you. A man to a woman."

She bit her lip, eyes burning. "Okay."

"Hannah?"

She wiped off a sudden tear and her voice cracked. "I'm just a little homesick. That's all."

He took her into his arms, cradled her head. What a tender monster he was. If she only knew. "When we get to Japan, I'm going to buy you something spectacular."

"I don't want anything."

He stroked her hair. "You're a good girl. Don't worry. I'll take care of you."

Freedom Star Aviation
Near Sacramento, California
0920 Hours Local Time

Mad Dog and Kat were racing away from the hangars in their rented SUV as he spoke frantically on the phone to Wolfgang, who was back on Cebu Island in the Philippines. Wolfgang was at the "Pound," the colonial style mansion with guest house they had turned into their living quarters and offices. As always, he was a little dense, and Mad Dog's voice grew more tense. "That's right, the nightstand. The one on the left. See it now?"

"Yeah?"

"Wall safe is right behind it." Mad Dog gave Wolfgang the combination and waited while he worked it.

"Okay, I got it open, but I don't see any case like you're telling me."

"Look again."

"Boss, there ain't jack shit in here. Some papers and crap, your two pistols. No case."

"All right. I'll be in touch, thanks." He thumbed off the satellite phone. "I don't fucking believe it."

"So he took the necklace, too?"

"He knew I had it. I even told him I put it in that safe, in case something happened to me."

"Oh my God."

"Yeah, oh my God."

"So he stole thirty million dollars from our IPG accounts, dumped the money into his own Swiss accounts, and then he's got the balls to steal that jade necklace, too? What's it worth?"

"Over ten million."

Kat rolled her eyes, shook her head.

"That's what you get when you trust somebody."

"No, it's not. Not always."

"You know, when I hired him, I did every background check known to mankind. I worked with him for years. I trusted him with everything: my money, my life. Christ, he was my friend! An uptight motherfucker, but my friend! We've been through a lot together. I could tell you stories."

"Shit, does he really think he can jet off with all that money and hide from us?"

"I don't know. I just . . . I'm blown away. I don't understand it." Mad Dog pulled the SUV to the side of the road, sat there a moment, clutching his heart. "Chest pain like you wouldn't believe."

"Don't have a heart attack, come on."

"Don't have a heart attack? I'm out forty million dollars! I'll have a fucking heart attack if I want to!"

"It's only money."

"People died for that fucking money. We got no business without that money. It's over."

"We'll have to start from scratch."

"Bullshit. I don't think he's spent the money yet."

"What? You think we can find him? Ask for it back?"

"Oh, we'll find him. And when we do, God help him . . . " Mad Dog threw the SUV in drive, got them back on the road.

Kat's gaze went distant, and once more she shook her head. "I just . . . I can't believe he wanted to rob us. I think he's in trouble. I think he's in very serious trouble."

"I hope you're right, for his sake. Then I won't torture him first. I'll just kill him."

Kat waved him off. "All right, enough whining. I'll try to call Waffa. See if he knows anything."

"Who else? What about Albert and Patrice at MI6? You know, maybe he owed them something. Maybe it all has to do with them. He called in a huge favor when he had them rescue us from the border. Maybe his deal involves stealing our money."

"We should talk to them, if they're willing."

"If they don't talk, then we know we have to dig harder there. If they're not involved, and they want to help their buddy, they'll tell us everything they know. But I need to go there myself, throw my name around, get people nervous."

"Try calling first, okay? Just to make sure those guys are still in London."

He snorted. "No shit. And you're not talking about the wasted time, sweetheart. Price of airline tickets is nuts."

She nodded, narrowed her gaze, pressed the satellite phone closer to her ear. "I got Waffa's voice mail . . . Uh, hey, Waffa, it's Kat. Give me a call back. It's urgent." She gave him the number and hung up.

Waffa Zarour ran an Internet café in Ramallah, ten miles north of Jerusalem. He bought, traded, and sold information like a vendor at a flea market, and Mad Dog was always astounded by the length and breadth of his intelligence. If there was one man on the planet who could find Bibby, it was Waffa.

"Let's get ahold of my friend Big Booty at J-SOC."

"Big Booty?"

Mad Dog grinned crookedly. "Don't ask. Get out my laptop, address book is in there. She can hook us up with some more intelligence assets and see if there are any special operations that might tip us off."

"That's a long shot, but we'll take it."

"After you talk to her, we'll call MI-6." He checked his watch. "It's still only five-thirty there. I want flight schedules to London. We might have to go to Chicago and Boston first. Maybe we can get something straight to New York, then go from there."

"I'll see what I can do."

They drove in silence for a few minutes, as she made the calls, groaned over voice mail recordings. Finally, she said with some astonishment, "I have Albert Mc-Mullen on the line. Here you go." She handed him the phone.

"Hello, Albert? Yes, it's Michael Hertzog."

"Oh, yes, Mr. Hertzog, I know who you are. Alastair spoke quite highly of you."

Mad Dog wasn't used to hearing Mr. Bibby's first

name. He hesitated a moment, then answered, "I never had a chance to thank you for helping us cross the border into A'stan."

"That's quite all right. When Alastair needs a favor, Patrice and I will always be there. We owe him our lives. Besides, we had some other opportunities nearby that also deserved our attention."

Interesting. Bibby never mentioned that he had saved anyone. Then again, he rarely spoke of his work with MI-6, except to say that the bureaucrats had ruined most of it. "Well, I'm glad it worked out for everyone. Now the reason I'm calling does concern our mutual friend. Albert, I'm going to be frank with you. Bibby has, shall we say, borrowed a large sum of my money, and now I'm having difficulty contacting him."

"It's ironic you should say that, because we're having the same problem."

"Really?"

"Yes, when he came to London, he demanded to see Galina Saratova's father, the colonel who defected to us. His name is Boris Sinitsyna. He was an NKVD colonel and political officer assigned to the Russian Embassy here."

"I know about him."

"Well, I sent one of our transition team members to escort Alastair for the meeting."

"And?"

"And he spoke alone with the colonel for about thirty minutes. After that, we had lunch. And after that he said he wanted to run some errands. That was the last we heard of him."

"Have you questioned the colonel?"

"No, we've had no reason to do that."

"You didn't find it curious that he wanted to speak to an old Russian who'd just defected?"

"Given the circumstances, no. We presumed he was working for you, gathering more information regarding your former employer, who just happened to be working for Moscow Center."

"Don't remind me. Can you set up a meeting for me with the colonel?"

"I believe we can do that—clandestinely, of course— but he's a difficult man. You might be wasting your time. And there's no indication that he would know where Alistair is."

"Right now that old Russian is the only clue I have. My partner Kat and I will catch a flight to London. We should be there late tonight. I'd appreciate you setting up a meeting for us. If it turns out that Bibby is in trouble, he'll need our help."

"Absolutely. Let me give you my cellular number. Call me once you're in London."

Mad Dog had Kat jot down the number, then he said good-bye.

"You were wrong about the old Russian," Kat said as she inputted the number into their satellite phone's contact list. "He's not our only clue. If Waffa doesn't get back to me soon, when we get to London, I'm going to Ramallah to find him."

"Alone?"

"Divide and conquer."

"Alone?"

"Mr. Hertzog, I've been doing this much longer than you. While you were yelling at privates to get their shit squared away in the Marine Corps, I was already a mercenary."

"You were a bodyguard, give me a break."

"I'm going."

"Have fun. I hear they treat women like gold in the Middle East."

"If it makes you happy, I'll shave my head and wear a strap-on."

He made a face. "I still can't believe this is happening."

"You know, if we knew more about Bibby, about his personal life, we might put something together. But he's always been so evasive. He's an expert on downplaying his whole life."

"Yeah, and maybe he's been plotting this from day one. You know, the perfect little crime, and we'll never get him. The day I hired him was the day he decided to rip me off. He's been laying low, waiting for the right time."

"Sometimes you think you know people—"

"But you don't."

Mad Dog got on the freeway and floored it. Bad idea. Within ten minutes he had involuntarily pulled over. And yes, he had chest pains again.

But the steel-faced cop writing out the ticket could have cared less. "Here you are. You can take care of this online. Next time, slow down."

Mad Dog spoke through his teeth. "Hey, I just lost forty million dollars today, okay?"

The cop smiled. "Forty million, plus another two hundred and ten dollars right there. Have a nice day."

Chapter 2

....

Svetlanov and Hannah had been riding for nearly twenty hours and passed through two time zones, adding a couple of hours to their watches.

Had it been a pleasant ride? Well, it'd had its moments, but now he was about ready to strangle her. First-class accommodations notwithstanding, her mood swings had worn him down to a nub, and it would be a great relief to leave the train for a little while.

They had just crossed the calm waters of the Kama River and were pulling into the station at Perm, an industrial town nestled at the foot of the Ural Mountains. The train clacked and rattled to a slow and hissing stop, the provodniks shouting their announcements.

Hannah said she wanted to wash up, so Svetlanov donned his heavy jacket and hat and went out alone into the early evening air.

The old babushkas stood on the platform, near tables shaded by brightly colored umbrellas. They sold smoked fish and hot potatoes in bags, and other traditional Russian foods that made Svetlanov's mouth water. The buffet service was a thriving business, found at nearly every stop, and he had already learned that the restaurant car was for the uninformed. You bought your food from the babushkas, carried it back, and had the provodniks cook it for you, if, of course, you were leaving five-hundred-ruble tips.

Gorlach and Mykola were already out on the platform, lighting up cigarettes.

"Smoke?" asked Gorlach, offering up one.

Svetlanov shook his head, then fixed a penetrating stare on the slightly older man. "You want to fuck my girlfriend."

Gorlach's eyes widened, and Mykola swallowed.

Svetlanov took a step closer to Gorlach's right hand man, drew in a deep breath through his nose. "You do!"

"No," said Gorlach. "It was—"

"Are you saying she's ugly?" Svetlanov asked, turned to him.

"No!"

"Are you saying she's ugly, and that's why you don't want to fuck her?"

"We think she is a very pretty girl," said Mykola, shivering through his words.

Svetlanov grabbed the man by the collar. "And you want to stick your rotten cock in her, don't you?"

"I don't!"

He shoved Mykola away.

"Sergei, please, it was an accident!" hollered Gorlach.

Svetlanov stared at them a moment more, then broke into a fit of laughter.

The two fools didn't know whether to laugh or apologize again, then succumbed to Svetlanov's chuckling. He smacked each of them on the back, and they finally began laughing, too.

Then, suddenly, it hit Svetlanov. He rushed toward the train, crying, "I'll be right back!"

Inside the carriage, he bolted down the corridor, reached their compartment and rifled through his knapsack, where he kept the two bars of soap with the rest of his toiletries.

And yes, she had gone into his things, taken one of the bars, and was now in the washroom.

With visions of the diamonds being washed down the drain, Svetlanov charged down the corridor, nearly knocking over another of his men. "Get out of my way!" he cried.

He had no breath by the time he reached the washroom, where Hannah glanced sleepily at him. "What's wrong with you?"

Hornsea on Bridlington Bay
England
1755 Hours Local Time

They pulled up in front of the bungalow, and Mad Dog took a moment to massage his eyes before getting out of the Peugeot. He could never sleep on planes, so he'd been awake nearly twenty-four hours. The lack of sleep, coupled with the stress, seemed to have sucked about ten years off his life. Maybe eleven.

Albert McMullen had picked him up at the airport. Nice chap, if too well groomed and effeminate. He made small talk during the ride, but Mad Dog barely listened.

Meanwhile, Kat had left for Ramallah to find Waffa.

She and Mad Dog fought once more over her going alone, and she'd left in a huff and was already in the air.

Damn it. She could take care of herself and had no tolerance for his ego or possessiveness. But he was genuinely concerned. If she got herself killed, he'd never live it down. Shit. He loved and hated her independence. What the hell could he do but let her go? He found it hard to sit still as he imagined her wandering in congested and dangerous areas.

"Mr. Hertzog? Are you all right?" Albert asked. "You look . . . quite awful."

"You look gay, but I don't want to be politically incorrect or judgmental about it. Let's go see this old fucker."

Albert winced. "Fuck you, too. Now, when we get inside, I suggest you mind your manners."

"I'll do my best. You said he speaks English?"

"Yes, he's fluent, but it won't matter if he decides not to talk. There's nothing we can do. I won't allow you to threaten him. I want to be clear about that."

"Define 'threaten.'"

Albert snorted, then got out of the car.

Mad Dog followed, tripped on the stone walkway but caught himself before falling.

"You weren't drinking on the plane, were you?" asked Albert.

"Maybe a little."

"Just remember the favor I'm doing you here. Don't fuck it up by embarrassing me. This man has become a valuable source of information, and he'll continue to help us."

"Oh, I doubt you'll be embarrassed."

Albert rang the bell, and the old Russian answered. Mad Dog liked him already: military boy, Russkie through and through, silver crew cut, still in great shape, a study in geometry—

Which made him feel a half ounce of guilt for bursting through the door, seizing the old man by the neck, driving him back into the kitchen, forcing him across the kitchen table, shoving him even farther back into the wall, then wrenching him down, onto the floor, pinning him so that he could wrap both hands around his neck.

"My God, Hertzog!" shouted Albert.

Mad Dog lifted the colonel by his neck, banged him back down on the floor. *"Where the fuck is he? You know where he is, you old fucking commie! Tell me where the fuck he is right now, otherwise I'll choke the fucking life out of you. Talk, motherfucker! Talk! Where is Alastair Bibby?"*

Well there it was: diplomatic relations, mercenary style.

Albert had rushed into the kitchen, grabbed one of Mad Dog's arms and tried to pull him off the old man, but Mad Dog's death grip was permanent.

"You can't kill him!" cried Albert.

"Watch me." Mad Dog glowered at the Russian, whose face was now crimson, eyes threatening to pop from his skull. "Where the fuck is he?"

The colonel's voice came low and thickly accented. "I'll tell you. For a price. Otherwise, kill me. I don't fucking care, asshole."

Something jabbed Mad Dog in the side of his head. Slowly, he turned to find Albert brandishing a pistol.

"He's worth much more to me than you are," said the Brit.

Mad Dog raised his brows. "Point taken. But this motherfucker is going to deal."

"Let him go."

"No."

"I'm warning you, Hertzog. I have no qualms about shooting you, especially after your accusation about me being as bent as a nine-bob note, understand?"

"Not really."

Albert took a deep breath and growled, "Let him go."

Mad Dog tightened his grip. "He knows where Bibby is. And he's about to tell me, right here, right now."

British Airways Flight 163
En Route to Tel Aviv
1805 Hours Local Time

Her ass had become shaped like an airplane seat, yet here she was again, back on another plane for a five hour ride that would feel like an eternity. At least she was on a nonstop flight to eternity.

Consequently, she had time to kill. Hated that. Kat's mind raced. She wished she could make some calls, but security restrictions prevented her from using the satellite phone. The plane did, however, have a brand new wireless network, though she wasn't allowed to use Internet phone services. Lovely.

Another check of her e-mail came up empty. For some reason, Waffa had gone underground. Or maybe he was . . . she didn't want to go there. She loved the man.

A lifetime ago he had helped her start her business, found her the rich and forward-thinking Arabs who needed her protection and got off on having a sexy, powerful woman in charge. She'd met him through a mutual friend in Washington, and they quickly became friends. Waffa planted the idea in her head that she could get in the VIP protection business. He was one of the few who had believed in her from the start.

Sure, many potential Middle Eastern clients couldn't handle the fact that she was female, which limited her clientele, but she didn't want to work for those assholes anyway. The more progressive types embraced her, understood the power of a black widow, understood how those who judged her a weak female were the ones who fell hard and fast. Cunning was as devastating as large caliber weapons.

So where was Waffa? she wondered.

She'd even tried contacting his wife via e-mail, but even she hadn't replied.

There was another message from Billy Pope, who said that he tried to call and had gotten her voice mail. He didn't want to interrupt Mad Dog with this news, thought it might be better if she broke it to him.

Mad Dog's old friend and mentor, Gunnery Sergeant Daniel M. Forrest, III, USMC, retired, had just passed away.

Kat put a hand to her mouth in shock.

She knew how much Michael loved and cared for old Dan, had witnessed their father-son relationship. Mad Dog had practically been raised by Dan since the age of thirteen, and when Dan became ill and could no longer take care of himself, Michael had assumed the responsibility, put him up at the house, treated him like a king.

Daniel Forrest *was* the United States Marine Corps to Michael.

But the old man's time had finally come. He was seventy-six, had diabetes and complications, and, according to Pope, went to bed and slipped away. A beautiful death. A fitting death for a solider.

But Michael hadn't been there to say good-bye, and his heart would be broken.

Could he handle the news, given their current situation? *God, why'd it have to be now?*

No, they wouldn't tell him. At least not yet. She fired off a reply to Pope, told him not to say anything. But Pope wanted to know about arrangements, and she couldn't give him an answer. Only Michael knew what to do.

God, she was torn. If they didn't tell him and they went ahead and either buried old Dan or had him cremated without Michael's consent, that would be worse. Michael would feel that he'd been robbed of the opportunity to pay final tribute, and he would blame them.

So they would have to tell him. Soon. Maybe they could keep old Dan at a funeral home or the coroner's office until the situation with Bibby was somehow resolved. How long would that take? She'd need to call Pope the moment she landed and discuss it with him.

What else could happen? Some nut job could try to blow up her plane? Jesus . . . the negative thoughts were moving in and setting up house.

Kat glanced across the aisle at a little Indian girl seated next to her mother. That was beauty right there. The future. She slapped her computer shut, closed her eyes, and tried to get some rest.

Hornsea on Bridlington Bay
England
1808 Hours Local Time

"He's in Russia. But that's all you get for free," said the colonel.

Mad Dog squeezed the old man's neck and shook him. "Russia's a big place. Can you—"

"Hertzog, you're out of time," said Albert. "If you don't let him go, I'll shoot you . . . maybe in the leg, the arm . . . I won't do you the favor of killing you."

Mad Dog locked gazes with the Brit. Oh, yes, he'd seen that look before. Albert would fire. It was just a question of which limb he'd target.

And really, his little talk with the colonel had already been successful. The old man had admitted that he knew where Bibby was. Details would emerge as the negotiations continued.

So Mad Dog relented, relaxed his grip, climbed off the colonel then rose to stand near the sink. Not one to miss a moment of irony, he abruptly leaned down and offered his hand to the man he'd just been choking.

And surprisingly, the colonel accepted. "I would have killed me, if I were you."

"And if I were you, I would've offered me some fucking tea before inviting me in to attack you."

The colonel grinned and looked to Albert. "This one, I like."

"Are you mad?" asked Albert.

"No, that would be me," answered Mad Dog.

The colonel raised his brows. "I hope you have money, because if you want to know how to find your friend, it's going to cost you a lot."

Mad Dog raised his chin to the Brit. "Albert, would you mind leaving us alone?"

"Bloody hell, I will. I'm going to stand right here, with this pistol."

"I won't talk with him here, and this room is secure," said the colonel.

"Albert, I'll give you fifty bucks if you go outside."

"You fucking Yank! You think this is funny? This is a powerful and important man!"

"Yeah, and he still has to piss, shit, and fart like the rest of us, so why don't you shut the fuck up and go outside?"

"I can take care of myself," said the colonel.

The Brit shook his head.

"Albert, don't waste my time. Don't waste his time. You really think I'm going to kill him now, after he's teased me with the bait? Come on, you're smarter than that. He just wants money for the information I need. We'll work it out. You go bye-bye."

"Why did I know it would come to this?" Albert drew in a long breath, swore under his breath, then ventured toward the front door, saying, "I'll be *just* outside."

Once Albert was out of earshot, Mad Dog turned to the colonel and said, "Fucking Brits. They're all so uptight. Still pissed about the Revolutionary War, I guess."

The colonel cracked a grin as he lowered himself into a chair at the kitchen table and rubbed his sore neck. "I told him I like you. But I didn't tell him why."

"Why?"

"Because you are a fucking idiot."

Mad Dog threw up his hands. "Okay, we've established that. Now, business time. You know Bibby's in Russia. You know why he's there. You know exactly where he is."

"I do. But why do you believe me? Is it because, well, you are a fucking idiot?" The colonel smiled.

Mad Dog didn't. "Yeah, I was a fucking idiot to believe your daughter, to take that fucking job, to let her set me up, to let half my fucking boys get killed. Yeah, I was a fucking idiot."

With a growl, the colonel slammed his fast on the table. "You're not here to talk about my daughter!"

"Or how she sent me and my friends off to die, without a fucking conscience."

"You know nothing."

"I know how she helped the motherland, all right, didn't she? Fucking mole."

The colonel closed his eyes. "This talk is over."

"I'll tell you when it's over."

The colonel opened his eyes, looked back toward the stove. "Would you like that cup of tea before you leave?"

"Would you like me to choke you again?"

Lowering his head, his gazed locked on Mad Dog, the colonel replied, "You wouldn't survive it."

"Listen to me, asshole. That fucking Brit has thirty million dollars of my money. And you're going to help me get it back. Or you're going to die."

"Why should I help you? And how do you know I have the information you need? I could be lying."

"What do you want?"

"I want a million dollars."

"Fuck you. I just told you I'm broke."

"When you get your money back, you will give me the balance. I only require a quarter million up front. Now, let me give you the information you will need to transfer those funds into one of my accounts."

"Accounts? Didn't your government freeze your assets when you defected?"

"Of course. But since then I've acquired some . . . let's call them operational funds."

"So you defected, you come here, and what? They're letting you rip them off? Letting you rip me off?"

"It's business, Mr. Hertzog. That's all. I have information that they want and information you want. Everyone pays. If you believe otherwise, then you are a fool."

"Why did Bibby come to you?"

"For the same reason you have. For the same reason everyone does. Information."

"How much did you charge him?"

"I'll be right back." The colonel rose, left the room, returned with a painfully familiar dark blue box. He lifted the lid to expose the necklace; translucent, emerald green beads gleaming across a bed of silk.

"That belongs to me."

The colonel slapped shut the case. "No. It was my daughter's. After she died, you hired a man to steal it from her, and Bibby returned it to me."

"So he bought information from you with a necklace he stole from me."

"A necklace you stole from my daughter."

"I don't believe this."

The colonel shrugged. "I didn't care where he got it. And it was payment enough for me."

"You know what that's worth?"

"I know exactly what it's worth."

Mad Dog rubbed his unshaven jaw in thought. "I'm surprised he didn't cover his tracks. This isn't like him."

"Well, the situation is unique, and I don't suspect he would've had the time to do that. He has a lot on his mind, what you call stressed out, huh?"

"What kind of trouble is he in?"

The colonel took in a long breath. "No more talk. I'm going to write down everything you'll need. You will come back after the transfer"—he smiled darkly—"and I will point you in the right direction."

"I need to coordinate this with my people back in the Philippines. That's going to take a little time."

"Don't take too long. You'll need to be back on a plane very soon."

Downtown Ramallah
West Bank
0115 Hours Local Time

Kat set her watch two hours ahead, then wove her way down the sidewalk, a knapsack slung over her shoulder. She reminded herself not to leave without getting some of Rukab's ice cream, which was based on the resin of chewing gum and had an incredibly delicious and distinctive taste. Ramallah was known for it, and Rukab Street was named after the ice cream parlor located on one end. Hopefully she would still be in the city when they opened in the morning.

Despite the late hour, there were still a lot of people on the street. Just a week before a curfew had been lifted, and the once war-torn outskirts of the city had grown quiet, allowing the young people to roam once again.

She hadn't been to Ramallah in a couple of years, and the place seemed more crowded than she remembered it. So many billboards, signs, and placards of every color, shape, and design hung aloft that you could barely see the windows of the tall office and apartment buildings lining both sides of the street. Groups of men sat in plastic lawn chairs outside shops, playing cards and other games in the warm night air, while the younger folks, particularly the males, flocked to the cafés like the one Waffa and his wife owned. They had simply called it "Café," and then after a year or two renamed it "Waffa's Cyber Café," so as Kat approached the storefront, she was taken aback by the shattered sign overhead and the large piece of plywood covering the front door. She pressed her face to the tinted glass, peered inside.

Computer monitors were smashed and lying across the floor. Wires coiled like snakes atop piles of glass and overturned chairs. Even the long sofas, where people once smoked and drank coffee, had been slashed apart and kicked over. More startlingly were the long scorch marks that climbed the rear walls. The long counter area was covered in soot, the ceiling above it collapsed, blackened pieces dangling like frayed skin.

She lost her breath as she stepped back from the glass and unconsciously looked around for an answer.

Life continued along the streets of Ramallah, and no one seemed to care about one small café that had been vandalized and set fire. She grabbed her phone, dialed Waffa again, got his voice mail. Then she leaned back on the glass and cursed.

Where the hell was her friend? She feared for his life. And now her own curiosity could get her into trouble. She composed herself. Time to go. Time to call Michael and tell him what she had found.

Two young men, both with short beards, approached her, and the taller of the two called in English, "So sorry, ma'am, but they are closed."

"Thank you," she snapped, and pushed past them.

"Wait, please," called the shorter one, his accent thicker than the taller one's.

"Sorry." She took three more steps, felt a hand lock onto her arm.

The taller one's expression darkened. "Don't go."

She reached into her pants pocket, then turned back, a credit card in her hand, one whose edge she had sharpened until it cut flesh like a razor. She slashed the man, who screamed—

Then she broke into a run down the street, drawing stares from those seated along the sidewalk.

"Kat! Stop!" hollered the man. "We can take you to see him!"

Breathless and chilled, she slowed, whirled around, started back toward them, the tall man clutching his bleeding arm, the other shaking his head at her and saying, "He told us you would be difficult."

She lowered her voice. "Waffa sent you? Bullshit. Why didn't he tell me?"

"He can't."

"Bullshit."

"They've tapped all of his lines."

"What are you talking about?"

The tall one grew impatient. "Come on, we'll take you to see him."

"I don't believe you."

"He said you wouldn't. So he told us to show you this."

The shorter man reached into his breast pocket and produced a photo of Kat and Waffa, one she had taken and given to him, one that Waffa said he kept in his wallet, one on which Kat had written the words: *For My Teacher. Thank You.*

Unless they had killed Waffa and removed the photo from his wallet, they were working for him.

She returned the photo, then glanced around. "Take me to see him. But are we being watched?"

"Of course. We'll lose them."

"Who are they?"

"Enemies."

"Oh, that's helpful. Are they the same ones who burned down the café?"

"Yes," said the shorter one.

"Waffa must've pissed off the wrong people, all right."

The shorter one nodded.

"You cut me very bad," said the tall one, removing his palm from his forearm to reveal all the blood.

"If you would've just told me."

"We did."

"Yeah, a little late. Well, I don't have anything to bandage that in my pack. We'll have to get you something, though. For now, we'll use part of your shirt."

Three taxicabs later, with the switches made in the narrow alleys between apartment buildings, Kat found herself being led into the basement of yet another apartment building, the narrow stone staircase dust-covered and slippery.

They reached a large metal door, the kind you'd find on a meat locker, illuminated by a single bulb dangling from the ceiling.

They had bandaged the taller man's arm in one of the cabs. He identified himself as Rashad and the shorter man as Nazir. Now, Rashad told her they had to go, but if she rapped on the door and called for Waffa, he would come. Abruptly, they both left.

Oh, God. Kat raised her fist, thought better of it, then reached for her cell phone. She figured she'd finally call Michael, having been too nervous while in the cabs. She dialed the number—

When the metal door swung outward.

She yanked her credit card free.

And Waffa, pistol in hand, frowned at her. "Hello, Katharina. Did you want to go shopping?"

She sighed and rushed to the short man, his curly hair wired with gray, his hooked nose glossy with sweat, his smile warm and inviting. They hugged for a long moment, then she pulled back and said, "Oh my God, Waffa, what happened?"

Chapter 3

······························

Hornsea on Bridlington Bay
England
2345 Hours Local Time

Mad Dog was about to rap on the door when the colonel opened it. "You kept me waiting for too long. Maybe now I've changed my mind. Maybe now I will go to bed."

"You like money, old man?"

"Of course."

"Then shut the fuck up and let's make a deal."

"No manners, you Americans. No manners at all." The colonel accepted the documents Mad Dog offered, then led him into the bungalow and to the kitchen, while Albert once again waited outside.

"FYI, Colonel, I had to print out bank transfers, make my own, and we grabbed some fish and chips on the way back. Sorry it's past your bed time."

"You smell like fish. Well, that delay might have cost you more than you know."

"Oh, yeah? Talk."

After a snort and roll of his eyes, the colonel examined the papers and nodded.

Mad Dog tensed. "Do we have deal?"

"Your associate is headed to Krasnoyarsk, a big city on the Yenisei River. There he will board the Rossiya Train Number 2, which is headed to Vladivostok. It's a very long ride. He's a couple of days ahead of you, but you can still catch him if you don't stop for fish and chips again. You will need to board the train at Khabarovsk, which is the next to last stop before Vladivostok."

Mad Dog saw a pen lying on the counter. He took it, then tore a piece of paper from one of the bank statements. "Give me the names of those cities again. I don't know what part of Russia they're in, and I certainly can't spell 'em."

The colonel complied, and once Mad Dog finished, he asked, "So what's Bibby doing on a train?"

"Riding, of course."

"Don't fuck with me, Colonel. If he's traveling a long way, why didn't he just fly?"

"He needs to be on the ground. I will give you more information as needed." The Russian dropped his voice. "You will give me your satellite phone. And we will stay in touch."

"I paid for all the information up front."

"No, you gave me a deposit. And I'm giving some information, not all."

"So, if I had the entire million, you'd tell me everything?"

He smiled amusedly. "Probably not. Keeping a few secrets sometimes keeps oneself alive."

"Motherfucker."

"We say *yebanat*. Your phone, please?"

"If I want to talk to you, I'll do it through Albert. You're not getting my phone. I'm sure they're not letting you make outside calls, either."

"Well, then, you'll get nothing more from me until you pay the entire sum."

"I have enough for now."

"Maybe. But if your associate reaches Vladivostok and you fail to intercept him, then only I know where he's headed from there."

Mad Dog hesitated. "You already know we won't catch him, don't you?"

"No, you might."

"No, we won't. That's how you guarantee your back end. So stop fucking with me. Where's he headed after that?"

"Mr. Hertzog, you can catch him, but even then he won't tell you everything you need to know. You will call me, you will transfer the rest of my money, and I will tell you the entire story, the one he will never tell you."

"Why don't I just beat the fucking shit out of you and be done with it?"

"Because these nice Brits won't let you, and because I'm an old man without much to lose. I've had a good life. And I will fuck you over and die before telling you, and you'll never know. Believe me when I say that your associate has many secrets."

It all came down to trust. And that was the goddamned problem. Well, he'd already paid a quarter million. He was in up to his chest. "Colonel, just tell me this much— is he in some kind of trouble? Is that why he ripped me off? I don't want to kill him, and what you tell me could make the difference."

The old Russian took in a long breath, closed his eyes

for a moment, then said, "If I were in his position, I might do exactly the same thing. But thank God I'm not."

"What position is that?"

"Mr. Hertzog, you don't have time for this. I suggest you book yourself on a flight to Moscow. From there you can catch another flight to Khabarovsk."

"All right, but even if I catch up with the train, Bibby won't be traveling under his own name. He's an expert at getting docs, IDs, passports, you name it. How am I supposed to find him?"

"There will be several stops before you reach Vladivostok. Most passengers like to get out and stretch their legs for a short time. I'm sure he hasn't radically altered his appearance. And I'm sure you'll meet up with him on the platform somewhere."

Mad Dog raised an index finger to the old Russian's face and decided it was time to issue his bluff: "One of my men is a former Navy SEAL, a computer expert who can withdraw the money from your account as quickly as he deposited it." Billy Pope was good but not that good. "So I hope for your sake that your information is accurate. You already have enough pain in your life. You don't want me to bring more."

Mad Dog started for the door, knowing his words had little effect—except to make him feel slightly better.

"Mr. Hertzog? Wait a moment."

Mad Dog glanced curiously at the man.

"I know my daughter hired you, and you blame her for the deaths of your men. But did you ever get a chance to talk to her? I mean other than business?"

Mad Dog's tone softened, if only a little. "As a matter of fact, I did."

"What was she like?"

"Excuse me?"

"I spoke to her on the phone all the time, but I never got to really know her. I never knew she was working for Moscow Center. And when she went to America, she was lost to me forever. What kind of woman was she?"

Mad Dog was about to say, *She was a complete bitch,* but held back. The colonel was merely a father now, still grieving the loss of his daughter, still trying to connect.

Maybe a little personal information would gain him more of the Russian's trust, which in turn might gain him more information about Bibby down the line. "Your daughter was very beautiful and very persuasive. She was good at what she did. I was impressed when I met her. She told me that she bought that necklace because she had read about my experiences in Burma. She learned about *fei-ts'ui* jade. She was . . . a little quirky . . . like me. And again, she was very beautiful."

The colonel frowned, and Mad Dog understood why. He shouldn't have told the man that he'd wanted to fuck his daughter. "Was she a kind person?"

"That's tough to answer."

The colonel lowered his gaze. "I'm sorry, Mr. Hertzog. I just . . . did you know her own people killed her?"

"They weren't her people. They were Americans. My people. And they couldn't afford a security leak like that. Couldn't afford the media circus. She made her choices. She lived by them. And she died by them." Mad Dog sighed, then headed for the door.

"Good luck, Mr. Hertzog."

Luck? Shit. He'd need a lot more than that.

"You didn't think you had any privacy in there, did you?" asked Albert, who was waiting for him on the walkway. "He thinks the room is clean, but we're monitoring it again."

"I don't give a flying fuck what you chaps think about any of this bullshit. Just get me to the airport."

"Fuck you, Hertzog. Call yourself a cab." Albert stomped off toward his Peugeot.

"All right, man, come on. You said you'd do anything to help Bibby. Well, help me find him by driving me to Heathrow."

Albert rolled his eyes. "Okay, that is, if you don't mind driving with a homosexual."

"Gee, can you make a man who's just lost millions feel any worse?"

"Do I really look gay? Because I'm not gay. I've fathered two children."

"I don't care. Just drive."

The colonel watched Hertzog and Albert drive off, then stepped outside and called out to "Charles," the security man posted between the bungalows across the street.

MI6 kept the colonel under constant surveillance, but he had already struck a deal with the unusually friendly Charles: Cuban cigars for the occasional use of the man's satellite phone. It was a fine arrangement, but the colonel was running low on cigars and had thought he could use Hertzog's phone instead, but the bastard was too smart for that. So he would exhaust his cigar cache, then find some other way with which to bribe the underpaid guard.

Charles thought that he was merely making personal phone calls, not doing business, because the colonel and his friends had a very simple code. He'd reminded Charles that he was risking his job by doing this, but Charles shrugged off the risk. Foolish boy.

After taking his cigars, the young man handed over his phone, saying, "Who we calling this time, Colonel?"

"My uncle again. My cousin's friend is going to see him. It's a bit of a surprise."

"Oh, yeah?"

"He wrote me a letter," the colonel lied. "Your bosses let me read it."

The colonel dialed the number, waited, then, finally, his "uncle" answered. Of course they spoke in Russian, though the colonel suspected that Charles knew what they were saying.

"Hello, Uncle. Sorry to call before nine. How are you?"

"Fine," answered the man on the other end. "But one less glass of vodka would have helped."

"Or one more!" The colonel chuckled.

"Dear nephew, tell me why you've called."

"Some news. Our cousin's friend is coming to see you. He says he can't make it to Irkutsk in time for the big birthday party."

"Oh, that is too bad."

"Yes, but he will try to meet our other friends in Khabarovsk."

"I understand."

"You know, when he finds out how young those boys are and what wonderful birthday presents they have, he's going to be very jealous. He won't want them to get to Vladivostok."

"No, he won't. But maybe we can convince him to stay with us for a while. I think he might understand. And I'm sure it'll all work out for us, so long as everyone has a good time at the party."

"Yes. I just wanted you to know, Uncle."

"Thank you for calling. You are a fine nephew, and I look forward to seeing you very soon."

"Yes, that would be nice. Good-bye."

The colonel returned the phone, and the security man nodded and said, "Something big is going down in Irkutsk, eh?"

"My uncle's sixtieth birthday party. Over a hundred people have been invited."

Charles was hardly naive, but he didn't seem to care. "Sounds like quite a party. Too bad you can't attend."

The colonel drifted back toward his bungalow. "Yes, too bad. Enjoy your cigar."

Hunting Lodge
Southern End of Lake Baikal
Near Irkutsk, Russia
0805 Hours Local Time

Major Viktor Zakarova sat up in bed and rubbed the corners of his eyes.

Ekk knocked on the half-open door, then raised his chin. "Sir, I heard your phone ring."

Zakarova ignored the remark and instead asked, "Have you checked the train schedule?"

"Still on time."

"Good. Now I just got off the phone with Sinitsyna. He says the Brit has a friend who's come looking for him."

"Because the Brit stole the money he's using to pay us."

"Exactly. I'm sure the man in pursuit is Hertzog. If you recall, he founded IPG. Sinitsyna has done us a favor, though. Hertzog won't be in Irkutsk. He's headed to Khabarovsk."

"Then we've nothing to worry about."

"You young fool. You don't see the larger picture. If those warheads fall into the wrong hands—American or British hands—they could be traced back to us."

"But Hertzog is a mercenary."

"And an American. A former United States Marine."

"So you believe he would turn over the weapons to his government?"

"I'm not sure."

"I understand. We can send people to Khabarovsk to tie up the loose end there."

"The colonel already has people in place, but if they fail, we'll have to be ready."

"I think I understand where this is going. The warheads will never reach Vladivostok."

"No, they won't. And they won't be handed over to the Americans or Brits, either, of course. In the end, they will be loaded back onto our truck and be returned here."

"Meanwhile, we'll have a handsome reward for our efforts."

"And more candy to sell at a later date."

"Sir, this sounds like a brilliant plan. But we're going to need more time to consider the logistics."

"Ivan should be here soon with our man from AL-ROSA. Once he arrives, feed him, then we'll decide what our plan of action should be after Irkutsk."

"Yes, sir. But what about Sinitsyna? Will you send that team to England to rescue him?"

"The old colonel believes he's the mastermind behind all of this, only because he's made the right connections over the years, gathered the necessary intelligence, connected us with the necessary middlemen. But our assets are much greater than his. He's never understood that."

"So you're leaving him there to rot? I thought he was your friend. You told me—"

"I know what I told you. I might honor our deal eventually. However, if for some reason everything goes terribly wrong, the old colonel might confess his sins to the Brits, who've already paid him well."

"Is it too late to hire an assassin?"

"No need, Ekk. One of the colonel's guards works for

us. He's a corrupt soul who learned how to steal when he lived in St. Petersburg. He's got a penchant for cigars. I give the word, and he'll kill Sinitsyna immediately."

The lieutenant stood in awe. "You are the master-mind!"

"No, I am just a soldier who needs coffee, and God help you if it is bitter."

Ekk winced.

Somewhere in Ramallah
West Bank
0210 Hours Local Time

Kat and Waffa sat in a small, makeshift living room with just one small window allowing faint neon light from the street to filter through. She had begged him to make some coffee, and now sat in a small recliner as they waited for the drip pot to fill.

"Waffa, you've always been so careful and so discreet. What the hell happened?"

"One word: Hezbollah."

"The party of God," Kat said under her breath. She couldn't have been more sarcastic. "They tore up your café?"

"Yes."

"Where's Melissa?"

"Hiding. Like me. Safe now."

"I'm sorry. I'm really sorry."

"It's okay. I always knew that someday it would come to this. I've traded for too long and worked with too many scumbags. But you know? I think this is it, Kat. I think I'm going to leave Ramallah forever."

"But this is your home. You told me you would never leave."

"I know. I owe more to Melissa. You know she's pregnant."

"Oh my God. Congratulations."

"Thank you. So you know why I must go."

"Why don't you come to the Philippines with us? It's beautiful there. We could set you up as a liaison for IPG. Melissa would love it."

"That sounds good. I'll think about it."

They sat a few moments in silence as the coffeepot finally grew full and Waffa poured them a couple of mugs.

Kat took hers, breathed in the strong java, then took a long sip. "I've been awake for over twenty-four hours."

"I can see that."

"Waffa, I didn't just come to say hi."

"You never do."

She frowned. "Come on, that's not fair. You know how much I owe you. Everything."

"What do you need? I'm not sure I can help you now, since I'm hiding down here for a while, but we'll see."

"It's about Bibby."

Waffa glanced down into his mug. "How is that bird anyway?"

"He's flown off with thirty million of IPG's money."

For a few seconds Waffa didn't react. Then he suddenly burst into laughter. "That son of a bitch."

Kat's satellite phone began to ring. It was Michael. She sent his call directly to voice mail. "Waffa, we're looking for him. Any thoughts?"

"Well, you might try the Crown and Greyhound in London. That's one of his favorite pubs."

"Come on, Waffa. You know where he is. He's like me, one of your best friends in the world."

Waffa sat there, sipping his coffee, staring off into the distance. "You've put me in a difficult position."

Kat sighed. He had just admitted he knew something. "I'm sorry, Waffa. Is he in trouble?"

"Oh, yeah."

"How bad is it?"

"It's bad."

"Why didn't he come to me or Michael?"

"He would never do that. He's a very private man. No one gets too close, you know that."

"No one except you."

"Yeah, well, our friendship cost me a lot."

"What do you mean? Does Bibby have something to do with the café getting torched?"

"Indirectly, of course. I made a few bad deals, too."

"Please, Waffa, I'm begging you. Tell me where he is."

Waffa closed his eyes. "I made a promise."

London Heathrow Airport
Terminal 3
0214 Hours Local Time

Mad Dog called Kat once more, and once again the call went directly to voice mail. He wrung his hands, called Wolfgang back on Cebu Island.

"How's it going, boss?"

"Don't ask me that shit. Just get your ass on a plane. I need you in Vladivostok yesterday."

"Vladivostok? Where the fuck is that?"

"Read a map, asshole. It's in Russia."

"Oh, shit, it's going to take me forever to get there."

"I don't care. I need you. Pack a sat phone, spare batteries, small ruck. That's it."

"Weapons?"

"I'll have to set you up when you get there."

"What's the deal?"

Mad Dog filled him in regarding Bibby's little train ride.

"So why's he going there?"

"I don't know. But we gotta catch him before he gets to Vladivostok."

"Boss? Honestly, this sounds fucked up. Maybe the old Russian is dicking around with us."

"We got nothing else to go on, so it's worth a shot."

"All right. I'll get to Manila, see how many damned planes it'll take to get to Darth Vaderstock."

"Vladivostok. Please try to show up at the right place. Call me when you get there. I'll want you in position at the train station."

"What if there's more than one station?"

"I'll find out and call you."

"So Billy's gonna sit this one out?"

"Tell him to man the fort. I'll be calling. I'll need him. See if he can get a list of everyone on board the Rossiya Train Number 2 currently headed to Vladivostok. See if he can ferret out which alias Bibby might be using."

"Roger that, boss. You talk to Kat?"

"Not yet. She's sending my calls to voice mail. And oh, yeah, tell Dan to give Billy a hand, all right?"

"Uh, okay."

"Something wrong?"

"No, no. See you in Siberia. I've never said that before."

"Yeah, and actually meant it." Mad Dog hung up, dialed Kat again. Right to voice mail. "God damn it, answer!"

She needed to get her ass on a plane to Moscow ASAP if she was going to help. He'd already bought his ticket. If she could get on a nonstop flight from Tel Aviv, they'd both be in Khabarovsk in five to six hours.

Somewhere in Ramallah
West Bank
0420 Hours Local Time

Kat finally gave up on Waffa. Two hours of talk had yielded nothing but his apologies for not talking.

"Well, I wanted to get some ice cream before I left, but it's a little early."

"Stay longer."

"I can't. I have to go." She rose, and he did, too. They hugged.

"I hope you respect my decision."

"Yes, I do. I just hope what you're doing doesn't get someone killed."

He nodded. "Me, too."

Kat gave him one more hug, then he let her out, told her that Rashad and Nazir would meet her in the alley and give her a lift to the airport. She mounted the staircase, reached the top, then opened a small door and emerged outside—

To find both of Waffa's men lying in blood pools, their throats slashed.

Someone grabbed her from behind, and even as she whirled to free herself, she pulled out her credit card and slashed away, hitting a cheek, a neck, then moving her other hand toward cold metal, a gun in her assailant's hand.

To her right a pair of men wearing balaclavas covering all but their eyes rushed into the basement, pistols drawn.

She dropped the credit card, got both hands on the pistol. "Waffa! Get out! Get out!"

Chapter 4

....

Somewhere in Ramallah
West Bank
0425 Hours Local Time

The silenced pistol went off with a thump, the round striking the stone wall behind them.

Kat slid her leg around the man's leg and tripped him to the dirt, even while maintaining her death grip on the gun.

Christ, he wouldn't let go. She fell on top of him, slammed her knee into his groin. He gasped, tried to roll, but she held him back, muscles tensing. In a few seconds he would break free.

Fuck it. She moved one hand, lunged forward, got her teeth on his hand, bit down and drew blood, grimacing over the sickly sweet taste.

He screamed, released the gun, which she wrenched away then put to his head.

Bang, point-blank shot.

As a blood mist settled on her arm, the guy jerked once more, then his jaw dropped and his tongue slid limply between his teeth.

She stole a breath and climbed off of him, raced toward the basement, stumbled down the stairs.

Two thumps came from silenced pistols, followed by a triplet of loud fire, an AK-47, shots ricocheting off the wall on either side of the entrance, brass casings chinking off the floor, the stench of gunfire thick in the room.

The big metal door was wide open—

And there was Waffa, lying on the floor in a pool of blood, the rifle tucked under his arm, his two attackers splayed across the floor to his right. He'd been shot twice in the chest, near his heart. He was panting, barely able to breathe, his lungs no doubt filling with blood.

Kat ran forward, put a bullet in each guy's head before nearing Waffa.

He's dying . . .

She broke into tears as she crouched beside him, cradled his head.

He glanced up at her, coughed up blood. "You know what to tell Melissa."

"Yeah, but how will I find her?"

"She'll find you."

"Okay."

"And I'll tell you about Bibby. Everything."

But Kat couldn't have cared. He had minutes left, maybe less, and there wasn't a god damned thing she could do about it. He opened his mouth . . . and then . . . he was gone.

She rocked him gently for a moment, the force of gravity tripling, pinning her to the floor, the lightbulb flickering, a massive void opening deep inside her.

Then, struck by a bolt of self-preservation, she set him down, rose, and charged out of the room.

*   *   *

Two minutes later she was running through the predawn streets of Ramallah, her clothes bloodstained, her eyes red and swollen. She had yet to spot a taxi. The sat phone rang. She stopped at a corner and answered.

"Where the fuck have you been? Jesus Christ!"

"Shut up!" she told Michael. "Just shut the fuck up!" She was crying through her words.

"Kat, calm down. Tell me."

"Waffa's dead."

"Are you all right? What happened?"

"They, uh, they torched his café. He was hiding out—"

"Who torched the place?"

She tried to explain through her labored breath, her tears, her swirling thoughts. Her pulse began to race. More Hezbollah would be coming for her.

She knew she wasn't being paranoid. Kill a few thugs, wake up a mob, and they wouldn't be quick with her.

"Hold on!" She spotted a lone cab moving slowly down the empty street, flagged down the driver, jumped in, told him to take her to the airport.

"Waffa knew where Bibby is, but he never told me," she told Mad Dog from inside the taxi. "He wanted to at the end, but—" She choked up.

"It's okay, Kat. I got it out of the colonel. Cost us a fortune, but Bibby's in Russia, on a train. We can catch up with him, but I need you in Moscow. Get a flight to . . . shit, if I can pronounce it, Sheremetyevo Airport."

She sniffled, rubbed her eyes. "Okay, I'll call you when I get to the airport in Tel Aviv. I'll let you know how soon I can meet you."

"Just hang on, okay?"

"I think this all has to do with Bibby. Waffa getting killed, everything. It's all his fucking fault!"

"Easy. Deep breaths. You get to the airport, you get the fuck out of there. You meet me in Moscow."

"Okay." She hung up.

The driver, a lanky bearded man who had horrible teeth and was blind in one eye, said in broken English, "You want to go to hospital? You have injury."

"I said the airport. I don't have injury."

He glanced back at her again. "Okay, but still, you have injury, maybe, inside . . . " He tapped his heart.

"Yeah, okay, you're right. Just please drive."

She threw her head back on the seat, closed her eyes a moment, then just sat there, breathing, not realizing that she was so emotionally and physically spent that her body couldn't take any more.

Within a minute she was fast asleep.

She awoke to a hand on her leg, which immediately made her jolt. The driver smiled. "Airport is here. Time to go." She swatted away the asshole's hand and burst from the cab.

After paying him, she reached into her knapsack and withdrew the pistol she'd stolen from the guy who attacked her. She handed it to the driver. "Tip," she said.

He took the gun, looked it over. "Nice. Not so good to bring on the airplane."

"No," she said. "Not so good."

Then, out of nowhere, it dawned on her that she hadn't told Michael about Dan's death. Okay, she would wait until she met him in Moscow, tell him in person, be there for him when he needed her.

The driver tucked the pistol under his seat, then waved good-bye.

As Kat headed toward the terminal, her satellite phone rang. She didn't recognize the number. "Hello?"

"Kat. It's me."

Her jaw nearly hit the pavement. "Bibby? Where are you? What the fuck are you doing?"

"I assume you're trying to find me."

"No, shit! How could you do this?"

"I can't explain. Just don't come looking for me, please. I don't want that on my conscience, all right?"

"Waffa's dead. Did you know that? Now you've got that on your conscience!"

"Oh, God."

"Bibby, what are you doing? For God's sake, what is it?"

"Don't come, Kat. You'll regret it."

And he was gone.

She just stood there, dumbfounded, the concrete sucking her down, and there was no escape.

"Excuse me?"

She glanced up.

It was her cab driver. "I want to take you to hospital."

After a weak grin, she shook her head, took off running for the bank of glass doors and the ticket counter beyond.

**Ninoy Aquino International Airport
Manila, the Philippines
1025 Hours Local Time**

Tommy Wolfgang boarded the plane bound for Seoul, South Korea, not feeling one bit guilty about spending Mad Dog's money to buy himself a seat in first class. Fly five hours in coach? Sca-rew that.

Didn't matter to Wolfgang that the company had just lost thirty million. Well, it kind of did, but the way he figured it, if Mad Dog went out of business, they'd all find other work. Not too many assholes in the world were willing to do the kind of shit they did. Or at least he liked to believe so. Hell, they could all go work for one of the big outfits. They even had their own websites.

Ah, maybe not. That would suck. Like Mad Dog always said, working for the big companies was just like being back in the military. Same red tape. Same bullshit.

All right, time to relax, he told himself, but he wasn't looking forward to the second leg of his journey: another two hour flight from Seoul to Vladivostok, with a two hour layover in between.

Air travel: It was a violation of God's laws, and all human beings were going to hell for challenging the Almighty. If God had wanted people to fly, he would have shoved tail rotor assemblies up their asses and booted them from tree limbs with the command, "Fly!"

All of which was to say he wasn't a happy flier, never had been, never would be. Especially flights out of Manila, where you glanced over your shoulder and into the eyes of some asshole Islamic militant who'd spent his weekend banging hookers and building bombs. Sca-rew that shit, too.

He wasn't suspicious. Not him. Wolfgang craned his neck. Which one of those assholes back there was plotting to blow up the plane? Had to be at least one of them on board. *Fuck . . .*

After a few more deep breaths, he settled into his seat, stretched out his legs. It could be worse, he told himself. He could be trapped inside a sunken refrigerator with no way to get out. He shuddered off the childhood memory.

The flight took off, and once they reached their cruising altitude, Wolfgang fired up his computer, thought of doing some research, but instead played a game of solitaire while he maintained surveillance on the cabin. He chatted briefly with the attendants, didn't even flirt, ate his bologna sandwich he'd packed in advance, then got off in Seoul after a pretty good flight, no complaints,

thank you. *Though, honey, you're a flight attendant . . .
smile a little more . . .*

He sat around the airport in Seoul, looking at all the
shit they had for sale and wondering why Korean men
were so damned short. He left a message for Mad Dog,
then finally boarded an old Tupolev-154 operated by
Vladivostok Air. The cabin on the Tù-154 was run-down
and noisy, but the seat felt pretty good. It took a long
time to reach cruising altitude, but he figured the piece
of shit wouldn't crash, at least not until they made their
final approach.

So he took a little snooze, woke up, added three hours
to his watch, and then, *thump-thump, whoosh,* they
landed. Some old Russian broad fell down in the aisle on
the way out. Vodka . . .

Wolfgang got off and looked around at the bare-bones
airport, like something out of the 1960s. He'd been to
Russia before, but never this far east. Everything looked
third-worldish. He lifted his voice and said, "What a
dump! Where the hell can I get a cup of coffee?"

An old man and his wife who had been seated a few
rows back shook their heads at him and muttered something in Russian. He smiled back, which got them even
madder, then he reached for his sat phone and started
off.

Rossiya Train Number 2
Trans-Siberian Express
En Route to Vladivostok
1335 Hours Local Time

Erik Gorlach had lied to Svetlanov when he said he
didn't want to have sex with Hannah. Mykola had lied as
well, and as Gorlach leaned back in the easy chair, he

imagined himself with his boss's girlfriend, and thought what a wonderful time they would have.

In fact, for the past two days he had repeatedly fantasized about her, and now, as they neared the city of Omsk, he pictured himself in yet another scenario where he was her master and she begged for him.

"What are you smiling about?" asked Mykola.

Gorlach shuddered. "Nothing."

"I don't believe you."

"Did you tell Bratus to come back here?"

"Don't change the subject."

"Did you tell him?"

"Yes, I did. He'll be here in a moment."

"Good." Gorlach pulled out his cell phone, called Svetlanov. "He's on his way."

"What's going on?" Mykola asked.

"Why don't you go get us some tea?"

"I'm not thirsty."

"I am. Go!"

Mykola frowned, slid open the door and started into the corridor just as Bratus, a much heavier man, slid into the room, with Svetlanov pushing in behind him. Bratus had deftly fired the RPG round that pierced the armored car's windshield. He was very good with weapons, if not with reading people.

"Okay," said Svetlanov, dropping an arm across Bratus's shoulders. "Let's talk."

The big man looked confused, nodded, and dropped down into the easy chair. "Do you have a special job for me?"

Gorlach drew in a deep breath, eyeing Svetlanov, who leaned over Bratus and said softly, "Why do you want to steal from me?"

"Steal from you?"

"Yes. Gorlach tells me that you've been plotting with him to steal my diamonds. Is that true?"

Bratus looked to Gorlach, his expression a cross between fear and the recognition that he'd just been betrayed. "He's lying! He's the one who wants to kill you! He recruited me!"

"No, he's been working for me, testing all of you. And you know, Bratus, I can't have employees who are not honest, not loyal, especially when temptation is all around us."

The man nodded, swallowed, began to rise—

But Gorlach had moved quickly, and slapped Bratus back into the seat. During the past day, Gorlach had tried to persuade the others to help him kill Svetlanov and steal the diamonds. Only Bratus had come forward.

"You don't look well," Svetlanov told Bratus.

"Oh, let's get this over with." Gorlach thumbed the switch on his blade and with a quick thrust drove it home, into Bratus's heart. "A terrible waste of time and training."

Svetlanov sighed in disgust. "His heart wasn't in it," he said, then laughed at the bad pun.

Bratus gasped, reached for Gorlach's hand, but his grip faltered and he slowly went limp.

"Don't make a mess," said Svetlanov. "Wrap him up like a Christmas package. We'll dump him off at the next stop. I've made arrangements with the provodniks."

"Good."

"Make sure the others learn what happened. This will send a powerful message to them."

"Of course. That was our idea from the start."

Svetlanov placed a hand on Gorlach's shoulder. "You are a cruel and evil man. I despise people like you."

Gorlach wasn't sure how to respond.

Then Svetlanov added, "But I need you. And I will reward you."

As Svetlanov left, Gorlach withdrew his blade and turned, seeing Mykola enter the cabin with tea in hand. His eyes bulged.

"Put that down and give me a hand!" ordered Gorlach.

"You've killed Bratus!"

"You're next if you don't help!"

Svetlanov returned to his compartment, where he found Hannah reading her book. If she wasn't doing that, she was listening to her iPod, repainting her nails, or blogging on her laptop.

She looked up. "Where did you go?"

"For a talk."

"Was it a good talk?"

"Yes."

"I'm bored."

"I know. Should we have a talk?"

That shocked her. "Well, yes!" She tossed her book aside, some piece of crap by a man named Sartre, and rose from the bed. "What do you want to talk about?"

Svetlanov glanced to his small bag, inside of which lay the two bars of soap containing the diamonds. Yes, he had caught her before she washed with one of them, and she still thought it strange that he'd become so angry. He told her that he got rashes if he didn't use his special soap and didn't want her touching it.

He came over to the bed, forced her back down. "I was wondering if you love me yet."

She narrowed her gaze on him. "You're testing me."

"Why not?"

"You shouldn't."

"No, I mean why don't you love me yet? Because if

you did, you would have said, 'Yes, of course, why do you ask?'"

"I don't love you yet because—"

He gripped her chin, raised his brows.

"Because you scare me."

"Me?" He released her chin, then stroked her cheek. "I'm not that way."

"What's so important about Irkutsk?"

"What do you mean?"

"I heard you talking to Gorlach. What's going to happen in Irkutsk?"

"Nothing important. Don't worry about it."

"I am. We're not going to a wedding, are we?"

Svetlanov stiffened. "Hannah, do you think I would lie about all of this?"

She shrugged.

"All right," he said, lowering his voice. "I have some business in Irkutsk, and it might be a little complicated. But don't you worry."

"I am worried. Make me feel better." She grabbed him by the head and pulled him down on top of her.

Sheremetyevo Airport
Moscow
1050 Hours Local Time

Mad Dog had been in Moscow for two days, spending one night at a nearby hotel, then taxiing back to the airport. His flight out of Heathrow was delayed because of a mechanical problem, and Kat's flight out of Tel Aviv was delayed nearly twenty-four hours because of a bomb scare, followed by yet a second bomb scare. Kat had been freaking out on the phone. He'd never heard her like that before, and she'd unnerved him. At least she was supposed to land within a half hour. Hopefully, they wouldn't bust her chops too much going through customs.

At the same time, he'd been keeping tabs on the train. Once Kat arrived, their flight from Moscow to Khabarovsk would take about seven hours, and the train was still nearly four days away from reaching there. They'd have plenty of time to prepare. Shit, they could even have fish and chips and curse the exaggerating colonel while they were at it. Mad Dog even thought of jumping the gun and trying to intercept Bibby at Krasnoyarsk, where the Brit was supposed to board in about twenty hours. They'd check the flights to see if that might be possible.

But then again, he had already made arrangements with an old arms dealer buddy to have Wolfgang armed in Vladivostok and the weapons delivered to them in Khabarovsk. Wolfgang was already in place, so worst case scenario was that he alone would have to capture Bibby.

Yep, that was worst case.

At the moment, Mad Dog was seated opposite a bank of duty free shops and stalls, most of them devoted to the sale of Lay's potato chips and alcohol. A few of the stands were shaped like boats, painted bright blue, with large wagon wheels affixed to their sides. Women dressed in brightly colored aprons spent more time arranging and rearranging their displays than selling anything.

He checked his watch. Shit. More time to kill. He'd been wrestling with calling someone who might provide significant help, but he could already hear the laughter ringing in his ears.

Aw, hell, he had nothing to lose. His pride, along with his thirty million, was already gone. He dialed the man's sat phone number, doubted the asshole would even have the thing turned on. Waste of time.

Eureka. It rang. And small miracle, Mr. James Moody, a model representative of the Central Intelligence Agency, a hero for all ages, answered with, "Hertzog? Is that you, you fuck? Why the fuck are you calling me? Do you know what time it is here? Jesus Christ!"

"Where the hell are you? A'stan?"

"No, I'm in New York."

"Then fuck you. You're only eight hours ahead of me. It's dinnertime."

"Where the hell are you?"

"Moscow."

"Oh, shit. I don't want to hear this."

"I got a little job for you, if you're interested."

"I told you I'm not retired yet, and I'm not taking any work from you. I'm tired of bailing you out."

"Hey, dude, if Bibby's friends from MI6 hadn't come along, you'd be lying facedown in the Amu Darya."

"That's speculation. You strike that shit from the record."

"Listen, Jimmy Judas, one back-stabber to another—I'm fucked. I need help. Can you throw me a bone?" After a moment of silence, Mad Dog asked, "You still there?"

"Yeah, I'm just waiting for the shock to wear off. I can't believe you're asking for my help."

"Help doesn't include sarcasm, all right, asshole?"

"Well, there you are again, calling for Jimmy *Jesus*. But you forget that I still hate you for how you fucked me over back in A'stan, ruined everything I had going there by stealing all that money, which you used to start your company. I had warlords in my pocket. I had control of the situation."

"That's water under the bridge."

"Under the bridge? Shit, you pissed on my boots."

"What do you want from me, an apology? Fuck off."

"This from the shitbird calling for help."

Mad Dog opened his mouth, thought better of his reply. "Look, just hear me out. Bibby's taken off with thirty million of my money."

"Whoa, that's a nice piece of change, and technically some of that money is mine."

"Just shut up. Now listen. Bibby's on a train here in Russia, Trans-Siberian, and he's heading to Vladivostok. I have to catch up with him, find out why he took my money, and force his sorry ass to give it back."

"What did he do? Transfer it into one of his personal accounts?"

"Yeah."

"So you guys play the same game. Transfer it back."

"Bibby's got it locked tight. He's the expert."

"So it's clear he hasn't spent the money yet."

"No, it's not. All we know is he made the transfer. If he's already spent the money, then I'll probably kill him. Bottom line: I want him alive, then I'll be the judge, jury, and executioner."

"Don't admit that shit to me. And like you said, he saved my life. Saved yours, too. And hey, you got intel links. Call in your favors. Maybe he's just screwing you over and building his retirement. I mean I heard your benefits package sucks. Can you blame him?"

"No, that's not it. He's in trouble. It's got something to do with Saratova's father."

"That Russian colonel being held by the Brits?"

"Yep."

"No, shit? This sounds more interesting. Maybe I'll do a little digging for you—if I find the time."

"You'll find it. And hey, more bad news. You know Waffa Zarour?"

"Everybody knows Waffa."

"You mean *knew*."

"Oh, don't give me that shit."

"Just happened a couple of days ago."

"You gotta be kidding me." Moody's voice cracked.

"We think he was killed by Hezbollah agents. No confirmation yet."

"Those motherfuckers."

"Kat thinks that Waffa died because of something he did for Bibby. We're not sure. But this sounds bad—which is why I'm calling in more muscle."

"Well, I'm glad to hear you call it that. I might be an old fucking spook, but there's some bad-ass firepower at my beck and call, eh?"

"Don't pat yourself too hard on the back."

"I won't. So now you want me to be your bitch? I don't know, Hertzog. Waffa was a good guy. If Bibby fucked him over, then maybe I'll help you get Bibby, whether he saved our asses or not."

"Why don't you hop on a plane and meet us out here?"

Moody snorted. "I'll do a little pointing and clicking, but you're not getting my ass to Russia. I'll call you back if I get anything earth-shattering. If I do, I'll sell you the intel real cheap."

"I knew I could count on you, Moody."

"You did?"

"Fuck no."

"Hertzog, do me a favor. Don't get whacked over there because I need someone like you to make me feel good about my life, okay?"

"For you? Anything. Roger that. Fuck you. Goodbye."

"Fuck you, too."

"Call me back."

"I will."

Mad Dog thumbed off the phone, then grinned. Well, that had gone better than expected. He felt his spirits lift a little as he went off to meet Kat at the gate.

Seeing her would make him feel better still.

But when she came down the ramp and passed through the doors, looking tired and drawn, she barely glanced up at him, as though she couldn't.

"Kat?" He marched right up to her, slid his arms across her shoulder and hugged her tightly.

"Michael."

"I missed you," he whispered in her ear.

She pulled back. "Please, let's sit down for a few minutes. There's something I need to tell you."

Chapter 5

....

Near Ground Zero
Church Street
New York City
2017 Hours Local Time

I t took CIA agent James Moody all of thirty minutes to set up a meeting with one of his colleague's informants, a Mr. Abdul-Mujib Abdulhalek.

When the bony, bearded man with a severely hooked nose wasn't driving a cab or flying back and forth to Lebanon for the CIA, he was going to Mets games, which disappointed Moody, a lifelong Yankees fanatic who couldn't understand why anyone would root for the Mets when you had God's chosen ones playing right here in New York.

So Moody and his misguided baseball fan informant met on the street, then walked a couple of blocks to a brand-new Starbucks.

Moody bought black coffee. Abdul-Mujib ordered some expensive, multisyllabic latte that even some English-speaking employees had trouble pronouncing, let alone a Lebanese immigrant. Nearly six bucks for it, too, shit, and of course, it was on his tab.

They sat. Moody wasted no time. "I need to know who killed Waffa Zarour. Do you know?"

"I heard about his café in Ramallah, but I didn't know he was killed. I heard he'd gone into hiding."

"Well, they found him. Hezbollah?"

"Could be. Waffa had many enemies, but he had more friends, people who would protect him. I'll find out who did this. If it was Hezbollah, then maybe it has something to do with the meetings they've been having in Tehran."

"What meetings?"

"Oh, they have had many these past few months. Waffa was passing information between them and the Iranians. Maybe he learned something he shouldn't have learned."

Moody nearly choked on his coffee. This was major intel, big stuff, and he couldn't believe that he hadn't heard about it already. "Does Rica know about this?" Moody was referring to his colleague who had more direct contact with Abdul-Mujib and was currently in Tel Aviv.

"Rica knows, but it's all very sensitive. We don't know why they've been meeting. Also, we know that Hezbollah has sent two spies to Haifa and more to Tel Aviv, and they have been sharing information with that third group in Tehran."

"Well, it's more than fucking coffee that's brewing." Moody lifted his head at the loud hiss of the cappuccino machine.

"I will find out who killed Waffa, but I need something."

"How much?"

"No, not money. You have already paid for this information. I need for you to come with me to the game tomorrow. I want you to watch the Mets kick the living shit out of Atlanta, the same way they are going to kill the Yankees in the World Series this year."

"You got tickets?"

The man smiled; it was an unfortunate smile. "I got two."

"Well, you got a deal! Except the Mets are going to get their asses kicked. Atlanta's got Rodriguez on the mound. Your boys don't have a prayer."

Abdul-Mujib raised his brows. "Say this with me. Slowly. Let's . . . go . . . Mets."

Moody cracked a broad grin. "Screw . . . you . . . Mets! Yankees rule! Kiss my ass!"

The Lebanese man shook his head vigorously. "You are very confused. Tomorrow, you will see the light."

"Nope, I'll just see some Mets ass-spanked pink."

Hertzog Residence
Holbrook, New York
September 22, 1976
1140 Hours Local Time

Thirteen-year-old Michael Hertzog, Jr. sat on the sofa, eating salami stacked on a hard roll and smothered with mustard. It was a good sandwich, not a great one. Only Dad knew how to make the great ones.

They had just come back from Dad's funeral, and Mom was busy with Aunt Rosemarie and Grandma and Uncle Jeff and Tommy, and all the other neighbors and friends from work who had come for the party afterward. Mom told him it wasn't a party, but Michael knew damned well that when you had food, liquor, and loudmouthed guests, you had a party. They were relieved that Dad had died. It had taken him two years, and during that time, Mom's hair had turned gray.

Dad had been a big, strong guy, a New York City cop, and it was hard for Michael to see him lying there, all scrawny and bald and pale and having a hard time just smiling.

That wasn't the way he wanted to remember his father, but part of him clung to that image, to the feeling of Dad's hand clutching his shoulder, to the sound of Dad's voice: "Michael, you're going to be okay. You're already a man. I taught you how to be a man. And you're going to be a great one. You're a leader. Never forget that."

"I'm a leader," Michael whispered to himself, then took another bite of his sandwich.

"What do you got there?"

Michael looked up. Dan Forrest was hovering over him, all sharp angles of navy blue with red trim. He was about Dad's age, and his mother lived next door. Michael had known Dan all his life, and always admired how perfect he kept his Marine Corps dress uniform.

"You mean the sandwich? I got salami."

"Any good?"

"Pretty good."

"You mind if I sit down?"

Michael shrugged.

Dan took a seat, though he never looked comfortable, never seemed to be at rest. He was now a gunnery sergeant, whatever that meant, and he had been to war, to Vietnam, Dad had said. Michael had always wanted to ask Dan if he'd ever killed anybody, but had yet to build up the nerve.

"I'm sorry about your father."

Michael nodded. "Everybody keeps saying that. But they didn't kill him. The cancer did."

"You want to go outside and play some catch? I got a football in my trunk."

"Okay."

They slipped out of the crowded house and wandered into the backyard, where Dan threw him some of the highest passes he had ever caught. It was great. After a half hour they took a break and sat on Dan's back porch. Dan brought out two bottles of beer, which scared Michael.

"Can I have Coke?"

"You never had beer before?"

"I took a sip once."

"Well, you drink this. Today we drink to your father."

Michael took the beer in his hands, the glass so sweaty that he nearly dropped it. "Mom was saying it was good that Dad got to see the bicentennial celebration."

"You're babbling. Don't be nervous. It's just a beer."

"Okay."

"Yeah, your dad was in the Navy. He loved his country. He wanted the best for his family." Dan held up his beer and motioned for Michael to do likewise. "To Michael Hertzog, Senior, one of the finest men I've ever known."

They tapped bottles, then took long sips. Michael wished that the beer tasted sweeter, but it wasn't too bad. He also wished for something else, something far more important:

"I wish my dad didn't die."

"Me, too. But that's what God wanted, so we accept it."

"Are you going to be my dad now?"

"What, and marry your mother?"

"I don't know."

Dan grinned, took another long swig of beer. "Later on, you want to go to the movies? There's a new one with Clint Eastwood. Just came out."

"Okay. But is it for adults?"

"Don't worry about it. I'll get you in."

Dan took him to see *The Outlaw Josey Wales* that evening, and he was struck by the story and by Clint Eastwood's performance. There was one line of dialogue that rang in his ears during the ride home:

When things look bad, and it looks like you're not gonna make it, then you gotta get mean. I mean plumb, mad dog mean. 'Cause if you lose your head and you give up, then you neither live nor win. That's just the way it is.

On the way home in the car, Michael kept repeating those words over and over so he wouldn't forget them. And when they got home, for some reason he started crying, maybe because he'd been holding it in all day, he wasn't sure.

Dan came over to him, put both hands on his shoulders and said, "It's okay to cry now, kid. Because I know you're tough, tough as your dad, tough as us Marines."

Sheremetyevo Airport
Moscow
Present Day
1220 Hours Local Time

Mad Dog's eyes burned, but it wasn't okay to cry this time. Or at least that's what he wanted to believe.

Kat kept asking him if he was all right.

After the third time he hollered, "God damn it, stop asking!"

"Sorry." She whirled away from him.

He grabbed her, and she tugged free. "Look, it's just—"

"I know." She faced him, pursed her lips. "What do you want to do?"

He stood there. He should say fuck the money and go home and bury the man who had been his father.

Or he should just hold off a little while longer. Or maybe he could go himself. No, he couldn't leave this up to Kat and Wolfgang. He had to be involved. It was his company, his money. If one of them died trying to recover it, he would never forgive himself.

But he felt terrible for not rushing home to pay his last respects.

"Michael?"

He shuddered out of his thoughts. "Do me a favor. Call Pope. Dan's will is in my safe, same one Wolfgang was in. I made all the arrangements. He'll be buried at Arlington. Tell Pope he's . . . he's going to have to take care of it."

"Okay."

While she did that, he went to the rest room, splashed cold water over his face, glanced at the man in the mirror.

Worn-out. Tired. Pathetic.

When things look bad, and it looks like you're not gonna make it, then you gotta get mean. I mean plumb, mad dog mean.

He took out a picture of his father that he kept in his wallet, held it up, saw how much he now resembled the man. Then he removed another photo, one of him and Dan in the Philippines.

You couldn't hang on for just a couple more weeks, you old fuck? I should've given you an order not to die before I left. I barely said good-bye.

He went back out, met Kat, who finished speaking with Pope, then said, "Billy's got us covered. He wanted you to know how sorry he is."

Mad Dog bit his lip, sighed.

"Anyway, the security guys at the Pound will give

him a hand, plus all the folks from the bank and the airport."

Mad Dog nodded. She knew just what to say to make him feel a little better. He started off toward the ticket counter, got on line, checked his watch.

"The colonel rushed us here," she said. "We have time. We don't have to get on the plane yet." She took his wrist, led him away from the line of people.

He swore under his breath. "What are you doing?"

"Let's go to a hotel. Spend the night. Get up in the morning and fly out. We'll be fresh. Like you said, Wolfgang's already in Vladivostok."

"And we're going to trust *him*? Shit, he's just insurance. Probably moping around there trying to get laid."

"Listen to me. Waffa's dead. Dan just passed away. I need sleep. Look at me."

He did. Her clothes were bloodstained, her hair a mess, her face sunken in. Jesus . . . she was right. They'd both been going nonstop for what felt like a week.

The spirit was willing, but the flesh had been beaten down so hard that he, too, couldn't take much more.

Her bloodshot eyes widened. "*Look* at me."

"I am. Okay."

With her hand still attached to his wrist, he led her outside, where they called a taxi, climbed in, told the driver which hotel.

A few minutes into the ride he began muttering to himself, and she asked what he was saying.

"Nothing. Just a line from an old movie."

"Why are you thinking about movies?"

"I don't know."

"Michael . . ."

"All right, so on the day we buried my father, Dan gave me my first beer, then he took me to the movies."

"Oh, yeah? What did you see?"

"Clint Eastwood flick. *The Outlaw Josey Wales*."

"I haven't seen it."

"You probably weren't even born then. Anyway, there's a line in the film . . . " He quoted it to her.

"So is that why they call you Mad Dog?"

"No, *they* didn't start calling me that. *He* did."

Hunting Lodge
Southern End of Lake Baikal
Near Irkutsk, Russia
21 Hours Later
1340 Hours Local Time

Major Viktor Zakarova stared at the truck carrying the two warheads.

A brilliant flash pierced his eyes, then the ground heaved as pieces of his flesh were torn from the bone.

And then he was pulverized, part of a massive detonation whose fallout would kill many more.

The history books would call him a criminal. Call him evil. A terrorist.

He returned his gaze to the truck.

A fine layer of snow had already collected on its cold hood. He craned his neck skyward, opened his mouth, caught a snowflake on his tongue.

His satellite phone rang. *Ah, the Brit.* "What is it you want now? I'm terribly busy, you know."

"I'm in Krasnoyarsk and I've just boarded the train. Do you know what carriage they are in?"

"No, I do not. I suggest you remain quiet and comfortable. If you attempt to do anything, they will, shall we say, ruin all of your plans. Do not make contact. Do you understand?"

"I will call you again, when I'm closer."

"I know you will."

The Brit hung up, and Zakarova glanced up again, caught another snowflake, as Ekk approached. "Sir? The train has just left Krasnoyarsk."

"Yes, I already know."

"Was that the Brit?"

"Yes, he's boarded the train."

"Then we'd better get moving. We don't want to be late."

Behind Ekk, their man Ivan and the diamond expert from ALROSA were already headed toward one of the trucks.

"In just a few hours we're going to be very wealthy men," said Ekk.

Zakarova nodded.

"You cannot smile over this?" asked Ekk.

"I look around, and this is paradise for me. The mountain, the lake, the country. Hunting and fishing. No amount of money can replace this."

"Okay. Then we will leave you here. And I will accept your share."

Zakarova moved forward and with a broad grin gave Ekk a jab to the stomach. "Oh, you will? I don't think so."

Ekk held up his hands in surrender. "I'm not ready to lead this group yet."

"No, young man. You are not. Are the men armed?"

"Heavily."

"Good answer. Let's go."

Train Station
Vladivostok
1545 Hours Local Time

Wolfgang figured he'd spend half of his free time doing a thorough recon of the train station and its environs. He picked out several sniper positions, and was presently searching for some ambush and choke points.

The main station appeared to have been designed by Disney engineers. It was an alabaster white affair with fancy windows and spires and all kinds of castlelike shit. Real regal looking. There were names or a name for that kind of architecture, not that he knew anything about that. He could tell you exactly how to blow up the place, not design it.

Out front lay a bus terminal and a parking lot jammed with taxis and private cars. Two foot bridges took you from the station to the buses and lots, and Wolfgang had already noted how he could lay low behind the railings and spring upon any unsuspecting British motherfuckers who might've stolen thirty million dollars. Who knew? There could be more than one of the bastards. He needed to be ready.

The other half of his free time was spent warding off the pimps on the street who were trying to foist their prostitutes on him.

Damn, those punks took all the fun out of hunting down a woman, seducing her into bed. The skanky bitches in their little harems weren't worth his time, and he pitied them.

Adding insult to injury, his first attempt at actually picking up a woman had left him red-faced and frustrated. She turned out to be a tourist herself and assumed him to be a misguided schmuck looking for hookers.

He tried to explain that he was looking for a "nice girl, not a hooker," but she told him to "Fuck off" in perfect English, as they do in South Jersey, where she told him she was from.

Wolfgang shifted away from the bridge and back into the station, where he spotted a beautiful blonde with legs like sticks of butter pecan ice cream melting toward him. She wore a tight leather jacket and her hair was pulled back. She wore no makeup and didn't need any.

Oh, yeah, she was hot, and he was a heat-seeker. Wasn't a countermeasure in the world that could stop him. "Hello, I need some help. Can you help me?"

She faced him, stopped, frowned.

God, he wanted to jump her. But he was a gentleman—at least until they got back to his hotel room.

"What is problem?" she asked, her smoky, heavily accented voice sending a lighting bolt into his groin.

"I need some help to learn Russian. I'm going to be here for a few days. Can you help me? Please?"

She glanced at him like he was out of his mind, then uttered something, pinched his cheek, and sashayed off.

A short man with a slight paunch and thick gray moustache who'd been standing nearby with his newspaper glanced up and chuckled.

"What'd she say?" Wolfgang asked him in broken Russian.

"She said you have a nice chin, but your penis is probably too small," he replied in English.

"Bullshit."

"I learned English in school. My translation is good. And my dick is bigger than yours. Maybe I should go talk to her."

Wolfgang drew back his head, dumbfounded. "Fuck you."

The short man grinned even wider, lowered his voice. "Hey, motherfucker. I'm Yury Melnickov."

"You are? Fuck, dude, I'm not supposed to meet you for another hour."

"Dude, I like to see who I'm dealing with, and you are . . . well, you are a very entertaining man."

"You spotted me a mile away, didn't you?"

"Yes. Dumb-ass ugly American bothering women. Mad Dog told me that's how to find you."

"So, you going to show me what you have?"

"Yes, my car is out back. I will take you to where I keep my shop. I hope you have brought the cash."

"I have the deposit. The boss will pay you the rest when you see him down in Khabarovsk."

"Very well."

They moved away from the station, the decaying Soviet-era apartment blocks rising like gray and black teeth in the distance.

A group of about ten Russian sailors came toward them, all pimple-faced and peach-fuzzed.

"They come for the prostitutes," Yury explained.

"Poor guys. Those girls are nasty."

"They don't care. They get what they are looking for."

"Know what I'm looking for? A USP45CT. It's a compact .45 caliber handgun developed for SpecOps."

"That's an HK weapon."

Wolfgang grinned and nodded.

But Yury frowned. "What do you think I am, a fucking arms dealer?"

"Uh, excuse me, *yes*!"

"For what you assholes are paying, I should sell you arrows and slingshots!"

"Damn it, dude, what do you have?"

"You'll see. I don't think you'll be disappointed."

"Got any explosives?"

Yury stopped near his little car. "He didn't say anything about them . . ."

"I'm just curious. I might do a little shopping for myself."

"Well, if that's the case, then yes, I can offer you a few good choices."

"You have a gift card program? They come in handy during the holidays."

The Russian chuckled under his breath. "Of course. And we have a very good layaway program and a reward points card for frequent shoppers."

Wolfgang got a kick out of that. The guy knew his shit and was witty to boot.

Yury thumbed his remote and opened the car doors. "Now get in, my ugly American friend. I will show you Yul Brynner's old house."

"Who?"

"My God. The star of *The King and I* and *The Magnificent Seven*. He played the pharaoh in *The Ten Commandments* with Charlton Heston. He grew up here in Vladivostok."

"You mean the bald guy? 'So let it be written, so let it be done'?"

Yury made a face. "Yes, the bald guy."

Ararat Park Hyatt
Room 427
Moscow
0950 Hours Local Time

Mad Dog bolted upright in the bed. "Jesus Christ! What time is it?"

"It's nearly ten o'clock," said Kat. "Relax. The train is days away from Khabarovsk."

"I had a dream we missed it."

"Well, we didn't. I'll pull up the schedule on my computer."

The satellite phone rang. Kat answered. It was Wolfgang. She handed the phone to him.

"What's up, Wolfgang?"

"Hey. Your buddy Yury is a real character."

"So are you. Everything go okay?"

"Oh, yeah. He's the candy man. And the candy man can."

"Remind him he's supposed to meet us in Khabarovsk. Tell him I'll call when we get there."

"Where are you now?"

"Still in Moscow."

"You get delayed? Customs?"

"No, we're just exhausted."

"Well, the train's not even in Irkutsk yet. Did Pope find out if Bibby's on board?"

"Haven't heard from him yet, but now I'm guessing Bibby's got those tracks well covered."

"What a fucking traitor. I never trusted that asshole. I knew there was something about him."

"Keep an open mind."

"If you say so. Anything else you need me to do while I'm waiting?"

"Stay out of jail. Don't pick up any diseases."

"Roger that. I'll talk to you soon."

"Wolfgang?"

"Yeah, boss?"

"You knew Dan passed away. Why didn't you tell me?"

"Uh, I don't know. You got a lot on your mind. I figured Kat was the one."

After a long, awkward moment to consider that, Mad Dog said, "All right. Thanks."

"You're pissed?"

"No, not all. Be good." Mad Dog hung up, lifted his weary gaze to Kat. "Last night was the first time we slept together and didn't have sex."

"Get used to it."

"We're not married yet."

"You're proposing?"

"I thought I did that already? You said no."

"I said nothing. You never asked."

"Second thing that goes. Where's my Viagra?"

"We might've lost thirty, or is it forty million, including the necklace? But we haven't lost our sense of humor."

"If I don't laugh, I'll cry." Mad Dog rubbed the sleep grit from his eyes. "Let's get Pope on the horn. I want an intel update. See what Big Booty has for us, too. And did I tell you I called our bestest buddy with the CIA?"

"You did? Why?"

"I told him the truth, and I asked for help."

"Are you kidding? He won't help us."

"Don't be so sure. I think he's coming around. I think after all these years he's beginning to like me."

Kat put her hand on his forehead. "Yup. You're feverish, delusional. Very sad."

He pulled her in close, was about to kiss her, then said, "What if Bibby gets away?"

"He won't."

"How you can be so sure?"

"Because I know you. You'll hunt him across the entire planet if you have to, because it's not about the money anymore. He was a good friend who lied, and that broke your heart."

"Oh, don't fucking put it that way."

"It's true."

"No, it's not. He stole my fucking money!"

"And broke your heart."

"Yeah, whatever!"

"When you catch up to him, don't kill him. Make him tell you why. He owes you that. He owes all of us that."

Mad Dog drew in a long breath and made the promise to himself. "I will."

The sat phone rang. The number quickened his pulse. "Speak of the devil," he told Kat, then thumbed the button to answer. "Hey, asshole, do you know what time it is here?"

"Listen to me, Hertzog. No fucking around. I have an informant in New York. His people say it was Hezbollah that killed Waffa. His information has already proven very reliable."

"Waffa knew they were after him. No big surprise there."

"Yeah, yeah, but you told me Bibby's on a train, heading to Vladivostok. My informant tells me that last week Hezbollah sent two agents to Krasnoyarsk. And that's a stop along the Trans-Siberian route."

"Did you say Krasnoyarsk?"

"Yeah, did I mispronounce it? Or does that mean something to you?"

"That Russian colonel in London? Saratova's father? He told me that's where Bibby was boarding the train."

"So maybe Bibby and Hezbollah are on board? Are they working together?"

"I can't believe that. I won't."

"There's one other story coming out of Moscow. You're there. You should've seen something about it."

"We've been holed up in our hotel room, trying to de-lag. Haven't watched TV or read a paper."

"So you don't know about the diamond heist?"

"No. Tell me."

"Twenty million in polished stones were taken from a courier. Really sophisticated attack on the armored car. A few witnesses guessed it was the Russian mafia. They pulled it off in broad daylight. Seems to me the timing on all of this is way too coincidental."

"Maybe Bibby's trying to buy the diamonds? Maybe he's trying to pay off Hezbollah? Maybe he and Hezbollah are trying to get the diamonds from the mafia?"

"We already have a copy of the train's passenger list. Langley will coordinate with the FSB in Russia to see if they can identify any known Russian mafia members, and if they can, then there's a good chance those rocks play into all of this."

"Good deal. You'll call me back?"

"We haven't discussed my fee."

"I'm fucking broke."

"Then why did you check into a five-star hotel?"

"Why are you keeping fucking tabs on me?"

"Just shut up. I'm working pro bono here."

Mad Dog hung up and looked at Kat. "Shit. Even Moody's helping for free. That means there's more to this than he's saying."

"I told you what Bibby sounded like on the phone."

"Come on. Let's get the hell out of here. We have a plane to catch."

Chapter 6

· ·

Southern End of Lake Baikal
En Route to Irkutsk
1635 Hours Local Time

The truck carrying the two warheads rolled down the uneven and unforgiving mountain trail, its rear end fishtailing now and again as it hit ruts and challenged the occasional mound cutting across the path.

Major Victor Zakarova rode in the second truck, along with his man Parshin and the driver, Ekk. Off to their left lay Lake Baikal, visible through the tall stands of trees whose limbs were already growing white and beginning to sag.

He checked his watch. They were not making good time, because the snow had begun to fall much more heavily and the road was now icy and slick. Worse, the heater did a poor job of warming the cab, and Zakarova repeatedly covered his face with his gloved hands and exhaled to stave off the chill.

They came around another bend, and abruptly the ground grew more tortuous, switching back twice, then shifting once more, always descending.

Ekk switched on the windshield wipers as the wind picked up, blowing snow fiercely across the hood. It was only half past four in the afternoon, but the storm cast the entire mountainside in gloom. For a few moments Zakarova lost sight of the truck ahead—

Then suddenly it came up on them.

"He's stopped!" cried Parshin.

Ekk's voice cracked as he slammed on the brakes. "What's he doing?"

Zakarova reached for his cell phone, already knowing there was no time for him to make the call or time for Ekk to stop the truck.

"Cut the wheel!" Parshin yelled.

"Don't hit him!" warned Zakarova.

The tires locked, and even as Ekk veered to avoid the truck, they slid across the ice, sideswiped the tail end of the other truck, then caromed toward a stand of trees.

Ekk rolled the wheel once more, battling against the slide as Parshin and Zakarova screamed that he do it, and the truck spun around, coming to a sudden and pulse-pounding stop without hitting a single tree.

"Sir, are you all right?" asked Ekk.

Ignoring the lieutenant, Zakarova vaulted out of the truck as Ekk threw it in Park, before jumping out of the truck himself. Zakarova ran back toward the road, squinting through the snow. What he saw sent a shudder down his spine.

The truck carrying the nuclear warheads had lurched forward, hit yet another patch of ice, and begun sliding down the trail, the driver unable to stop. They were still skidding as Zakarova reached the road. He watched in horror as the truck turned lazily to the left, broadsiding a pair of trees standing closest to the trail edge. The concussions and shattering glass echoed through the mountains and seemed to cut into Zakarova's gut, even as the wind cut across his face.

"Get down there!" he ordered Parshin, his breath thick in the air. "Ekk? Bring the truck around!"

As Zakarova backhanded snow from his brows, he started for the truck, eager for the driver's explanation for stopping dead in the middle of the trail during a snowstorm.

Rossiya Train Number 2
Trans-Siberian Express
Nearing Irkutsk
1640 Hours Local Time

Gorlach couldn't help but sense that a man sitting in the back of the restaurant carriage was watching them. He leaned over to Mykola and said, "Do you see him back there?"

"Which one?"

"The skinny one with glasses."

"Yes, I see him. He's an Indian or an Arab. I will go talk to him."

"No, you fool. Let's wait until he leaves. Then we'll follow."

Mykola nodded, then glanced down at his plate. "Why is the food so expensive and so horrible?"

"We should have listened to Svetlanov. He buys all of his food on the platform."

"But he has the provodniks cooking it for him. What do we have?" Mykola shook his head in disgust.

Gorlach leveled his index finger on him. "We have you."

"Oh, really?" Mykola folded his arms over his chest. "I will not cook, especially for you. Get a wife."

"He's getting up," said Gorlach, his gaze never leaving the skinny man, who was paying his bill.

"I don't know. Maybe he is gay. He thinks you have a nice ass." Mykola chuckled heartily.

But Gorlach was in no mood. "I think our friends in Lebanon have sent someone to keep an eye on us. Let's go see if I'm right."

"Okay."

They rose, and Mykola paid the bill while Gorlach headed down the aisle, after the man, who wore expensive slacks, and a long, black leather coat tied tightly at the waist.

Gorlach gave the man enough of a lead, paused as he moved between carriages, then quickly followed, opening the door and shuddering as an icy blast of air struck his face, along with the snow.

Gorlach seized the ice-cold door handle of the next car and hurried inside.

For a second he lost the man. Then . . . there he was, moving quickly down the aisle, squeezing past several women. If he didn't hurry, he knew he'd lose him.

He picked up the pace, shifted past the women, realized that the man was moving outside again, to the next carriage. So far he hadn't looked back, but Gorlach assumed his luck would soon run out.

Taking a deep breath, he broke into a jog down the aisle, drawing the cries of a provodnik who ordered him to slow down, then cursed in his wake.

Reaching the door, Gorlach wrenched it open, started for the next one—

When a hand lashed out, seized his arm and yanked him to the side, His senses were assaulted by the cold, the snow, the racket of the train, the sudden and needling pressure on his forehead: a gun!

And then another surprise.

He was not being held by the skinny man in the leather jacket but by another man with thicker spectacles, a shaved head, deep blue eyes, and pale skin.

He was about a head taller than Gorlach, and when he spoke, it was not in Russian, but in English, with a heavy British accent.

"Does Svetlanov have the diamonds?"

"Ya tvoyu mamu yebal pakimis tye smotrel i plakal kak malinkaya sukam," responded Gorlach through his teeth.

He had just told the Brit, "I fucked your mom while you watched and cried like a little bitch."

Apparently, the Brit understood him, and in Russian, responded, *"Poshol nahuj!"*

"Fuck you, too," Gorlach said in English, then shifted his gaze to the right, to the tracks speeding by, the blinding snow.

"You'll die if you don't answer me."

"Who are you?" Gorlach asked.

"Where is Svetlanov right now? Is he with his girlfriend?"

"I don't know. You'd better kill me."

Just then Mykola pulled open the door, and Gorlach fell back, toward his colleague, even as he was reaching around to the back of his waistband, where he'd tucked his pistol.

The Brit's weapon thumped and flashed.

Gorlach looked back, saw blood dripping from Mykola's head a second before the man collapsed. Then he turned back to face the Brit, or rather the Brit's pistol as the man brought up an arm—

He fired, but Gorlach only felt a sharp pinch in his arm as he reached for the man and wrapped his hands around the Brit's wrist, trying to pry the gun free. The

Brit exploited that moment to pull him up, turn him sideways, then force him to edge of the railing between carriages.

Gorlach felt a knee in his groin, then a powerful shove sent him toppling over the rail—

And into the air.

He fell backward, gazing up into the swirling clouds of snow, his arm now on fire, his breath gone, the train rattling so loudly that it became the only sound in the universe, muting even his pulse.

Oddly, his thoughts did not turn to his own safety, but to the fact that he had remained loyal to Svetlanov, that if he hadn't, he and Bratus could have stolen the diamonds, taken off, and he would not at that moment be plunging through air, headed toward perhaps his demise or worse, a broken back that might leave him paralyzed.

Yes, for a few moments he had entertained the notion of stealing the diamonds, though he'd thought that his loyalty to Svetlanov would never wane.

Another second of just the train thundering by, and he sensed the ground coming up on him fast. He gasped—

Then hit the snow-covered earth and broke into a roll down a slight embankment.

In that instant, he knew he wouldn't die, that his arms and legs worked, that he could come out of the roll. And after several more revolutions he did, sat there a few seconds, then got onto his hands and knees and looked up.

The world tipped on its axis, then leveled off. The train continued to clank on by, and he knew he had only seconds to get up, try to catch it.

The snow was blinding now, the wind lashing at him so hard that for a moment he thought it might knock him back down. He rose unsteadily to his feet, took a first step, nearly collapsed, then cursed at himself and began to run.

Trying to catch a moving train always looked easy in the movies. But as he drew closer, its sheer size and speed, along with the fact that only a few handles whipped by upon which he could gain purchase, left him feeling hopeless.

He screamed a promise to the Brit: *"Nu vse, tebe pizda!"* as he ran to keep alongside the train.

Yes, indeed. The Brit was fucking dead.

Southern End of Lake Baikal
En Route to Irkutsk
1651 Hours Local Time

"I stopped because I had to," shouted the driver, standing near the truck's door. "The engine just stalled! These trucks are very old!"

"Why didn't you call?" Zakarova demanded, drawing more fear into the driver's eyes.

"I thought I could—"

Zakarova raised his pistol, ready to execute the man—

"Sir!" cried Ekk. "We need everyone now. I mean in case those young punks try to play games with us. Every man!"

After flicking his glance between the driver and the lieutenant, and after considering the lieutenant's words, Zakarova slowly lowered the pistol.

But he took a step closer toward the driver. "You want an equal cut of the money, but why should we pay for your incompetence?"

"I'm sorry, sir."

"Do you think ten percent less would be fair?"

"Yes, sir."

"And we'll get nothing if you can't get this truck started!"

"The damage to the doors is only cosmetic," cried Parshin, coming around from the back side of the truck. "The warheads are fine."

"Then let's get moving!" hollered Zakarova.

While the driver rushed back to the cab, Ekk came toward Zakarova and dropped his voice. "Sir, I didn't mean to challenge you. I'm just worried—"

Zakarova whirled and put his gun to Ekk's head. "Do you think ten percent less would be fair for challenging me? *Do you*?"

Ekk's gaze turned cold and for a moment he did not answer. Zakarova was about to ask him again when the much younger man suddenly brought up his hand and locked it onto the pistol. Zakarova struggled against the lieutenant's grip, which was more powerful than his.

The other men broke off from the truck and moved toward them, their noses red, mouths falling open.

"Sir, I do not think ten percent is fair," said Ekk, his voice burred by exertion. "For either of us. Please let go of the weapon."

"So that's the way it will be?"

"Yes. That is the way."

"Okay." Zakarova abruptly relaxed his grip and allowed Ekk to take the pistol. "Will you shoot me now? Or later?"

"Without you, sir, we would have never smuggled out the warheads. Without your plan, we would have nothing."

Zakarova nodded.

"We owe you that much. It's true that we are not soldiers anymore. We are just mercenaries, arms dealers, thugs trying to make some money. But we don't have to behave like them. We are and will always be soldiers."

"You're right, young man. My temper makes me forget." Zakarova placed a hand on Ekk's shoulder. "I would not have killed you."

Ekk raised his head toward the driver. "And him?"

"Maybe."

The lieutenant pursed his lips. "I thought so."

"Sir?" cried Parshin, looking up from the truck's engine, the open hood angling over his head. "I think I know what the problem is. I can fix it."

"Well don't tell me! Just fix it!" said Zakarova.

"Oh, no," groaned Ekk, turning his head toward a pair of approaching headlights, the beams revealing the thick falling snow, the coughing and humming of a truck engine growing louder.

"Hunters?" Zakarova asked.

"Who else could it be?"

"We're the only ones who know, unless there is a traitor among us."

"No, this is just unfortunate," said Ekk. "What if they stop? If they ask questions?"

"They will stop," said Zakarova.

"Why?"

"Because they will have to." He shifted to the middle of the road and began waving his hands.

"Then, sir, it is a good thing that your weapon is still loaded."

Zakarova sighed deeply. "Yes, Lieutenant. It is."

Rossiya Train Number 2
Trans-Siberian Express
Nearing Irkutsk
1654 Hours Local Time

Gorlach thought both of his arms might have been pulled from their sockets as he caught the rail and let the train tear him from the ground as though God were scooping him up from the world of mortal men. So much noise, so much power, left him bleary-eyed and numb.

But he'd done it! He was attached to the train, if not on it yet . . .

He swung one foot up toward the metal step, missed, swung again, missed again. So he just hung there a moment more, realizing that his wounded arm would give out.

A look down at the tracks blurring by stole his breath.

There was just too much pain, noise, and that terrible throbbing in his arm.

He shut his eyes. It was over.

Someone shouted, the words incomprehensible. Before he could open his eyes and look up, hands were locked around his wrists and he found himself being hauled up by a burly provodnitsa with a shock of curly red hair bursting from her skull and whipping like fire in the wind. She was a nightmare in a blue uniform, all right, but handled him as though he were stuffed with feathers, a rag doll easily tossed back onto the train.

He was immediately in love with her.

For all of three seconds.

"Welcome aboard," she said. "And now you are going to be arrested for trying to hitch a ride."

"No," he cried over the din. "I was thrown overboard by another passenger. I have my ticket. My friends are inside. They will vouch for me. Call the police!"

She pulled him inside the carriage and shut the door behind them. His nose was running, his arm growing hotter.

"You're hurt." She reached toward him.

He recoiled. "Must've cut myself when I hit the

ground. Please, come with me. I don't want trouble. My friends will vouch for me. We have to see them."

"No, you stay here while I make a call."

As she shifted back to her room at the end of the carriage, her gaze still trained on him, he bolted off down the aisle.

Her shouts got lost in the voices of other riders who stuck their heads out from their open doors. One man cried, "You're dripping blood everywhere!"

He hadn't noticed, looked down, and swallowed back a rush of bile.

At the end of the carriage, Gorlach shoved an old man, a provodnik with a thick white beard, out of the way and yanked open the doors to the next carriage.

He raced on through yet another carriage, hearing the provodnitsa crying for him to stop. She was an ogre, an unstoppable bitch.

But he would reach their carriage well before her. He hustled down the next aisle, through the next carriage, and then headed straight for Svetlanov's room. The door was locked, and he rapped hard and shouted for his boss.

"Why do you want?" came the man's muffled voice.

"Open the door! Trouble!"

Two carriages ahead of the young Russian mafia men sat Hezbollah agent Charel Najjar and his partner, Abdo Fahed. They were both in their thirties, with closely cropped hair and well-groomed beards. They wore casual business attire and attempted to be as nondescript as possible. They had come a long way from Lebanon and were exhausted, hated the food, and were about to go mad from boredom—

When one of the young Russians, a man they had earlier identified as Gorlach from the intelligence photos they had been given, came rushing past the open door of their room, a screaming provodnitsa in pursuit.

Fahed immediately rose from his bed and rushed into the aisle, betraying his inexperience.

Now, as Najjar rose to follow and reprimand his partner, he realized something serious had just occurred. A trail of blood stretched off down the aisle, toward the rear door.

"Come on," urged Fahed.

"Wait."

Najjar tugged his partner back into their room, where they shut the door and removed their pistols from their backpacks.

Fahed furrowed his brow. "What's happening? We're not even in Irkutsk yet?"

"I don't know. But we're going to find out."

"Should we call them? Maybe they will want to speak with Svetlanov?"

Najjar stroked his beard in thought. "Not yet. If they are fighting amongst themselves, then that is not our problem, so long as the deal is made."

"I understand. But the major has sent someone to negotiate earlier than expected. Maybe they're trying to double-cross these young punks."

"Well, if that's the case, then we should be ready."

"We might need help."

"It won't come before we reach Irkutsk. Maybe Vladivostok. I don't know, either."

Fahed shrugged. "Let's go."

Najjar nodded and motioned that they head out to see if they could eavesdrop on the Russians.

Many of the passengers were leaving their rooms to look at the blood, while one of the provodniks asked them to return so he could clean the floor.

Ignoring the man, Najjar led Fahed down the aisle.

They rushed out of the carriage and into the next one, following the blood trail all the way. But when they opened the door to reach the Russians' carriage, they were blocked by a well-groomed young man, another provodnik, whose expression was steel.

"Please let us pass," Najjar said in broken Russian. "Our friend might be in trouble."

"This is a private carriage. No one comes through here. Go back to your room."

Najjar stole a look over the provodnik's shoulder, saw the injured man, Gorlach, standing in the hall, outside Svetlanov's room, shouting something and rapping on the door.

Fahed cleared his throat. "You must let us pass."

"It's okay," Najjar told the provodnik. "We'll see him later at the next stop."

He motioned for his partner to leave, and the provodnik nodded.

They turned back toward their room, passing a tall, lean man with thick glasses and a shaved head who was just turning into his own room. The man looked red-faced, flustered, though Najjar thought nothing of it. His attention was drawn to yet another provodnik, shaking his head at them.

Najjar smiled. "I think we might be lost."

Svetlanov tugged up his boxers and unlocked the door, telling Hannah to pull up the covers to hide her breasts. She gave him a look, thrust out her breasts, then obeyed.

Gorlach nearly knocked him over. "Mykola is dead." The man could barely breathe, let alone speak.

Svetlanov noticed his bloody sleeve. "What happened?"

Before Gorlach could answer, a beast of a woman who had squeezed herself into a provodnitsa's uniform appeared in the doorway. "This man is going to be arrested for illegally boarding the train!"

"I have his ticket," snapped Svetlanov.

"I don't care. He says he was pushed off by another passenger."

"Please, come in," Svetlanov said, softening his tone. He ushered her into the room, then closed the door. "We obviously have a problem, but we don't want any more trouble. I don't know what happened to my friend, but if he did something wrong, we're willing to pay for his mistake." Svetlanov went to his pants on the chair, withdrew his money clip and a wad of cash that widened the old witch's eyes. He counted off the bills, thrust them into her hand.

"Okay," she said slowly. "But no more trouble from you!"

"Don't worry." Svetlanov smiled, and he could tell that his good looks—and more important, his cash—had charmed her.

She quickly left and began calming down the other passengers.

Svetlanov ushered Gorlach over to the chair, shouted for Hannah to grab some vodka. He tore open the man's sleeve to reveal a terrible gunshot wound, but at least there was a clean entry and exit.

"Who did this to you?" he asked.

"We thought we were being observed by an Arab or Indian. We went after him, but I think it was a Brit who shot me."

"A Brit?"

"Yes. He knew your name."

Svetlanov swallowed. "Hannah, get dressed, pour some vodka on his wound."

"What the fuck is going on?" she asked, her eyes growing teary.

"Just an old enemy," he told her. "Don't worry about it."

Two more of Svetlanov's men showed up at his door. He ordered them to search the train for a Brit, and Gorlach chipped in more of the man's appearance. "If you find him, bring him to me. Don't kill him."

They hurried off.

Gorlach muffled his scream as Hannah, having donned her robe, winced and poured vodka on his wound. "Do they have a doctor on this train?" she asked.

"Go ask Alek. If they do, get him back here."

Hannah set down the vodka and hurried out of the room. The second she left, Svetlanov dug out his satellite phone and made a call.

"What are you doing?" asked Gorlach.

"Shut up and try not to bleed too much."

"Thank you for the sympathy."

"You should have killed that Brit. Now we have a real problem."

"I'm sorry."

"No, you're not. But soon you might be."

Southern End of Lake Baikal
En Route to Irkutsk
1720 Hours Local Time

Major Zakarova was just calming down because they had both trucks back on the road and would still be on time for their meeting in Irkutsk, providing the warhead truck did not stall again. Parshin seemed confident that his repairs had addressed the problem.

Behind them lay another truck, the hunters inside shot to death. A sloppy loose end, but there wasn't time for anything more elaborate. At least they had driven the truck off the trail and let it fall into a ditch, where it would become buried in the snow. Perhaps it would take a long time for their bodies to be found.

The trail was beginning to level off, and soon they would be on the main road. Though it, too, would be snow-covered and slippery, it would at least be more level.

A rapid beeping jarred him from his thoughts, and he quickly answered his satellite phone, only to find an irate voice grating in his ear. "What the fuck is going on?"

"Who is this?"

"Svetlanov, old man! What the fuck is this?"

"What are you talking about?"

"A Brit killed one of my men, shot another on board the train. What do you know about this?"

"Nothing at all."

"Don't lie to me, old man. When you get here, I'll put a bullet in your head."

"I don't know anything about it. And if you think you can threaten me—"

"You don't think it's a coincidence that the colonel is being held in London and one of my men is killed by a Brit?"

"Maybe the colonel talked. I don't know."

"Well, you had better find out, because I will walk away. I already have diamonds I can move. You have warheads that mean nothing without me."

"Don't be so sure. I will see you in Irkutsk. We will be on time. Good-bye."

Zakarova hung up and smiled at Ekk. "Good news. The Brit has killed one of Svetlanov's men and injured another."

"I thought it was best for him not to make contact," said Ekk.

"Yes, I thought so, too. But he has just made our work a little easier."

"But now Svetlanov will have his guard up."

"He would have anyway. Now he has fewer men. We must take him out as quietly as possible. The Brit will think we are working with him. We will finish him last."

"That sounds perfect. But what about Hertzog?"

"He should already be in Khabarovsk. But I will confirm that."

"Well, then, you have two phone calls to make before we reach Irkutsk."

"Yes, I do."

Zakarova took a deep breath and began dialing the first number to a satellite phone in London.

Chapter 7

....

Mad Dog and Kat had flown out of Moscow and landed at Novy Airport. Then they checked into a hotel and crashed once more.

The plane trip had taken seven hours, yet the time difference between Moscow and Khabarovsk was the same, so they landed about the same time they took off.

Damned rotating Earth.

Now, as they sat at the hotel bar, Mad Dog wondered what the hell he was doing, sipping after dinner cocktails when Bibby was out there and thirty million was gone, along with the necklace!

He took a deep breath, tried to relax his shoulders.

What else could he do but sit there, get drunk, and wait for the freaking train to arrive?

He had already played out scenario after scenario, trying to justify why the man had lied, why it was "okay" for Bibby to take the money, why he shouldn't be upset

with him. He tried to find a reason so compelling, so
emotionally driven, that even he would have made the
same choice.

But he kept coming up empty. The fucker had stolen
his money. And he wasn't buying the broken heart crap
Kat was selling. His bank account was broken, not his
damned heart!

But admittedly, it hurt. Damn, he would have never
guessed something like this could ever happen.

Both Waffa and the colonel had indicated that Bibby
was in deep shit. Was he going to buy those diamonds to
somehow get himself out? Would he sell them to Hezbollah? For what purpose? None of it was Bibby. None
of it made sense. And thinking about all of it gave him a
serious migraine.

"The train should reach Irkutsk in about two hours,
1950 their time," Kat said. "It won't get here for about
two and a half days."

"So we wait. We recon. We wait some more."

"We should have just boarded in Irkutsk. The colonel's
time line is wrong. And we're not even positive that
Bibby is on the train."

"The colonel has nothing to gain by lying to us," he
said.

"Maybe he does."

"I can't think that hard. My head is throbbing."

"I don't know, I think—"

"Shit, Kat, I got no one else. That's why we've come
this far. Why the fuck are we talking about this?"

"Because—"

"Look, the colonel's not telling the whole truth, but I
think Bibby's on the train. And I think Moody put this
into perspective—the diamond heist, Hezbollah boarding
the train in the same city as Bibby was supposed to . . .

All of this is linked, and Bibby's right in the middle. So here we are. And we fucking wait. And we nail his ass when the train gets here. That's it!"

Kat's eyes grew teary, then she just shrugged, ran a finger over the rim of her glass. "Did he ever tell you anything about his personal life?"

"I know about his work with Colin Ricer."

"What a nut job that guy turned out to be."

"Yep. Waffa introduced me to Bibby."

Kat closed her eyes. "I know. Me, too. But I mean, did he ever tell you anything else? Like why he left MI6 or anything about his parents, brothers and sisters, anything?"

"No. You know how he is when you ask him. He said he left MI6 because of personality differences. I checked him out. I got copies of the reports. That's just what it said."

"Well, I didn't want to tell you this, but there was a rumor floating around a few years back. I heard it from Waffa."

"I'm surprised he didn't try to sell it to you."

"Don't talk about him like that."

"Just go on."

"Bibby was in Pakistan, trying to form a new intelligence network. MI6 gave him a lot of start-up money, over four million pounds. The operation failed. The money was never accounted for."

"They thought he took it?"

"Yeah. He didn't leave MI6. They went after him, tried to nail him, but they couldn't. So they forced him out, covered it up. That's what really happened."

"So there's a history of him stealing from his bosses. You could've told me that a little sooner."

"Let me finish. We were both in Ramallah a few years

back. We were drinking, and I don't know how it came up, but I asked about why he left and about the rumors I'd heard that he'd stolen the money."

"And?"

"He denied it."

"Of course he did."

"He denied it *at first*. Then he started talking about how complicated the whole operation was and how he was undermined by his colleagues, about how the great mechanism, as he called it, had broken down."

"So he took the money."

"Not for himself. He realized the operation was being executed the wrong way, that they would accomplish nothing by bribing the warlords, but that if he used the money to get supplies to the locals along some of the border towns, those people would become loyal informants."

"Did he go to them first with this?" asked Mad Dog.

"They turned him down."

"So he did it."

"Yup. Made the money vanish, got them help. Turned over the operation to his buddies, Albert and Patrice."

"According to them, he saved their lives."

"That's right. During that same operation. There was a supply convoy moving into the area, and a few car bombs went off, and Bibby helped Albert and Patrice get out before the main attack. He got shot in the leg helping them escape. That's about all I got out of him."

"That's more than anyone else has. What's your point?"

"It's the same point. Don't judge him yet."

"Sorry, honey, but I already have. Why didn't he come to me? Why didn't he trust me?"

She just stared at her glass.

Mad Dog's satellite phone rang, startling him. It was Pope. "What do you got?"

"Something strange, boss man. Just got a call via satellite from a woman named Melissa in Ramallah, says she's Waffa's wife and is working with one of his couriers. Waffa told her to call us if he was killed."

"Okay . . ."

"She says Waffa was trying to help Bibby and Simone, and that he just found out yesterday Simone was murdered in Toulouse. Waffa believed Hezbollah assassinated her, and his little network is worried about something big going down."

"Whoa, slow down. Who's Simone?"

"According to this guy, she was—brace yourself— Bibby's wife. Full name's Simone Carlisle."

"Hold on." Mad Dog conveyed the news to Kat, who muttered a holy shit, then squinted in thought.

"Are you there, boss man?"

"Yeah. I want everything on Simone Carlisle. I'll get in touch with Moody, see if he can coordinate with you. You call me the second you got something."

"Did you say Moody, James Moody?"

"Long story, don't ask. He's playing with us today."

"Whatever you say, boss. Wish I were there with bandoliers on instead of sitting in this fucking wheelchair."

"You heal up, take care of Dan's arrangements, and get me what I need."

"Hey, Michael?"

Mad Dog was taken aback. Pope had never called him by first name. His voice cracked. "Yeah."

"We got your back. We always will. So don't worry. If that fucker stole our money, he's going down. I promise you that—and if I have to drag my shot-up ass on a plane to do it myself, I will."

"Thanks, Billy. Thanks. Talk to you soon." Mad Dog got off the phone, turned to Kat.

"Jesus Christ, now it's making more sense," she said.

"Oh, it is?"

"Maybe they had his wife. Maybe he was going to pay. Maybe he doesn't even know she's dead!"

"This is getting more convoluted by the second."

"Would you steal thirty million to save me?"

Mad Dog lifted his drink, finished it in one swig, exhaled through the burn. "I guess I would."

"You guess? Fuck you."

"Okay, I would. But I'd ask my friends for help!" Mad Dog checked his watch. "Where the hell is Yury? He's already a half hour late."

Kat shrugged, glanced away. "Simone Carlisle . . ." she thought aloud. "That's probably not her real name."

"No shit. Her name is Mrs. Bibby, the wife of a fucking ex-spy, ex-merc, soon to be assassinated thief!"

"She was in Toulouse."

"She could've been in Topeka for all I care."

"That's it! Carlisle. Toulouse. I knew I remembered something. Bibby once told me he was buying some real estate in Toulouse, an investment property. He got off the phone and said, 'That was Carlisle, my real estate agent.'"

"So he married his real estate agent?"

"Who knows? But he mentioned both the place and name once. I'm positive."

"You know a lot more about this guy than you're letting on. You sleep with him?"

She leaned toward him, eyes lit. "I should hurt you for that."

Mad Dog shrugged, lifted his phone, ready to dial Moody's number, when—

"Well, well, well, look at what we have here," cried

Yury Melnickov, entering the bar and raising his hands. "A couple of tourists. This is great, we can make a deal, I can rip you off, and we will smile, and you will never know what happened!"

Yury wanted to give Mad Dog a hug, but Mad Dog just took the man's hand and shook it hard. "Yury, it's good to see you again, buddy."

"Look at you. You are, as they say, bummed out, huh? It's okay. Yury's here now. There are no problems in the world that cannot be fixed with a nice handgun. Please, introduce this most beautiful woman." Yury took Kat's hand and went in for the kiss.

Kat grinned, let him kiss her hand, but then he held his lips there, breathed in her scent and moaned, which made her snap back the hand.

"Still a filthy dog, I see," said Mad Dog.

Yury winked. "A dog, yes. Filthy? No, no."

Kat grinned crookedly. "Yes, yes."

"Oh, please, forgive me," Yury said, throwing up his palms. "Let me make it up to you. Another round on me."

Hornsea on Bridlington Bay
England
0940 Hours Local Time

Boris Sinitsyna was about to sit down to his morning tea and scone when a knock came at the door. He swore under his breath, rose, then padded over. It was Charles, his boyish face screwed up into a frown.

"I'm sorry to bother you, Colonel, but might I come in for a moment?"

"Well, yes, but there will be no more bargaining for cigars."

"I know. I'm not here for them, although I wish you had not run out. Please . . . "

The colonel frowned himself, opened the door, and Charles passed into the bungalow, heading straight for the kitchen.

"What is this about?"

The young man took a seat at the kitchen table, leaned back and pillowed his head in his hands. "I just got a call from Irkutsk."

"It is my understanding that there are many people in Irkutsk who like to speak on the telephone."

The young man smiled, reached over, took the colonel's scone and brought it to his mouth.

The colonel snorted. "You've come to eat my breakfast?"

"No. Well, since I'm here, yes." He took a bite, hummed over the flavor, then smiled even more broadly.

"Who are you?" the colonel demanded.

"One of the many people in Irkutsk who likes to talk on the telephone is your uncle. And I just got off the phone with him. He's not a nice man at all."

"No, he is not."

"Do you know what he asked me to do?"

The colonel glanced back toward the living room, to the window that overlooked the backyard, where another of the MI6 agents was stationed. If he could just get that man's attention . . .

"Colonel, are you listening?"

"Yes. My uncle, he asked you to take good care of me, didn't he?"

"As a matter of fact, he did." Charles reached back with his left hand and, in a flash, produced his sidearm, training it on the colonel's head.

The colonel understood everything now, especially Charles's willingness to let him use the cell phone.

My God. Zakarova was better connected than he had

anticipated. He'd planted a spy within MI6's security force? That alone was an impressive feat.

Consequently, if that old war-horse wanted him dead, then he would have his way, because the colonel knew he could not alert the other guard at the moment. It seemed he had but one escape plan: strike a deal.

"You don't want to kill me, young man."

"No, sir, I don't."

"Then if we make a deal, you and I, you must promise that your loyalty will lie with me, not him. I'm certain I can pay you much more than he did. Much more."

Charles swallowed, took a long sip of tea, then said, "I know you can, Colonel. I take money from him. I take money from you. You take money from him, you take money from the American mercenary, the necklace from the Brit . . . everyone makes money. Everyone is happy. But I'm only loyal to me. Surely you can appreciate that."

"I do. How much do you want?"

"Two million pounds."

"Done. We will gather all of the bank information, and I will make the transfer to your account on the phone."

Charles set down the pistol next to the colonel's teacup, then lifted the cup and took a long sip. "You have to love technology. Our hands never get dirty."

"Sometimes, young man, you have to get your hands dirty. Sometimes, it's the only way."

Before Charles could move his lips to reply, the colonel reached out and threw the entire kitchen table out of the way, sending the pistol flying across the room.

With nothing between them, the colonel launched himself forward, seizing the young man's neck, knocking him back, onto the floor, and digging his fingers into that soft flesh.

Charles turned his head, trying to spot his pistol, but the colonel was fast cutting off his breath.

This wouldn't be the first time he, Colonel Boris Sinitsyna, had choked a man to death. The first time occurred in Afghanistan, seemingly a lifetime ago, and that Afghani rebel had the breath of Satan.

Charles began to foam at the mouth, his face flush, his eyes narrowed to slits. The colonel's grip was permanent.

As the young man began digging his own nails into the colonel's arms, he tried to bring his knees up, but the colonel sat squarely on the man's gut. The old training had never been forgotten.

The arrogance of youth . . . the audacity of youth . . . the sheer stupidity . . .

Those thoughts empowered the colonel, until the man went limp beneath him.

The back door opened. Immediately, the colonel threw himself across the floor, reached the pistol.

"Colonel? I heard something. Everything okay?"

After taking in a long breath, he replied, "No, Thomas. Please come here. I've fallen."

The other agent was about as young as Charles, humorless, and out to prove his worth to his superiors. He would have made a fine agent, had he not been foolish enough to walk into the kitchen with his weapon still holstered.

"Colonel?" Thomas turned his head, facing the colonel, who now sat up, Charles's pistol in his hand. Thomas glanced from the pistol to Charles's body and muttered a simple, "Oh."

And then the colonel fired, the gun much too loud, the smell much too pungent.

Thomas's head jerked back and he staggered a moment before collapsing.

"Look what this old man has just done," the colonel

said through a growl. "Look at this!" He grabbed a drawer handle, hauled himself to his feet.

His throat was going dry, his mind going blank. *No! Think, old man, think!*

He took Thomas's sidearm, took each man's cell phone, their wallets, anything that might be of use.

Before his defection, the colonel had been stationed at the London embassy for ten years, long enough to forge many strong relationships.

He shoved everything he needed into a small back-pack—most especially the jade necklace—then rushed out the back door, the hairs standing on the back of his neck. He had never been a fugitive before. The prospect was as unnerving as it was exciting.

With a shudder, he ran down the alley between bunga-lows, ducked behind a row of trash cans, then paused to make a quick call to Bartholomew and Kit, who would be shocked but would send a car, take him to their house. From there he could decide what he would do next. Of course, he needed to get back to Russia. He thought it might be interesting to confront Zakarova, who had probably come up with a plan to screw over the mafia, get the diamonds, and keep the warheads. If that turned out to be true, then there might be time to meet up with the major in Irkutsk. A phone call to Zakarova himself would confirm that.

Once he finished his call to get a ride, he darted out of the alley, toward the next row of bungalows, then began walking, just an average citizen out for his stroll. Never mind the backpack, the two pistols inside, the ten mil-lion dollar piece of jewelry.

He shuffled past an old woman walking her dog. "Good morning," he said in his best English accent.

"Good morning. Beautiful day," she said.

"Yes, it is."

Amur River
Khabarovsk, Russia
2005 Hours Local Time

Yury was at the wheel of his little blue car, Mad Dog riding shotgun, Kat in the back.

They followed a road parallel to the Amur, one of the largest rivers in all of Russia. Lights from office buildings and smaller docking facilities dotted the shoreline, and the river assumed a black lacquer sheen in the waning moonlight. Traffic was light, the air cool and fresh against Mad Dog's cheeks. He let his hand drift out the window and ride the waves of wind.

Yury was saying something about taking a tour along Muravieva-Amurskii Street, which was lined with restaurants and souvenir shops, but Mad Dog had to interrupt him. "I know you're proud of your country, Yury, but we're not on vacation! I've got an ex-employee who's screwed me over, and the last goddamned thing I want to do is buy some Russian souvenir that was made in China, for God's sake."

"You are an angry man," Yury said, glancing in the rearview mirror. "And life is too short. You tell him, Kat."

"I already have."

"Listen, you will have some time to kill. And if you spend all of your time having wild sex, well . . . maybe you should spend all of your time having wild sex."

Mad Dog sighed. "I see you've been hanging out with Wolfgang."

"This man is a bad influence." Yury reached an intersection, made a quick left, then said, "My son should already be at the hotel. We're almost there."

"So it's Yury and son, arms dealers?" Mad Dog asked.

"I have three boys. They all help. Viktor is my oldest. A good boy."

"I'm sure."

"Ah, there it is. Right up there."

As Mad Dog peered up through the windshield at the twelve-story building whose lights checkered across the shadows of the dark street, another pair of lights stole his attention:

Headlights.

Coming up fast behind them.

"What is this?" asked Yury.

And without warning the car plowed right into them, the thud whipping Mad Dog's head back, the plastic bumper and headlights shattering, the trunk bowing, obscuring all light coming in from the back window.

Yury had slammed his head on the steering wheel, and Mad Dog wasn't sure if he was conscious.

"Michael!" cried Kat.

Mad Dog was about to call Yury's name when the driver behind them gunned the engine, pushing them farther to the right, tires squealing. There were more muffled thuds as the wheels hit the curb, then they were catapulted onto the sidewalk, the other car's engine wailing loudly, their smashed trunk rattling and shaking.

The coldest chill Mad Dog had ever felt in his life shot through his spine and took root in his gut. He had been in combat situations, been in far worse, but the knowledge that someone was trying to kill him, someone who might have been hired by a once close friend, was almost too much to bear.

Yury pushed back from the steering wheel, blood dripping down his face. He screamed something in Russian, then threw up his hands.

They barreled straight for the brick wall of a long office building, the headlights wiping past the concrete, a man in a long overcoat throwing himself out of the way—

Just as they made impact.

Chapter 8

....

Aeroflot Flight Su 212
Somewhere Over the Atlantic Ocean
Destination: Vladivostok
1505 Hours Local Time

Agent James Moody had planted his bedraggled butt on an airplane, not because he felt badly for Mad Dog or even because he wanted to gloat over the meathead's massive sucking chest wound that was his now about-to-become-bankrupt company. No. He'd gotten his bedraggled ass on board the plane because of what he read in the intelligence report he'd ordered on Simone Carlisle.

The information was still incomplete, and the Agency had yet to uncover any definitive proof that she was, in fact, the wife of Mr. Alastair Bibby, but a number of other red flags sent Moody directly to the Web to buy his ticket:

Police in Toulouse had searched Carlisle's apartment, where she was murdered, and uncovered multiple pass- ports in multiple names, along with exotic jewelry and a small amount of crack cocaine. Moreover, her cell phone records showed many calls to the Philippines as well as to one of Bibby's satellite phone numbers.

But the clincher was the real estate company she was working for, a company already identified by Interpol and the Mossad in Israel as a front for Hezbollah operations.

Now, there was no proof that Simone knew what was going on at her company, but in the world of espionage, there weren't any coincidences. She either knew what they were doing and was threatening to expose them, or perhaps she discovered what was going on, was taken hostage, and Bibby had failed to bargain with them.

Whatever the case, two Hezbollah agents were now on board that train bound for Vladivostok, along with Bibby himself, if the old Russian in London was to be trusted.

So what did this all mean? Moody wondered. Shit, he was dying to find out. And along with the real clincher came the real kicker: He was on vacation, doing this all on his own time, his own dime, wanting to get into some serious shit because, damn, he got off on it. And it seemed that if he kept close enough to Mad Dog Hertzog, the shit always flew. Even old farts like him never lost that craving for the juice.

Moody knew that his days at the Agency were numbered, and he figured he'd play pretend mercenary for this operation, see how it all unfolded, then make a decision about actually signing up with the asshole he loved to hate.

Oh, hell, he couldn't believe what he was thinking. And he couldn't wait to surprise the meathead when he landed.

Just a few hours ago, his new buddy in New York, Abdul-Mujib Abdulhalek, had called. He still had a trace of sadness in his voice since his beloved Mets had their asses handed to them by the Braves, final score 13–1. Moody had been in his glory, watching those poor Met bastards get pounded while devouring his pretzel, hot dog, and beer. He tried to talk more trash to Abdul-Mujib, but the guy wouldn't allow him to gloat further. He cut in to say that at least six Hezbollah agents had been sent to Fushiki, Japan.

Moody wasn't sure what to make of this piece of intelligence, and Abdul-Mujib wasn't sure, either, but Abdul would follow up.

A flight attendant came by, and he accepted a warm towel, placed it over his face, and leaned back for a nice snooze. He turned his thoughts to Russian women, Fabergé eggs, and a nice bottle of vodka.

Amur River
Khabarovsk, Russia
2009 Hours Local Time

"The glove compartment," Yury groaned. "Get my other pistol in there!"

"What?" Mad Dog hollered as the safety glass continued to rain down on him.

"My pistol!"

Mad Dog's brain wasn't working, at least for a few seconds, then it kicked in like a lawn-mower engine after a few pulls on the cord. He fumbled in the dark, his hand finding the weapon.

Gunfire pinged and ricocheted off the car, and one of the tires suddenly blew out.

Yury reached under his seat, produced another gun, tugged open his door, then burst from the vehicle, screaming something at their assailants, unseen in the rising smoke of the collision.

"Kat, get down!"

"No shit," she groaned. "I already am. The fucking colonel set us up!"

"Or Bibby!"

Two more rounds cut into the car, and Mad Dog wasn't sure if he'd been hit.

Another pair of shots thundered.

Yury let out a bloodcurdling cry.

And that was it.

Mad Dog became a being of pure action and reaction, of pure instinct, became a guy half his age wearing a United States Marine Corps uniform. He ran into the light. Literally. Squinted, turned, saw a man to his left, fired!

Then, a flinch later, he dropped to his knees, rolled as two rounds came in from somewhere above. He shoved himself beneath the car, saw a pair of legs on the other side, took aim, fired. The guy screamed.

Mad Dog pulled himself up, circled around the back of the car, saw the guy hunched over, gripping his leg, his pistol hand coming around to take aim at him—

And he fired!

But the sound was odd, as though two shots had gone off. *What?*

He looked to his right, saw a young man in a dark wool coat standing there, his pistol arm extended. The kid fired once more before lifting his shaved head, hoop earrings dangling. "Hertzog! Come with me!"

"Who are you?" Kat hollered, pulling herself out of the shattered car.

The kid glanced sidelong at Kat. "I'm Viktor, Yury's son, come on! The police will come!" Viktor ran over to his father, who had been shot repeatedly in the chest, scooped him up and struggled toward another small car idling near the curb.

"Wait!" Mad Dog shouted. "Kat, search that guy. I got this one."

"No time," argued Viktor.

"Kat, just do it."

Mad Dog went through the pockets of their first attacker, while Kat did likewise with the other guy. Both were young, no more than thirty, with crew cuts and sharp builds. They could easily have been military men.

"I got nothing over here," she said.

"Same. Let me check the car." Mad Dog tugged open the driver's side door, went through the glove compartment, then checked under the seats. Nothing. And it was obviously a rental car. He popped the trunk, found a pair of small suitcases, opened them.

Bingo. Clothes and a wallet in each, with military IDs. He grabbed the cases, then he and Kat took off after the kid, leaving the two dead men and the smoking cars behind.

Sirens went off in the distance.

"What about the car?" Mad Dog asked Viktor. "They'll trace it back to your father."

"No, don't worry," the kid said, lowering Yury into the backseat. "They won't."

"If you say so."

The kid then spoke in Russian to his father, and though Mad Dog didn't understand much, it sounded as though he had just assured his father that everything would be okay.

"Viktor, your father is dead."

The kid glared at Mad Dog. "Just get in the car! I carry on his work! And we will get revenge!"

Mad Dog hopped in the front seat and Kat climbed in the back, just behind him.

"Hopefully, he doesn't blame us," she whispered in his ear as Viktor hit the gas and they tore off.

"Get out those IDs," he told her. "Call Billy back home. Those guys were Russian army."

Rossiya Train Number 2
Trans-Siberian Express
Nearing Irkutsk
1850 Hours Local Time

Svetlanov paced his cabin, thinking aloud, swearing, second-guessing himself, while Hannah had pressed herself into one corner on the bed, her knees pulled into her chest, her head buried in them. Gorlach, whose wound was hardly life-threatening, was back in his cabin. Svetlanov had lied and said they would get him medical attention soon. Though he considered Gorlach a faithful employee, he was a liability now, and if Gorlach couldn't get the job done, he would send him to the same cold grave as Mykola.

They would be in Irkutsk in one hour. Svetlanov had already arranged for three more men to meet them at the station. Not including Gorlach, he now had ten men working for him, ten men who would ensure they took possession of the warheads and kept the diamonds.

Svetlanov's father was in Vladivostok making more arrangements, and he had called to say that everything was set and he'd heard from their "friends" in Fushiki, who looked forward to their meeting.

The pressure was on, all right, and that rogue Brit could ruin everything. He'd sent two of his men off to find the Brit. No luck thus far, and they were running out of time.

"Hannah? Are you going to talk to me? Or are you going to sulk for the entire trip?"

"What do you expect?" she asked, not looking up, her voice muffled by her lap.

"I expect you to look at me." He crossed to her, dug his hand under her chin, forced her head up. "Look at me."

Her bleary eyes and red face struck a pang of guilt in him, but only for a moment. "You're in trouble, aren't you?" she asked. "Just tell me."

"We've done a lot of business in Moscow, and I told you, when you become successful like we have, you always make enemies."

"People who want to kill you?"

"Sometimes it comes to that."

"You've been lying to me, haven't you? This whole trip has been a lie."

He sat on the bed, grabbed her wrists, lowered her voice. "No lies. I'm so sorry about all of this. When they catch this man who shot Gorlach, it'll be over, and we can just think about each other. Maybe even talk about the future."

"What do you mean?"

"I mean our lives together. I want a wife. I want a family."

"I do, too. But I don't want to rush anything. I want us to be sure. But you can't lie to me. You can't hold anything back. No secrets."

"Okay."

She widened her eyes, took his hands in her own. "No secrets."

"Okay."

Svetlanov smiled as she pulled him toward her, thinking he was about to get a long kiss, but she just hugged him tightly, pushed her mouth to his ear, and asked, "Why are those bars of soap so important? I've never seen any of those rashes you told me about."

He moved her away and smiled. "I usually don't get them this time of year. But I have to be careful. You always have to be careful."

"Oh, uh, okay."

Something in her tone bothered him, and now he felt compelled to go to his knapsack, where he'd stored the small bag and the soap. He repressed the compulsion and said, "I'm sorry for overreacting. But when the rash comes, it is so itchy that it drives me insane. The soap is the only thing that can help. I'm sorry."

"It's okay. Now, if you'll excuse me, I have to go to the bathroom."

He moved back, let her rise and pass him. "Put on your coat. The carriage is cold, and there's quite a storm outside. Lots of snow."

She nodded, slid into her coat, buttoned it up, then pushed open the door and hurried into the aisle.

With a chill, he shut the door after her, then collapsed onto the chair, reached for the open bottle of vodka and let a long sip warm his gut.

His cell phone rang; it was one of his men, reporting on the search for the Brit. Still nothing.

"He didn't jump off this train. He's still here. And you have less than an hour to find him. Do you hear me!"

With a grunt, he hung up, tossed the phone onto the bed. He looked to the knapsack, figured he had time before she returned. Should he bother? Was he that paranoid?

He pushed forward, rose with a groan, dug through the knapsack, produced the small bag—

And discovered it empty.

Her name exploded from lips. "Hannah!"

His fingers dug into the door handle and he tripped trying to get outside. He bolted up the aisle. "Hannah!"

Alek appeared from his small provodniks' quarters,

his frown deepening as Svetlanov neared him. "What's wrong now, sir?"

"Did you see my girlfriend? Is she in the bathroom up there?"

Alek shook his head. "The door is wide open."

Svetlanov arrived and saw for himself. "You didn't see her?"

"No, I'm afraid I was in my room."

"That bitch!"

"Sir, can I do something—"

Svetlanov was already charging down the aisle, banging on doors to alert the rest of his men.

Utter panic gripped his body and his thoughts. Had she found the diamonds? Was she playing some trick on him? Had someone else found them, and their conversation about the soap merely been a coincidence? Was she working for someone, perhaps Zakarova? Had he been set up by the major and the old colonel? Or maybe Hannah was working with this mysterious Brit?

Svetlanov trembled with rage as his men poured into the aisle behind him. He whirled to face them. "Find Hannah. Now!"

Najjar was lying on his bed, staring out past the open door and into the aisle, when the young woman hustled by. He might've thought nothing of it, but something about her struck him. He rose, went to the door, watched her heading toward the next carriage. That coat, yes. She was Svetlanov's girlfriend. Why was she in such a hurry?

He turned to his partner. "More trouble."

"What?"

"I see his girlfriend. She looks like she's running. Maybe scared."

Fahed shrugged and yawned. "Maybe they had a fight."

"Get your jacket. Let's go."

"We're not here to chase after some Russian's girl-friend."

"Anything that interferes with delivery of the war-heads is our business."

"I'm tired. You go."

Najjar drew his sidearm, pointed it at Fahed's head.

"Okay," said Fahed. "I am not tired."

They fled their cabin, charging down the aisle after the girl, Najjar in the lead.

"Shouldn't we walk?" called Fahed.

"We'll lose her."

"And maybe we lose our cover, too."

Hannah Lamoureux's eyes burned as she faced head-on what she had been denying these past months: Svetlanov was a criminal, part of the mafia, and he was on the train to make some kind of exchange of diamonds.

She had heard about the diamond theft, and never in a million years thought he had anything to do with it. Yet his reaction to the soap had deeply troubled her, and so, while he was busy with his men just after Gorlach was shot, she decided to examine the bars herself, broke one in half, and discovered the diamonds inside. She had tucked both bars into her small purse and took the purse with her to the bathroom. She wasn't sure why she'd stolen the gems. She didn't actually want them. Maybe she was trying to get back at him for all the lies, make his life miserable, make him realize that she was important, not just a bitch on his arm.

And maybe hurting him was the only way to do that.

But what now?

He would chase her to the ends of the earth. That was the kind of man he was.

As she passed from one carriage to the next, she glanced into the cold, dark night, snow whipping hard, coming down sideways, the train vibrating, her heart about to burst.

She thought of jumping off.

But again, where would she go? Where could she hide?

Oh, what a fool she was to think she could hurt him. Yes, she could get his attention, but she couldn't hurt him. And maybe she didn't want to anymore. She just wanted him to say he was sorry and mean it. She could almost accept what he was doing, if only he would be honest with her.

She stopped dead in the aisle of a carriage and just stood there, shaking. Footfalls drew closer. She glanced up, saw two dark-skinned men approaching her. Something about them wasn't right. She took a deep breath and walked straight toward them, then around them, heading back the way she'd come. She would just tell him the truth. She would explain to him how hurt she was, and maybe he would listen. There was nothing left to do.

"Uh, excuse me, miss?" said one of the dark-skinned men behind her.

She froze, turned around.

Oh my God. He was holding her purse. She'd been so lost in thought that she hadn't even realized it slipped from her hand.

"Yours?" he asked in heavily accented English, perhaps assuming she was from the UK.

"Oh, yes, thank you." She took the purse from him. "I really appreciate it."

"It's okay." The guy was practically drooling over her.

Hannah smiled, then quickly turned back, heading away.

"Be careful," he called after her.

"I will.".

She opened the door at the end of the aisle, crossed to the next carriage, opened the next door—

And there was Svetlanov, marching toward her, his face gaunt, twisted, almost unrecognizable.

"Hannah! Where did you go?"

He reached her, wrapped a hand around the back of her neck and squeezed hard.

"When I got up, I didn't have to go to the bathroom anymore. So I just went for a walk."

He released her, snatched the purse from her hand, opened it, dumped its contents onto the floor.

The bars of soap were gone!

"Where are they?" he cried.

"I don't know what you want!" Her eyes swelled with tears. "I don't know!"

"My soap! Where are my bars of soap!" He rifled through her pockets, ran his hands up and down her body.

"I don't know! I didn't take them! I told you I wouldn't take them!".

Either God had come down from the heavens to save her or she was already dead and experiencing this strange moment in the afterlife.

And now how could she tell him that she had run off with his diamonds, dropped her purse, and the gems might be in the hands of two strangers?

Play dumb, Hannah. Just play dumb. And when we get to Irkutsk, run away.

*   *   *

Back in their room, Najjar and Fahed shut the door and examined the two bars of soap. One of them was wrapped in a small scarf, since it had been opened and broken in half.

"These are the diamonds he was planning to use to pay Zakarova," said Najjar, picking though the pieces.

"Then he needs them for the deal to happen," Fahed said.

"Why do you think she stole them?"

"Because she is his fucking whore, and she did! That is no mystery!"

Najjar narrowed his gaze, shook his head. "I don't know. Maybe she is a spy. And I'm wondering if maybe our work here is finished. We have just received our payment."

"Allahu Akbar!" cried Fahed, his gaze lighting on the gems. "God is great! My brother-in-law will know how to move these. We're going to be wealthy men."

"But if we take these diamonds and run, our mission will fail. And we will be running forever. You know they will come for us. They will find us."

"So what are you saying? We have to give the diamonds back to Svetlanov? Are you mad?"

"We have less than an hour to do it."

"No, Najjar. We take the diamonds, get off in Irkutsk, and fly to Pakistan. We will go see my brother-in-law. This is what we will do."

"We can't. The mission is bigger." Najjar picked up the bars of soap, thrust them out toward Fahed. "We were not meant to find them."

A knock came at the door.

Quickly, Najjar shoved the diamonds under a pillow on his bunk. "Yes?"

"We have a gift for you." The voice was decidedly male, Russian, a provodnik no doubt.

Fahed went to the door, opened it, and there he was, a new provodnik they had not seen before, tall, head shaved clean, glasses, uniform neatly pressed. He thrust out a package toward Fahed, who reached out—

Then suddenly fell back, clutching his chest as he hit the floor.

Najjar burst from his seat, saw the package drop away from the man's hand, revealing a silenced pistol. "The gentleman traveling with the lady asked me to knock you up," said the provodnik in English—and with an English accent. Then he added, "Where are the diamonds?"

Not only did the question surprise Najjar, but so did the man's Arabic, which was barely accented.

With his palms raised, Najjar just froze, then said slowly in Arabic, "I don't know what you're talking about."

"I just killed your friend. You, too, will meet Allah if you don't tell me."

"Who are you?"

"Talk."

"No. You will kill me anyway."

"Yes, but it's easier if you tell me where the diamonds are first. I know you have them. I saw you pick up the purse and take them out."

"I won't tell you anything."

"Then you die for Hezbollah."

Najjar closed his eyes, began whispering his prayers. A few seconds past, and when the shot didn't come, he snapped opened his eyes—

And saw the pistol flash.

Amethyst Hotel
Tolstoy Street
Khabarovsk, Russia
2135 Hours Local Time

They drove to a small row of apartments, parked in the lot, shut off the engine, and had been in the car now for thirty minutes.

Viktor whispered some prayers for his dead father, held the man's cold hand, and it was almost too much to bear.

Mad Dog and Kat were stunned into silence, and Mad Dog kept shaking his head over the fact that he had gotten yet another friend killed.

He and Yury had met during the first year of IPG's operations. One of Yury's competitors was selling weapons to the Philippine-based terrorist group Abu Sayyaf, and Yury was trying to thwart the man's efforts, not exactly because he hated terrorism but because *he* wanted to sell to Abu Sayyaf. Mad Dog intervened, turned Yury away from selling to the terrorists, and gave him a job supplying weapons to IPG and to the Philippine army and marines. Even Waffa had helped find more business for the Russian.

Yury Melnickov was a good man with a great sense of humor who had left behind a wife and those three boys, all because of . . .

Bibby? Sure, it was easy to blame it all on him, but the fact was that he, not Bibby, had called Yury, brought him into the snake pit, and gotten him killed.

"Okay. That is long enough." Viktor started the car, and Mad Dog asked him to drive back to their hotel. When they got there, Viktor sold them the weapons they needed and with a curt nod, his expression devoid of emotion, sped off for Vladivostok.

Pope called back to say that both of their attackers were, in fact, members of the Russian army, and he had all the details regarding their units and was working on more.

He told Pope to look for a more definitive connection between them and the old colonel, then called Albert in London, hoping the MI6 agent could arrange a call between himself and the old man.

"I'm afraid that's impossible," Albert said, his tone strangely ironic.

"What's the matter? You fucking Brits don't have a couple of tin cans and a string long enough?"

"Well, I shouldn't be telling you this, but given your current predicament, perhaps it will help, or at least put your guard up even higher. The colonel has unfortunately escaped."

Mad Dog broke out laughing.

"What's so funny?" Kat wrenched the phone away from him. "Albert? Hello, it's Kat. What's he laughing about?"

The Brit's voice sounded small and tinny, yet Mad Dog heard him repeat the news.

Kat gasped.

Mad Dog's eyes burned. "All I wanted to do was run my little fucking mercenary business. Make a few bucks, have some fun, and then have a nice retirement."

"Albert, did he have help?" asked Kat.

"We're not sure. If he didn't, then he single-handedly killed both of his guards. We're following our leads straight away, visiting every contact he has here. But we think he has a big lead on us and might manage to get out of the country before we can stop him. He's a master of forged documentation, and he has many friends here."

"Well, I hope that works out for you," Mad Dog said darkly. "Glad you boys are on the job."

"If you have any information, you need to turn it over to us. You know that."

"Well, I'm in Khabarovsk, and a couple of Russian army officers just tried to kill Kat and me, so we're thinking the colonel set us up. We're not even sure we should get on the train at this point."

"We'll send an agent."

"Not much time. If I were you, I'd send him to Vladivostok. That seems to be the trigger line for this shitfest."

Albert's tone grew as dark as Mad Dog's. "We'll be in touch, Hertzog."

Mad Dog hung up, crossed to the dresser and poured himself some vodka, took a sip, then checked his watch. "Train should be pulling into Irkutsk right about now."

"If you want, we can rent a car, drive along the route, try to pick up the train much sooner," Kat said, examining one of her maps. "There are a number of stops between Irkutsk and here. We might be able to reach Chita before the train gets there. We can buy new tickets and ride back instead of waiting around here. What do you think?"

Mad Dog finished his vodka, closed his eyes. "I'm half ready to call it quits."

"And what's the other half saying?"

"Drink more vodka. Go to bed. Wake up fresh. Rent a car. Find that asshole who stole my money."

"Come here." She sat up on the bed, pulled him close and gave him a long, deep hug, his face buried in her hair. "Thanks for saving my ass back there."

"It's a nice ass worth saving."

"Why thank you." She released him, covered a yawn. "Let's go to bed."

He nodded. "But tell me, are we just insane, running around like this?"

"Uh-huh." She smiled and pulled him down for a kiss, just as his satellite phone rang.

Chapter 9

....

It never ceased to amaze Wolfgang. No matter where you were, the ass end of the universe it seemed, you'd always find a Coca-Cola logo. He remembered when they were running that op back in Myanmar, which he preferred to call Burma, and he had charged into a hut in the middle of the jungle, and those scumbag kidnappers had hung a stolen Coca-Cola logo as a wall decoration.

So as he stood there, in the middle of the sidewalk, staring up at the Coca-Cola sign, he realized that the world had, in fact, been taken over by a soda company and that all humans had become slaves to their high fructose corn syrup habits. And that was his deep thought for the evening.

He tugged down his hat and tasted a few snowflakes before moving on. The damn cold was getting to him now. Maybe he'd go back to his hotel and get drunk, what the hell.

His satellite phone began to ring, so he ducked down an alley and took the call from Mad Dog. "Hey, boss. What's up?"

"I just got off the phone with Pope. He's sending some pics to your phone."

"Porno?"

"No, asshole. Pictures of the colonel. Remember the guy's name? Boris Sinitsyna."

"Why do I need to pictures of him? Isn't he stuck in the UK? MI6 has him, right?"

"Not anymore. The old fucker escaped. And I got a hunch he's headed your way."

"Why? Shit, you think he's meeting up with Bibby?"

"I don't know."

"Boss, this is a pretty big place. And he's probably traveling under an alias, so what do you want me to do? Try to find him? Forget it."

"When the train pulls into Vladivostok, you're going to check that platform. And if he's there, you're going to take him, understand?"

"How you want him? Pink in the center? Or cooked all the way through?"

"If you can take him alive, do it."

"Roger that. Yury hooked me up nice. I even picked up some small explosives, in case we want to go boom."

"Yury's dead."

Wolfgang felt a sharp pang in his gut. "Aw, Jesus, what happened?"

The words didn't connect at first: something about two guys, an attack, a car accident, a shooting. When Mad Dog was finished, Wolfgang glanced up into the snow-filled sky and cursed, his breath floating up and away.

"Listen, Kat and I are going to rent a car tomorrow, see if we can board the train sooner. I'll be in touch. And if Pope has anything else for you, listen to him, okay? I'm counting on you, Wolfgang."

"I know you are, boss. Don't worry. Talk to you soon."

Wolfgang tucked the phone in his pocket and closed his eyes. There stood Yury, pointing to the building behind him and saying, "This, you uncultured pig, is Mr. Yul Brynner's house. He was a great thespian, and one time, years ago, I actually got to meet him."

Rossiya Train Number 2
Trans-Siberian Express
Irkutsk
1951 Hours Local Time

Rows of tall, lantern-style lights illuminated the brick paver platform and cast the green outlines of the station in a misty hue.

Svetlanov moved away from the window as the train rolled slowly to a stop. "We're here. Come with me," he ordered Hannah, who'd been cowering in their room ever since he had confronted her.

"Where are we going now?"

"For a little walk. I want you at my side at all times. That's the way it is now."

"Can't I stay here?"

"Get your coat."

Svetlanov's pulse quickened and his eyes burned. The silenced pistol in his pocket felt too heavy, the coat tugging on his shoulder.

His cell phone rang. Gorlach. "Yes?"

"We're outside, with the other three."

"Very well. Do you see the trucks yet?"

"No."

"He didn't say he'd be late."

"No. He might already be near the loading area. I can't see with all the snow, but I will check."

"Do that. I'll be right out."

His men had spent the last hour moving from carriage to carriage in search of the two dark-skinned men who Hannah described, the men she believed now had the diamonds. One of the provodniks swore that he'd seen them, but now their room was empty, wiped clean, no traces of their presence, save for some small stains on the floor. Blood.

So thanks to his girlfriend, he had just lost a fortune in diamonds.

Consequently, he had every intention of killing her. But he would wait until it was all over. First he would rape her, torture her, make her pay in ways she could not imagine, and only after would he grant her relief.

He had once thought that she would make a suitable wife, thought he could teach her how to be a real woman who enjoyed serving her man, thought she could unlearn all of those lessons about being an independent woman fed to her by crazy liberal teachers. He'd had high hopes for Ms. Hannah Lamoureux.

But now, when he looked into her frightened eyes, all he saw was a pathetic bitch whose failure to trust him had placed him in a terrible situation. All those memories of the great sex they'd had meant nothing in the face of this.

He grabbed her by the arm, shoved her into the hall, and they moved together toward the exit.

Gorlach, still wincing over his gunshot wound, took two men down onto the tracks, where they crossed to the other side of the station to a row of maintenance buildings near a concrete loading platform. The snow was blowing hard and he could barely see through it until a pair of headlights were switched on, blinding all of them.

Out of the glare appeared a tall, clean-shaven man bundled in dark wool and wearing a cap. He jogged toward them.

Gorlach reached into his pocket, as did the others, but the man raised his palms and, out of breath, asked, "Are you with Svetlanov?" His Russian sounded native.

"Yes," Gorlach answered.

"We are around the back, waiting."

"Why didn't you call?"

"I thought we did . . . go get your boss. We'll meet you back there."

Gorlach nodded, and as he and his men returned to the platform, it dawned on him why the Zakarova party had not called: They reached the meeting place first and had already positioned their men, giving them the advantage. Svetlanov would not be happy.

There had been some discussion about him posing as Svetlanov, in case Zakarova attempted a double cross, but the good major had already done his homework and could recognize Svetlanov's face. He would deal only with the man himself. Svetlanov had assured all of them that he would be okay. Hannah would serve as a convenient shield should it come down to that.

What a shame. She was an incredible young woman, bold enough to rob the man himself. Gorlach admired and pitied her. She had romanced fire and would be burned. He'd pay a lot for just one hour with her.

Shaking off the thought, he increased his pace, even as he worked his cell phone, planning to get the others into their positions. He glanced up to the station, spotted Svetlanov coming down the platform with Hannah at his side, their caps already heavy with snow.

*   *   *

Major Zakarova sat inside the idling truck, watching as Ekk returned to the cab and hopped inside. "He should be here shortly."

"Good. Be ready to move out."

"All right. But isn't it strange that the Brit hasn't called?"

"Maybe Svetlanov took care of him. A pity. I would've liked his money."

"Me, too."

Zakarova's phone rang, and he knew the number. "Well, hello. Have you calmed down?" he asked Svetlanov. "Are you ready to do business?"

"I'm coming over now."

"Good. I've brought my expert from ALROSA to inspect the payment."

"Of course. That shouldn't take him long. I will see you in a few moments."

"Svetlanov, I hope you are a man of your word, because if a man does not have his word, he is nothing."

Only static answered; Svetlanov had already ended the call.

A tap on the glass to his right startled Zakarova, and there, standing on the truck's running board, was a bespectacled man pointing a pistol at him.

"Well, Ekk, it seems we've found the Brit."

"Major, I'll—"

"No, don't move."

"Yes, sir."

Zakarova slowly rolled down his window.

The Brit shoved his pistol into Zakarova's face. "Major, I'm sorry I didn't get a chance to call."

"And sorry for this rude introduction as well?"

"Listen carefully. I have the diamonds."

"You?"

"We'll talk more about how I've acquired them later."

Zakarova smiled. "You're a fool. Did you think I would trust an amateur thief?"

"And you trust Svetlanov?"

"He's a professional."

"I'll add another ten million to the diamonds if you take your trucks and drive away right now. Don't turn over the warheads to Svetlanov. You have no idea what he plans to do with them. You're soldiers, not terrorists."

"Why are you doing this? You're a mercenary. If you have the diamonds, as you say, you should be leaving the country by now."

"I have my reasons."

"Well, unfortunately, Mr. Bibby, I don't believe you."

Bibby reached into his pocket with a bare hand, held up a large stone, approximately twenty-five carat, between his thumb and forefinger.

"Costume jewelry, Mr. Bibby?"

"Have your man examine this stone!"

"I'm sorry, sir, but your time has run out." Zakarova raised his chin, and Bibby turned his head.

Three men and one woman were coming toward them, fighting against the wind and snow.

And suddenly Bibby hopped down and took off.

"I'll get him," said Ekk, opening his door.

"No, wait. I don't want Svetlanov to know there's a problem. Call Parshin. Tell him to find the Brit, kill him, then search him good. Let's get out, take Svetlanov into the shop, and we'll do our business inside."

"The others are already waiting."

"Good. Come on."

"But sir, what if the Brit—"

"I know, Lieutenant. We are all wolves now."

Zakarova opened his door, climbed down, then stood, waiting for the small party to arrive. As they drew closer, he recognized Svetlanov, who kept the pale-faced woman close to his side with a sharp, gloved grip on her arm. "Major. A pleasure to finally meet you."

Svetlanov thrust out his hand.

Zakarova hesitated, then finally shook it. "Let's get out of this weather. We've already opened the shop and turned on the heater."

"Excellent."

"But first you must introduce me to your lovely wife."

"Oh, she's not my wife. This is Hannah Lamoureux, my fiancée."

"A pleasure to meet you, madam." Zakarova shook her gloved hand, noted the intense expression on her face, her glower aimed at Svetlanov.

And at that moment Zakarova knew for certain that the painfully young, painfully cocky Svetlanov had no plans to make an exchange.

Zakarova led them to a door, which had obviously been opened with a crowbar, its lock busted outward. They moved into the dark confines, and Ekk switched on more lights to reveal a broad garagelike facility for working on locomotive engines. Machine parts lay across worktables, and perimeter shelves buckled under the weight of more parts, boxes, and tools. The place reeked of oil, grease, and fuel, but it felt good to get out of the storm.

Thus far, no one had drawn a weapon, but everyone had their hands in their pockets, including the girl.

The rest of Zakarova's party was already inside, with two of his men posted in hidden positions behind small cranes.

Their diamond expert from ALROSA, a stump of a man, frail, with a gray beard and heavy-rimmed glasses, came forward with an attaché case that he opened across a table to reveal its black velvet interior. Svetlanov had been fascinated with the man's trade and had asked him many questions about how he could tell real gems from fakes. The jeweler said it required the proper tools.

And so he withdrew an examination light from the case. It wasn't north light, the best light, as he had explained earlier, but it would have to do.

Next came a jeweler's 10x triplet loupe and a Mizar DiamondNite All-in-One diamond and moissanite tester. The nine-volt, handheld Mizar probe could differentiate in under two seconds the thermal conductivity levels between nature's finest and the best man-made moissanite crystal in the world. He attached the loupe to his glasses, then flagrantly waved his hands. "The stones, please!"

"Svetlanov?" called Zakarova, gesturing that he hand over the diamonds.

The young man, the "new Russian," wore a grin so dark, so sinister, that even Lucifer would have been envious.

Ekk looked to Zakarova, and there was no disguising the worry on his face.

Gorlach was in charge of a three-man team outside, and his job was to kill the pair of guards near the warhead truck, which was parked behind the buildings, about fifty yards away from the first vehicle. The truck's engine was off, the keys most likely in the major's pocket.

Both guards were heavily armed with AKs and bandoliers of grenades. One was posted at the driver's side door, the other near the truck's tailgate.

After sending his first man off to confront the guy near the door, Gorlach told his second man to move forward and then keep low near one of the tires. On Gorlach's signal, that man would gain access into the cab—first trying the door, then busting out a window if necessary—and then he would employ his high-tech toys to get the vehicle started.

Catching the guards by surprise and quietly taking them out would be the real challenge. Gorlach had brought along a large blade to keep things simple.

He skulked around the truck, sprang upon the guard near the tailgate, yet even as he did, he knew that given his gunshot wound he couldn't win the confrontation—

Which was why he'd given the blade to Latka, a friend of Svetlanov's father, who came in behind him and thrust the blade into the guard's heart.

But as Gorlach rolled over and glanced up, through more pillars of falling snow, he saw a man rise from the shop's roof, a rifle pointed down at him and Latka.

Gorlach began to raise his hands when Latka suddenly turned, about to fire—

A thump rang out, and Latka fell. Gorlach looked up again and saw the soldier still holding his rifle. He hadn't fired, and now swung around, appearing as confused as Gorlach.

Where had that round come from? Gorlach whipped his head, saw only more snow tapering off toward the shadows.

Another thump, and the guy on the roof dropped like a bowling pin.

Out of instinct, Gorlach rolled over, crawled on his hands and knees beneath the truck, glanced up and into the vacant eyes of his other man, who had fallen dead beside the guard. Both men had been taken out!

Was his third man already in the cab?

Gorlach's utter surprise found his lips: "What the fuck?"

Then hands were on his legs and he was being dragged out from beneath the truck.

Panting, he fumbled for his pistol, came up with it, but not before a boot knocked the gun out of his hand, a boot accompanied by a familiar voice: "Remember me?"

It was the Brit, eyes blazing behind his misty glasses, lips tightening into a grimace. "Do me a favor this time? Die."

Gorlach closed his eyes.

Svetlanov shifted over to the jeweler from ALROSA and reached into his inner coat pocket, as though for the diamonds. He even imagined the two bars of soap tucked inside the pocket and reasoned that it was just as well that they were gone. He was even more motivated now to take possession of the warheads.

Without them, there was nothing. Without them, his father would be beyond disappointed. Svetlanov feared that his father might kill him for such a failure, the same way his uncle had killed his cousin, who had lost the family over ten million dollars because he allowed himself to be duped.

And so Svetlanov reached into his pocket, keeping Hannah close, and in one liquid motion had the knife in his grip, let it flash, then drove it straight into the jeweler's heart.

He might as well have been impaling a piece of steak; the feeling was the same, with slight resistance and some scraping as he hit a rib.

Then he turned, placing the jeweler between himself and Zakarova's men—

Even as everyone in the room produced their pistols, arms extending.

"Oh my God," gasped Hannah. "Oh my God."

Zakarova looked at the young man to his right and cried, "Shoot him!"

And that's when Svetlanov rushed forward with the body of the jeweler still in his grasp, the young man firing a round into the dead man's shoulder.

Gunfire rang out again, some silenced, some loud and rattling the shop's rolling doors.

Svetlanov let the jeweler's body fall away even as he reached for and came up with his pistol. He fired a round directly into the young man's head, then faced Zakarova, who had a pistol aimed at his gut.

"Hold your fire!" the major cried.

Hannah had slid under one of the tables, knees pulled up, face buried, her entire body shaking.

"Ekk?" the major called, looking down at his fallen comrade. "Ekk?"

"He's dead, old man. Now hand over the keys to your trucks."

"I have a pistol to your gut, and two other men in this facility that you can't even see."

"You have nothing."

Abruptly, Svetlanov raised his pistol and took a step back from the major.

That was a signal to his other men, who had just slipped into the room.

Rounds drummed loudly, and the major staggered back a moment, his chest riddled, a final round punching his cheek and knocking him onto the floor, even as Svetlanov hit the floor himself, to avoid more incoming fire.

As Zakarova lay there dying, he glanced over to Ekk, whose blank face, so young, so very, very young, was just a meter away from his.

You're too young to remember the days when we trained because we loved our country, the days when we crossed the bridge into Afghanistan and fought with honor.

I know how that story ends, and I'm glad I wasn't there. I don't want to remember.

Old Russia will return!

We all have our dreams.

Yes, we do, Lieutenant. I hope you dream well. And I'm sorry that it came to this. You were a good solider. We both were. That's all that really matters.

Svetlanov threw himself across the floor, toward the table where Hannah was hiding, as more rounds ricocheted off tables and machinery.

He realized that the major did have two more men inside the building, and he was about to explode with rage if the rest of his men couldn't silence them.

All the noise was sure to draw the local police at the station. Gorlach had assured him that they had made the proper donations so those officers would look the other way. That wasn't very comforting, though, since there was always one or two who refused to be bribed, one or two who thought they could change the world with a badge and pistol.

"Hannah, come on," he grunted, seizing her arm.

"No!"

"Hannah!"

Suddenly, she rushed out from beneath the table, got to her feet and sprinted for the door, gunfire striking the wall a meter away.

While Svetlanov scrambled to his feet, she opened the door and vanished into the snow.

"Hannah!"

Three of Svetlanov's men were still trading fire with the last two soldiers as he broke from his cover and headed for the exit. He thought that if Hannah wound up getting him shot, then he would kill her right here, right now.

He reached the door, turned his shoulder toward it and rammed himself outside. Glancing to his right, to his left, he saw her racing around the back of the building, bound for the truck with the warheads.

If Gorlach's team hadn't taken out the guards back there, then she would be shot within seconds. He wanted to call the man, but there wasn't time.

Svetlanov raced along the wall, his Italian leather loafers providing no traction in the snow. He rounded the corner, saw the truck, and nearly fell as he hit a patch of ice.

Hannah had slowed near the truck, looking at the dead men lying near it, the snow already burying them. She stopped and whirled to face him, sensing his approach. "Sergei! What have you done?"

But Svetlanov's thoughts were whirling themselves, colliding, his heart slamming his ribs. Yes, the guards near the truck had been taken out, but so had his team! What was going on? He rushed up to her, grabbed her wrist. "You have no idea the problems you've caused me! No idea!"

"I'm not going. No!"

He grabbed her by the neck, slapped her across the face so hard that his hand smarted.

She screamed, then cried. Svetlanov squeezed her neck and smacked her again as his cell phone began to ring. Blood gushed from her nose as she fought against his grip.

He turned back for the building—

And came face-to-face with a gloved fist that made contact with his eye and sent him tottering back until he collapsed onto his rump, sending up clouds of snow. He literally saw stars, the ground listing as though he were at sea.

"Oh, oh, oh my God!" Hannah screamed, sounding more surprised than scared.

Svetlanov blinked, turned his head, realized he'd dropped his pistol as he glimpsed the tall man in a provodnik's uniform holding a gun on him.

"Daddy?" asked Hannah.

The provodnik glared over the rim of his glasses and in Russian cried, "Shut up! Just shut up!"

"Hannah, you know him?"

"Yes," she said, backhanding blood from her mouth and chin. "He's my father!"

Chapter 10

....

Svetlanov glanced to his pistol lying in the snow.

The provodnik Hannah claimed was her father lifted his silenced weapon a bit higher, fired a round in the snow between Svetlanov and the weapon. "Don't move," he said.

Svetlanov raised his hands.

"What the fuck are you doing here?" Hannah shouted in English, grabbing the provodnik by his jacket collar. "What the fuck? Have you been following me all this time? Jesus Christ, Daddy! Why? Like you give a shit?"

"Hannah, is he really your father?"

"No!" cried the provodnik. "Your little whore is on drugs! She's delusional!"

"Wait a minute! You're the Brit, aren't you! *You are*!" Svetlanov's eyes grew even wider. "Hannah, sweetheart, he is your father, isn't he?"

She nodded. "I don't know what the fuck he thinks he's doing here."

"Maybe he's come to rescue you from me, huh?"

"It's over now, Hannah," said the Brit. "Close your eyes." The Brit shoved Hannah aside, moved toward Svetlanov.

"No!" she cried, moving between them. "Are you crazy?"

"Go over to the truck. *Now!*" shouted the Brit.

"I won't let you do this."

"Neither will I," Svetlanov said, glancing over the Brit's shoulder at the two men hustling toward them, cutting through the clouds of falling snow.

The Brit glanced at Svetlanov, stole a look over his shoulder, then dropped to the snow, screaming, "Hannah, get down!"

As the Brit tried to target the oncoming men, Svetlanov dove for his pistol, came up with it, turned it on the Brit—

Only to find Hannah rushing up to him, screaming, "Don't you shoot my father!"

Svetlanov couldn't take his eyes from her. She would try to kill him with her bare hands if he squeezed his trigger. He didn't doubt that for a second.

"Hold your fire! Hold your fire!" ordered Svetlanov, then slid his arm around Hannah's neck, held her there, put his pistol to her head.

"Sergei, you want to kill me now?" she asked.

"Shut up," he growled.

Seeing his daughter, the Brit rolled and sat up as Svetlanov's two men arrived, covering him with their pistols.

"I'll kill her. Don't think I won't."

The Brit lowered his voice and said in English, "I know you will."

"Drop your weapon."

The Brit glanced at the two men, at Svetlanov, then tossed his pistol at Svetlanov's feet.

"Who are you?"

"I thought we've already established that."

"You shot one of my men."

"Actually, I've shot more than one."

"Get up."

As the Brit complied, Svetlanov faced his men, fired off orders, told them to get back to the shop, search for the keys, hide the bodies, then get the trucks moving toward the platform, where the train's loading crew was already waiting for them. He had arranged for the transfer days in advance, the loading crew paid handsomely for their work and silence.

"What's your name?" he asked the Brit. "It's not Lamoureux, I assume."

"My name is Tony Blair. Fuck you."

"Hannah, what's your father's name?" Svetlanov pushed the pistol harder against her temple.

"Go ahead, shoot me," she said.

"Hannah . . . " warned the Brit.

"Just kill me, you bastard!"

"Okay."

Hannah closed her eyes, sniffled, then suddenly said, "I'm sorry, Daddy. His name is Alastair Bibby."

"And who does he work for?"

She opened her eyes. "I don't know."

"Don't lie, Hannah." Svetlanov's voice turned darkly musical.

"He worked for the government. That's all we know. That's all he ever told us."

Svetlanov narrowed his gaze on Bibby. "You're professionally trained. I can tell."

"You're a bright young man with too much responsibility. Let me make this easy for you. Now that our mutual enemy Zakarova is gone, you and I can do business."

Svetlanov almost chuckled. "Oh, is that right? Come on, walk . . . "

He started toward the shop, holding Hannah close, the pistol still to her head. He kept near the wall, while his men got the warhead truck started.

"Can you pick up my weapon?" asked Bibby. "It's expensive."

Svetlanov made a face.

The Brit moved ahead of them, muttering, "One of my favorite pistols."

"You're a quirky one, aren't you?" Svetlanov said.

Bibby spun around, holding a diamond in Svetlanov's face. Not only did the stone surprise Svetlanov, but he hadn't noticed the Brit reach into his pocket to produce it. Or had he been holding it the entire time? "You see this?" asked Bibby. "You see what I have?"

Svetlanov frowned, tried to hide the fact that he had just lost his breath. "Hannah, you lied to me! You said there were two men. You said they found your purse!"

"They did," snapped Bibby before she could answer. "She didn't lie. They had the diamonds. I killed them and dumped them off the train. Now I have the stones hidden away. And you and I are going to strike a bargain."

"Hold that stone up to my nose."

The Brit smiled knowingly and complied. "They still smell like soap, if that's what you're looking for."

"My God. You do have them."

"Or maybe I just have one. You really don't know. There are too many unknowns here. Let's talk."

Svetlanov's eyes burned, and he told himself it was from the cold, not the stress. "All right. You give me the diamonds, and I let your daughter live."

"Or you release my daughter, and I tell you where I've hidden the diamonds. You kill her or me, and you'll only get one. That's it."

"But I'll still have the contents of that truck."

"Be careful. Zakarova was quite a cunning man. He could have bobby-trapped your little prizes."

"My problem. Not yours. Now tell me. All you want is her?"

"That's all."

"And you're obviously aware of what's on that truck?"

"I am."

"Then there is no bargain. You need to die." Svetlanov removed the pistol from Hannah's head, turned it on Bibby.

The Dog Pound
Talisay City
Cebu, the Philippines
1934 Hours Local Time

Billy Pope was just finishing his dinner when the estate's security chief, John Gonzales, called. This was not unusual, since Mad Dog had left Pope in charge of the small mansion and guest house, and the chief liked to check in at least twice before Pope retired for the evening.

However, what was unusual and had Pope rolling his wheelchair toward the main kitchen's back window was the chief's message: "Mr. Pope, I'm in the backyard. One of my men is dead."

"He's what?"

"He's dead, sir. You heard that right. It was Felix along the wall."

"How?"

"Stabbed, sir."

"You call the police?"

"Yes. The team at the front gate is heading back into the house."

The moment Gonzales finished, a thud echoed from the basement, then all power went out.

Pope rolled himself out of the kitchen, swearing over his still-healing gunshot wounds, his mind wanting to take him up the stairs and into his room, where he would retrieve his pistols.

Now he was stuck in the dark, either about to be robbed or worse.

"Power's been cut," he told the chief.

"I see that. We're on our way."

Billy Pope, former Navy SEAL turned mercenary, was used to being in dangerous situations—that was an average day at the office.

But being unarmed, in the dark, and stuck in a wheelchair was another story, one that could only have a shitty ending.

A door hinge creaked somewhere on the other side of the house.

Pope held his breath, thought of rolling himself forward, thought again.

He pricked up his ears, listened for footfalls.

This wasn't just a robbery. Couldn't be. Had he and Wolfgang pissed off the local terrorists enough to incite this kind of response? Maybe. Those Abu Sayyaf meatheads were known for going on the occasional rampage.

Or perhaps this had something to do with Bibby, with Hezbollah, with the diamonds Moody kept talking about. Pope was feeding Mad Dog information. Maybe these assholes wanted to put a stop to that, he thought. Cut off Mad Dog's intel at the source? If so, they had gone to great lengths, resorted to murder, which could only mean that Mad Dog and Kat weren't just up to their ears in serious shit, they were about to drown in it.

Pope heard the footfalls now, drawing near.

Trans-Siberian Express
Irkutsk Station
2034 Hours Local Time

Svetlanov stared down the sight of his pistol and into Bibby's eyes.

"You're going to do this?" asked Hannah. "You're going to shoot my father right in front of me?"

Svetlanov flicked his glance to her. "Yes. You don't know your father, Hannah. You don't know him at all."

"I don't know you, either. How many other lies have you told me?"

Svetlanov ground his teeth, then exploded. *"Shut up!"*

"Is my life worth twenty million or more?" Bibby asked. "Because, young man, that's what it'll cost you. And it seems you've lost your girlfriend as well. All you've got is your cargo, and I can make it very easy . . . or very difficult for you when you reach Vladivostok. Do you understand?"

Svetlanov could no longer hold his hand steady. He desperately wanted to shoot Bibby, but he wanted answers even more. "How do you know so much? You're working for someone! Who? Sinitsyna?"

"Maybe I am. The colonel and I have had several enlightening conversations. You don't know what our relationship is. I suggest you keep me and my daughter close, and when we reach Vladivostok, you will unload your cargo, I will give you the location of the diamonds, and she and I will walk away."

"No."

"Then you lose the diamonds. And when you reach Vladivostok, life will become quite unpleasant for you."

"You're bluffing."

Bibby's face was unreadable. "You'll never know, will you?"

"What I do know is that you love your daughter." Svetlanov grinned. Here was the right button to push. "I know you don't want anything to happen to her. She's so beautiful." He moved to Hannah, reached up to stroke her cheek, but she smacked his hand away.

Bibby's tone grew hard. "Don't play this game, young man. I've been at it for a long time. You won't like how it ends."

Svetlanov smirked. "Move."

Bibby nodded, turned forward and began to walk.

"And you, too, Hannah."

She shook her head.

"I said *move*!"

"You fucking bastard." She closed her eyes momentarily, took a deep breath, then hurried after her father.

They reached the edge of the building, and Svetlanov shoved his pistol into his pocket, keeping his grip on the weapon. "We're getting back on the train. All three of us. We're going back to our room, Hannah, where your father will remain our guest."

"Sergei, what's in those?" Hannah asked as the big truck carrying the warheads rumbled on, the crates labeled AGRICULTURAL MACHINERY covered with snow.

"Very expensive equipment. Not your concern."

"Would you like me to explain it to her?" Bibby asked. "I don't think 'expensive equipment' is an entirely accurate description."

"Just walk!"

Once on the platform, they wove through the other passengers, and Svetlanov frowned because Bibby didn't try to bolt off. Inside their carriage, Alek was a bit taken aback by Bibby's uniform.

"I've never seen you before," said the young provodnik.

Bibby answered in flawless Russian: "That's because I'm your supervisor, and I normally ride in plain clothes to see what kind of pathetic service you are offering our customers."

Alek's mouth fell open.

"He's lying to you, Alek," said Svetlanov. "He's just a friend playing a practical joke on me. The uniform isn't his, sorry."

"Sir, with all due respect, I think impersonating a provodnik is—"

"Oh, he knows, Alek," said Svetlanov. "He knows."

They moved through the aisle and into the room. Svetlanov closed the door behind them, withdrew his pistol and motioned for them to sit on the beds.

"You want to go to Vladivostok, don't you?" he asked Bibby.

"It's a nice city."

"Don't fuck with me."

Someone knocked on the door. It was Ustin, a stocky man with a double chin and bushy brows, Svetlanov's new right hand. He had joined the group in Irkutsk. "They're loading the crates now."

"That was fast."

"I tipped them extra, just as you said. They're taking care of the bodies for us, too."

"Very good. Call me when they're finished."

Ustin nodded, hurried away.

Svetlanov's cell phone rang. *Damn it.* His father was

calling from Vladivostok, and he needed to take the call. He would rather do so in private. He stepped out into the hall, closed the door. "Hello, Father. Good news."

The Dog Pound
Talisay City
Cebu, the Philippines
1940 Hours Local Time

Billy Pope was on the floor, crawling with only the use of his arms and barely one leg.

He had thrown himself out of his wheelchair, figuring he could take cover behind one of the sofas in the living room until the chief's men arrived.

Why couldn't he be more like Wolfgang, who liked to walk around with at least two weapons at all times? That skinny turd had those ankle holsters and always said that the extra weight helped him to develop strong claves.

Shit. Pope tucked himself between the wall and sofa, thinking, What am I doing? Am I going to lie down and die without a fight?

Fuck that. Just as he pushed himself away from the wall, the front door burst open and the chief's men came in, shouting, their flashlights flickering across the walls.

Exactly one second later everyone and his mother who had a gun started firing. Glass shattered. Expensive lamps and pottery smashed to the floor. Mad Dog would be pissed, and he himself was ready to piss his pants.

Someone groaned, slammed into the sofa, then rolled off and hit the floor with another gasp.

Then a pistol clinked and slid forward, just out of Pope's reach.

He forced himself out, keeping tight to the side of the sofa.

The wounded man—one of the chief's employees—was just to his left and clutching a gunshot wound in his neck, blood spurting.

Pope winced, forced the image from his mind, told himself to focus, focus, focus.

He grabbed the bleeding man's weapon, a .45 caliber pistol, then turned over, sat up, and tucked himself back into the corner.

The gunfire tapered off.

Silence, save for his pulse beating like a timpani drum in his head.

"Mr. Pope, are you all right?"

Pope was about to open his mouth—

But his training kicked in. If there was anyone else still inside, he'd be giving up his location.

"Mr. Pope?"

A triplet of gunfire from an automatic weapon echoed through the halls.

That wasn't an AK-47, he thought. Something much better, more expensive. No, these weren't Abu Sayyaf thugs. How'd they get exotic weapons into the country? Maybe they had black market connections—

And what the fuck was he thinking about that for? His ass was about to be waxed!

He wanted to call out to the chief, figured he'd dial the man's cell phone instead. Perhaps the ringing would distract the man or men inside enough for him to slip out the service door, about thirty feet away.

He hit the speed dial button, heard the chief's phone ring. Then he pushed away from the corner and, peering through the shadows, homed in on the sound.

There was the chief, slumped across the carpet.

A figure moved over him.

Pope crawled forward a few feet then stopped, propping himself up on his elbows. He took aim.

Rossiya Train Number 2
Trans-Siberian Express
Irkutsk Station
2042 Hours Local Time

The second after Svetlanov closed the door to take his phone call in the carriage aisle, Alastair Bibby reached into his pocket, withdrew his BlackBerry, and began frantically typing in a text message.

"He's going to kill us, and you want to play with that?" Hannah sighed and cursed.

Bibby finished the message, found Kat's satellite phone number and sent it off:

> LEAVING IRKUTSK FOR VLAD VIA ROSSIYA #2.
> IN CARRIAGE #7. PRISONER. HELP. BIBBY.

He'd told Kat not to come after him, but he needed her, along with Mad Dog. His years of training had taught him that he couldn't do this on his own.

Mad Dog would ask, *Why didn't you come to me and tell me your daughter was in trouble, tell me you were trying to save her from the middle of an international arms deal involving terrorists?*

And he would answer, *Because you would have said no. Because even if you agreed to help, we'd have to do it your way, not mine. Because I would have to reveal too much.*

In the beginning, when it was all for crown and country, it was clear. His fellow professionals warned him: never marry! A wife and children are an Achilles's heel.

A family was a distraction requiring a lifetime's balancing act—stealing, ever stealing, time and attention from the task at hand, requiring him to suppress and compartmentalize huge pieces of his life. The necessary lying and the emotionally draining need to remember those lies was an incredible burden, accompanied by the bitterness of always placing the people you loved second to the job.

He'd spent years reading the misunderstood and unspoken accusations of selfishness in his family's eyes. To preserve his own sanity, he'd spent his entire adult life adding layer upon layer of numbing isolation between himself and the two people he loved the most.

Yet at the same time, he would do anything to save them.

Anything.

Mad Dog would go on: *In order to protect your secrets, you stole from me.*

My fucking daughter's life was at stake!

I don't care.

And I'd kill anyone to save her.

Even me?

Even you.

Mad Dog had no children. He would never entirely understand.

And he, Mr. Stiff Upper Lip, Mr. Cool, Calm, and Collected, was thoroughly fucked now.

His pulse raced even faster as he reminded himself that he had no backup plan once they reached the end of the line, no help, nothing, save for the diamonds, Mad Dog's money, and his own negotiation skills.

What a fool he'd been! What a complete and utter fool!

He had convinced himself that he could strike a deal with Zakarova, outbid the mafia, send Zakarova back into the mountains, and rescue Hannah because as a father he had to believe that would work. As a father, he had to believe he could do something to protect his daughter.

But the plan had been shit! He had shuddered with the desire to act—to do something—when he should have thought things through more than he had.

He wanted at once to hug and strangle Hannah for what she'd done.

But it wasn't all her fault. He hadn't been a true father. He knew that. Simone had raised her. She had been the concerned parent.

He was selfish! And now he'd lost the only woman he had ever loved.

His dear Simone made a terrible mistake: She had gone to Waffa for help. How she had learned about Waffa was a mystery to him, but it seemed she knew a lot more about his business than he was aware of.

And according to another of his sources in Ramallah, she'd been asking about Svetlanov, and one of Waffa's men, a traitor, had gone to Hezbollah and tipped them off.

Hezbollah had sent agents after Simone, believing she knew about the deal and was going to expose them. His blood had turned to ice as he'd listened to the call.

"Your wife is dead. I'm so sorry."

He still hadn't brought himself to tears, and holding them in, holding all of it inside, was making him sick.

But he just couldn't grieve now. And he couldn't break the news to his daughter. In fact, he could still not believe it himself. The words would not come.

And most ironic of all, he would not have learned about Svetlanov's plan were it not for happenstance, had his daughter not noticed the handsome young Russian in a nightclub.

Bibby glanced at Hannah, barely able to catch his breath. He needed to tell her everything about Svetlanov:

"Listen to me. Your boyfriend plans to sell two nuclear warheads to Hezbollah, and they'll sell the warheads to Iran. The Iranians are going to nuke Haifa and Tel Aviv at the same time. This is the signal for what they're calling the final jihad. Your boyfriend doesn't care how many people die, so long as he gets his money."

"And you're here to stop him?"

"I came to get you out of this fucking mess."

"So, then . . . you're just like him. Selfish. You came for me. And you don't care how many people die."

"Is that a diamond in your nose?"

"Don't change the subject! You don't care how many people die!"

"Please, we're all we've got now."

She shook her head. "We're not."

"Young lady, you've no idea what I've done, no idea how hard it's been."

"And neither do you. I don't know why Mom . . . What did you say?"

Bibby frowned. "What?"

"You said we're all we've got. You mean right now?"

"Yes."

"I've seen that look. What are you not telling me?"

Bibby averted his gaze. *Lie to her. Just lie.*

"Did something happen to Mom?"

He closed his eyes.

The door slid open and Svetlanov and his exceedingly smug expression returned, his pistol directed toward Bibby. "Did you miss me?"

"Fuck off," Hannah snapped.

"And I thought we were in love," he replied with mock innocence.

"I trust it will be a very long ride to Vladivostok," said Bibby. "A very long ride."

"For you especially, since you'll be taken into another room, where my men will torture you until you tell us where you've hidden the rest of those diamonds. I'll take that one you have right now."

Bibby reached into his pocket, withdrew the stone, tossed it at Svetlanov's feet. "Old movie trick. When you bend down to pick it up, I go for your gun."

"So I bend down, never taking my eyes off you, and pick up the diamond," he said, doing just that. "Old movie trick, huh? From a bad movie, I think."

"Young man, you keep changing the plan. Again, if anything happens to either of us, this train will never reach Vladivostok."

Svetlanov's grin began to fade as he rolled the diamond between his fingers.

"Sergei, how could you do this?" asked Hannah.

"Do what? This is just business. And if you expect me to believe that you had no idea what my family does, then you're an idiot. You just didn't want to admit it. It's all just business."

"So's this."

Hannah sprang to her feet, lunged at him as Bibby screamed and Svetlanov tried to fend off her attack.

She got her hands around his neck, forced him back toward the door and began to squeeze, but Bibby latched onto her wrists and yanked her away, the force sending both of them crashing to the floor.

Yes, he could have shot her, Svetlanov thought. But he hadn't.

Instead, he rubbed his sore neck with one hand, aimed the pistol at her with the other.

Perhaps he was just waiting to say good-bye.

"I could shoot you right now," he began. "But I plan on fucking you a few more times before this trip is over. How does that make you feel, Bibby? Knowing that I'll be fucking your daughter in the next room, that she'll be crying and sore and begging me to stop?"

Bibby sat there, out of breath, fingers tensing with the desire to finish the job Hannah had started. "If there is a God, and He's looking upon you right now, He will know what to do, and I will offer to be His instrument of revenge."

Svetlanov snorted. "What is that? Shakespeare?"

"No. Bibby."

Chapter 11

....

Billy Pope shifted his weight from one elbow to the other, found the figure's head in his line of sight.

The pistol had very little recoil, and a split second later the figure slumped to the floor.

Pope just breathed, kept his aim on the body, waited for movement.

"Mr. Pope?" called another voice. "Mr. Pope? We got them! The house is clear!"

It was another of the chief's men. "I'm over here," Pope said wearily.

The young security guard reached him, all eyes glowing in the dark. "Are you all right?"

"Who were they?"

"Don't know."

"Help me over to that one." The guard helped him to his feet, threw one of Pope's arms over his shoulder, and they moved to the hall. "Flashlight?"

The guard handed over his light, and Pope directed it into the dead man's face, a Caucasian about thirty years old, closely cropped hair.

"Go upstairs and get me my digital camera."

"Sir?"

"Just do it."

"Okay. The police should arrive soon."

Pope wanted to take a photo of the man's face, run it through his database. He assumed the guy had no ID, and a quick search through his pockets confirmed that.

However, there was something on his forearm that caught Pope's attention: a tattoo of an Orthodox cross, with that extra horizontal line above and that extra diagonal line below. He'd seen such crosses atop the spires of churches in Moscow.

"You're a long way from home, aren't you?" he muttered to the corpse.

Amethyst Hotel
Tolstoy Street
Khabarovsk, Russia
2255 Hours Local Time

Mad Dog had already dozed off, and Kat was lying awake, watching him sleep, when her phone beeped. She had a text message, read it, and nearly fell out of the bed.

She shook Michael until he woke. "Jesus, what?"

"Read this."

He did. "Now the fucker asks for help?"

"You know, I had a feeling he would."

"Oh, you did? You share that with me?"

"No, but—"

"So now what?"

Kat's expression grew emphatic. "So now we come up with a plan to save his ass."

"Why didn't he tell us who's holding him?"

"I don't know."

Mad Dog's sat phone rang. "You got something for me, Billy?"

Kat moved in closer so she could listen in:

"Good news and bad news. Good news is, I think we can get the bloodstains out of the carpets and repair the bullet holes in the walls."

"What the fuck are you talking about?"

"Two assholes broke into the Pound, killed the chief and a few of his men."

"Jesus Christ! You all right?"

"Yeah," Pope answered, sounding as if he could hardly believe it himself. "We got 'em. I'm running the IDs. One guy I'm calling Boris has a Russian cross tattooed on his forearm."

"Hold on." Mad Dog covered the receiver. "What the fuck now?" he said to Kat. "Who sent those guys?"

"Well, if they're Russians, maybe they're mafia. I don't know. Could be the colonel again. Maybe he sent two teams."

"And now that old fucker's on the loose, shit."

"Billy, thank God you're all right," Kat said, loud enough so he could hear her.

"I got a fucking mess to clean up, I'll tell you that. Police are here now. I'll deal with this headache, just wanted to give you a heads-up. I called Moody. Still haven't heard back. Wolfgang got the pics I sent him. He's standing by."

"All right," said Mad Dog. "Just hang in there. Call Manila. Talk to our good friend the major, see if he can loan us a squad for a few days to keep watch."

"I was thinking the same thing. I'll check in again in the morning."

"All right. Stay in touch."

Kat grabbed Mad Dog's hand as he thumbed off the phone. "There's no way I can sleep. Not now."

"Me, neither. Guess that little nap will have to be enough. You want to pack up, get that rental car, get the hell out of here?"

She nodded. "But first I want to text-message Bibby."

"Now, think about it. He got off a message to you, saying he was a prisoner. They didn't confiscate his phone?"

"Good point. But are you saying that *he's* the one setting us up?"

"I don't know. I don't believe anything. I don't trust anyone . . . Shit."

"Trust me."

"You know what I mean."

She began typing in the message:

> COMING FOR YOU. HOPING TO BOARD THE
> TRAIN IN CHITA. KAT.

"Okay, here goes nothing." She sent off the message, then rose from the bed and started toward her small suitcase. "Have I told you how much fun I'm having?"

Mad Dog rubbed the corners of his eyes. "I don't know why you're here."

She raised her brows. "Dumb-ass love."

An hour later Kat and Mad Dog got the bad news from the young man behind the rental car counter: Traveling from Khabarovsk to Chita via "the road" was treacherous at best, since that corridor through Siberia was still under heavy construction, with long, long stretches of dirt and gravel and thousands of potholes. The kid said it would take them three to four days at best to reach Chita.

Bibby's train would be in Chita in about nineteen hours, according to Kat's map.

And worse, a massive storm front was pushing through, having already dumped a foot of snow on Irkutsk.

They might be able to charter a small plane, but they'd have to wait till morning and after the snowstorm had passed. The kid did, however, have another idea: Why not board the train heading back to Moscow? They still wouldn't reach Chita in time, but maybe they could get off at another stop.

"Look," said Kat, "we get on the train and we ride until we can't ride no more."

"But we need time to buy tickets and all that."

"We'll make the time."

They took a cab down to the train station, bought their tickets, and boarded the train.

"You know I like to travel," Mad Dog said, setting down his suitcase in their two-berth compartment. "But when this is all over, I just want to go home. Planes, trains, and automobiles. We won't need to ride bikes at some point, will we?"

"No bikes. Skateboards and mopeds, maybe." Kat checked her watch. Exactly 1:00 A.M. in the morning. "But at least now we both can sleep. I was dreading the idea of sitting in a car all that time."

Mad Dog nodded, and she went to the small window, glanced out at the rows of lights along the station, saw a young man hugging a young woman before she boarded a train across the platform.

The carriage grew eerily quiet, and Kat pulled back from the window, settled down onto the bed and closed her eyes. She felt Mad Dog sit on the bed, and he began to stroke her hair, which always sent her into a deep sleep.

"Kat?" he whispered.

"What?"

"Nothing."

She opened her eyes. "What?"

He pursed his lips. "It's just . . . what am I going to do?"

"About Bibby?"

"Yeah."

"We talked about this already. Stop thinking about it. Just shut up and shut down. Sleep. Who knows when we'll get another chance."

"You're right."

She gave him that look: *Of course I am.* Then she rolled over and pushed herself deeper into the pillow as the train lurched forward, the carriage shook, and then the steady and comforting vibration worked up and into the bed.

Rossiya Train Number 2
Trans-Siberian Express
West of Slyudyanka
2303 Hours Local Time

Bibby wondered if Kat had replied to his text message. He couldn't check to see because Svetlanov had finally ordered one of his men to search him, and they found his BlackBerry, although it was password-protected so they could not view any of his data, and he'd die before giving up the password. At least their delay in confiscating it had allowed him to call for help.

He sat on the floor beside Hannah, whose head rested on his shoulder. She was asleep, breathing deeply, while Svetlanov was slouched in the chair, staring at them and sipping vodka.

"The diamonds are on this train, aren't they?"

"Or not." Bibby smiled. "Have your men been looking for them? Did they search my room?"

"My men are very thorough."

"Two bars of soap. Small but not impossible to find. Your men are incompetent."

"You hid them outside the train, beneath the wheels or on the roof or somewhere."

"That would make them less convenient to find. But you assume I've been working alone. You assume no one close to you is capable of being bribed. You assume a lot. The diamonds could be on their way back to the UK for all you know."

Svetlanov was a cunning young man, but as Bibby had already noted, highly susceptible to suggestion.

"And I also assume you would never tip your hand to me," Svetlanov said. "You'll say anything to keep me thinking and keep yourself and her alive."

"You don't know me very well." They had bound his hands behind his back, and the electrical cord they used dug into his skin. Bibby rolled his wrists, winced, then added, "I don't have to say anything. Not anymore. You've already made your decision. You'll keep us alive because you want to sell those warheads, and you want to collect the diamonds. You went to a lot of trouble to get them, taking out an armored car. I read about it. An impressive operation."

Svetlanov grinned then caught himself. "Who are you? British Intelligence?"

"Your friend the major knew exactly who I was. It seems his intelligence is a lot better than yours. But alas I forget, you're just a glorified street thug, a punk in a silk suit. You deal drugs. You don't do this. Not this. You're in over your head. And it's just a matter of time before you will drown, young man. Trust me."

"What the fuck do you know about me, my family? Fuck off."

"Before I do, let me say this: Intelligence networks around the globe are now aware of what you're doing."

"Well, if they are, that wasn't your work. You came here to get your daughter, and you wouldn't have called anyone."

"Jesus, man, don't you have a bloody conscience? Do you know what's going to happen?"

"I'm letting the ragheads blow themselves up. And I don't fucking care. Not one bit."

"It'll all be traced to Russia and back to you. The unique residue and residual fallout from the detonations leave identifiable trace elements, an infallible chemical fingerprint pointing to the country of manufacture."

"I don't believe you."

"You should. It's as easy as tracing an oil spill down to the ship's tank that leaked it. But you could bail now. Walk away with the diamonds. Take those warheads and return them to the army, where they belong."

"Do you honestly believe I would ever do that?"

"Zakarova had no intention of selling them to you. His plan was to screw you out of the diamonds. He knew that placing those warheads on the black market would mean the deaths of thousands, including children. He knew that could never happen."

"Maybe. But it's too late for that now. My buyers would come for me, my father, all of us."

"So you've made a deal with the devil and there's no turning back."

"I don't want to turn back. I want my money. And maybe this is our way to change history."

Bibby closed his eyes.

And inside he screamed.

**Train Station
Vladivostok
0945 Hours Local Time**

Wolfgang wasn't sure whether to shake the man's hand or kick him in the balls.

He was leaning more toward the handshake.

But the ball kicking came in a close second.

"So what the hell's an ugly motherfucker like you doing in a Siberian shithole like this?"

He had rehearsed the line, a mouthful, because if he couldn't physically break the man's balls, then he'd do it verbally.

CIA agent James Moody, cheeks and nose bright red, extended his hand and said, "What am I doing here? I'm on vacation. But first I have to bail out your sorry asses—again. What else?"

"So the boss doesn't even know you're here?"

"Nope. Like I said, when I landed, I checked in, and Billy boy gave me your number. Let's go get some breakfast. Then we can talk about the local women."

They started through the waiting area, passing bundled up people sitting on benches and hunkering down against the heavy wind and cold. Damned snow was still falling.

"I thought you wanted a tour of the station," Wolfgang said.

"I did. Too fucking cold now. You armed?"

"Not at the moment, but I got some nice toys up in my hotel room. I'll hook you up."

"Good."

"So, you here about the colonel?"

"Who, Sinitsyna?"

"Yeah, he fucking escaped."

Moody stopped. "What?"

Wolfgang explained, then said, "Boss thinks he could show up here. I got some pics."

"I'll make a few calls myself, but MI6 must be all over it by now."

"Yeah. And we confirmed that Bibby is definitely on board the train. He contacted Kat. Says he's being held prisoner. Didn't say by whom."

"Idiot. We got diamonds, we got Hezbollah. We got a dead woman who might've been his wife. Be nice if he told us what the fuck he's doing . . . "

"Hey, don't look up, but there are two guys across the way. Look like businessmen. Very well dressed. They've been eyeing me since I came down here."

"Well, we look like a couple of ugly Americans, but being paranoid isn't such a bad thing in a Siberian shithole such as this."

"Let's recon the Russkies."

They walked by, and Moody said, "Mafia. Russian mafia."

"How the fuck do you know?"

"I work for the CIA. This shit I know."

"Then give me some schooling."

"Look at 'em. Imported suits, shoes. And the one guy's got a hole in his earlobe from his gang days in Moscow, got code numbers on the tag of his SUV back in the city."

"You're full of shit."

"And you ain't paying attention. We need to get pictures of those fuckers."

"I got my phone," said Wolfgang. "But I can't get close enough."

"I don't know what you assholes would do without me."

Moody turned back, started across the waiting area toward a tall column near the platform. The two "business" men were standing there, one checking his watch. "Take out your camera, act like a tourist."

Scanning with exaggerated turns of his head, Moody found the right place to stand, just a few meters away from the two men, and cried in English, "This is good. Right here!"

"Okay, Uncle Fester, calm down," said Wolfgang,

smiling. "I got a good shot." He held up the camera and clicked off two quick pictures, turning the phone slightly.

"Got it?" asked Moody.

Wolfgang nodded.

"I can't wait till the boys back home see this."

"More vacation photos?" Wolfgang asked. "They'll be bored out of their minds."

As they hurried away from the column and the two mafia men, Wolfgang had to grin. "You're playing on our team now."

"Temporary insanity. And hey, don't ever tell Hertzog this, but I've hated him so much because he's so goddamned good at what he does. He really pisses me off."

Wolfgang wriggled his brows. "I'll keep the secret, so long as you buy breakfast."

Moody made a face. "Cheap fucker!"

Irkutsk Airport
Irkutsk
0752 Hours Local Time

Colonel Boris Sinitsyna sat in the old domestic terminal, sipping black coffee from a plastic cup. A newspaper lay across his lap. Two hunters had been found shot to death up in the rugged hills near the southern end of Lake Baikal.

In an unrelated story, a man's body had been found lying along the Trans-Siberian train route. The man had yet to be identified but was a male Caucasian approximately thirty years old, shot in the head at close range.

The colonel took another sip on his coffee, grimaced, then checked his watch. He would be boarding his flight for Vladivostok in about twenty minutes.

There had been no communication from Major Zakarova in Irkutsk, and the only thing out of the ordinary there was some local police activity near one of the repair facilities, and employees at the station had told Sinitsyna that they thought thieves had broken into the shop to steal parts and shots had been exchanged with the police.

Sinitsyna could only assume that the deal had been made, so he had called his contacts in Iran and offered his services for a handsome fee. He would ensure that the weapons were delivered to Japan for the final exchange.

If Hezbollah failed to keep up their end of the bargain, the colonel would act on behalf of the Iranians to get the weapons transferred. Hezbollah had already reported that they lost contact with their two operatives on board the train, and Sinitsyna was not surprised. The Brit had no doubt neutralized them. So his own services were indeed justified.

And if push came to shove, if he found himself in a situation that was inescapable and he was about to lose his life, he had a chip up his sleeve.

Actually three of them—

All sitting in a hunting lodge in the middle of the snow-swept mountains.

The colonel believed that if Svetlanov had killed Zakarova and his men, he was the only man alive who knew where the remaining three warheads were stored.

Hopefully, it would never come to that. Another team of two Hezbollah agents—both Syrians—was supposedly already in Vladivostok. His strenuous objections to working with the Syrians disintegrated when he learned both were engineers capable of designing and interfacing for the Faja3 and the Zelga2 missile destined for Haifa and Tel Aviv, respectively. They needed the transit time between Japan and Beirut to work out the critical firing sequence for both the short-range and long-range missile. So he would fly off to Vladivostok, somewhat blind, and carefully monitor what happened there.

The colonel's friends in London, Bartholomew and Kit, had given him a flawless set of IDs and passports and loaned him the funds he needed via credit card accounts to travel without being traced.

Yes, it would have been nice to confront Zakarova, look into his eyes and say: *Your murder attempt failed. Mine won't.* He would have put a bullet into the old major's heart.

Everyone kills everyone, the colonel thought. Even the men who were trained to be fiercely loyal had become poisoned. He longed for the days of his youth, when honor meant something, when men had true hearts to serve.

The world, it seemed, had become a darker place, and the military establishments had become as corrupt as the governments that created them. It was a damned depressing worldview, but it motivated him, drove him to take what he needed, what he wanted, what he deserved.

After all, they had taken the most precious thing in the world from him: his daughter. And so he didn't care anymore.

The Brit had been right. He had become, in the end, a mercenary. It was a matter of survival.

Rossiya Train Number 2
Trans-Siberian Express
Skovorodino Station
36 Hours Later
1304 Hours Local Time

Svetlanov stood on the platform, smoking a cigarette and brushing falling snow from his face. The train was supposed to stop for about ten minutes in the town, but his men had called to say the local police were doing a thorough search of each carriage before allowing them to continue. He could only assume that they had found Mykola's body, thanks to the Brit, whose actions now threatened the entire plan.

He finished his cigarette, glanced up at the small station framed by the rolling hills, and hustled back into the carriage, into his room, where Ustin kept watch over Bibby, whose wrists had been freed.

Hannah sat in the chair, knees tucked into her chest, head buried—her usual pose. She'd barely said a word to him during the past thirty-six hours. And no, he had not kept his promise to Bibby to rape her. He had wrestled with the decision several times, and kept settling upon one fact: He really did care. He had actually seen himself making a future with her. And now this. He wanted to shoot himself for being so weak, for not treating her like a whore, but he just couldn't. He even imagined that when all was said and done, there might still be something between them.

I am a fool, he had told himself.

Ustin answered a phone call, then said, "They're on their way."

"Not a word from you when they come," Svetlanov warned Bibby.

"You're not going to turn me over?" asked the Brit, surprised.

Svetlanov raised his brows and said emphatically, "Diamonds."

Bibby nodded.

Tensing over the man's incredible calm, Svetlanov leaned down and locked gazes with him. "Aren't you nervous? Aren't you thinking that you're going to die?"

"Young man, if you've done what I've done, seen

what I've seen, you would know how ridiculous that question is."

Two police officers entered the room, both young and stone-faced. Svetlanov glared at them as they rifled through bags, searched under the mattresses, then patted down each one of them, including the groaning and disgusted Hannah.

All of the weapons had been hidden in with Alek, since the police would only do a cursory inspection of the provodnik's quarters. Moreover, the young man had access via his tool kit to the small air vents in the room, within which he had stored the guns.

"Has someone lost a watch?" Bibby asked the police in Russian.

Svetlanov's eyes widened.

"You'll keep your mouth shut," snapped one of the cops.

"Sorry, my friend is a little under the weather," said Svetlanov.

"And you'll close your hole as well."

The police finished their search, examined all of their IDs, then left the room.

"We'll be here for hours," said Ustin with a sigh.

Svetlanov left the room, headed down the aisle and reached Alek's quarters. He lifted his brow at the young man.

Alek sighed in relief. "No problems."

"Very good."

"Sir, you've placed me in a very uncomfortable position. And I'm not sure if—"

"I've paid you more money for this trip than you'll earn in a year. Remember that."

"I understand. I just wanted . . . I'm worried about the police."

"Don't be, my friend. We've done nothing wrong. You understand that a man in my position, a man with a lot of money, has to protect himself. Deals are made, enemies formed, and some seek revenge because of their own inadequacies."

"Yes, sir."

Svetlanov placed his hands on Alek's shoulders. "I think when we reach Vladivostok, you'll quit this job and come work for me."

"Sir?"

Svetlanov spun around, headed back toward his room while waving his hand. "We'll talk later."

Mad Dog stood inside the station, peering out through the window at Rossiya Train Number 2, sitting there on the tracks, uniformed police officers and detectives in heavy coats moving from carriage to carriage. They had a team of about a dozen men and had a lot of ground to cover. There was also a team of two men patting down those individuals trying to board the train. It was all quite rudimentary: no metal detectors or bomb-sniffing dogs or devices, just a quick, physical search.

"How do we get past them with our guns?" Kat asked, leaning in from behind him.

"I don't know, but this looks pretty haphazard," said Mad Dog. "They don't have enough men."

"What if we get caught?" she asked.

"You had to go and say it?"

"And what if that body they found turns out to be Bibby? He's not answering anymore."

She was referring to the newspaper article she'd spotted when they arrived at the station. She spoke better Russian than she could read, but understood enough to realize that Bibby could already be dead.

Mad Dog shrugged. "We don't know shit till we get on board and go through that carriage."

"You want to ditch the guns?" she asked. "There's no

other way. I mean, we didn't expect this kind of security for a fucking Siberian train."

Mad Dog closed his eyes. If they ditched their weapons, did that mean that his good friend Yury had died for nothing? He couldn't stand the irony of that. They needed to get on that train with their guns.

"Anyone taking their boots off out there?" he asked, opening his eyes.

"No," she said.

"Then let's go the bathroom. Ditch one, keep one in your boot. Best we can do."

She took in a long breath. "Okay."

Two minutes later they met outside the station, nodded to each other, then headed toward the line of passengers being searched. The wind was picking up, the snow beginning to fall more heavily again. Good. That might speed up the searches. The young cops patting people down looked as bored and miserable as newlyweds in a women's clothing store.

The female passenger in front of Mad Dog, who was no more than twenty-five, lifted her arms, and they patted her down, but the cop's face turned odd as he reached into her coat pocket and withdrew a pack of cigarettes.

She began to argue with him, reached for the cigarettes, then got shoved back by the other cop. The first one opened the cigarette box and removed a small bag containing a white, powdery substance.

And immediately the cop began blowing his whistle.

"Of all the fucking bad luck," Mad Dog grunted, turning his head back to Kat. "Here we go."

She glanced worriedly at him. *"Ya lublu tebya."*

"What?"

"Learn your Russian!"

Chapter 12

....

Rossiya Train Number 2
Trans-Siberian Express
Skovorodino Station
1312 Hours Local Time

Kat braced herself as two more cops arrived and hauled off the drug-carrying woman. She screamed about the bag, arguing that it contained legal medication for her headaches.

Mad Dog scowled at the woman and shook his head. How dare she try to smuggle drugs on board the train! Yes, he was playing it up for the other two cops about to pat them down.

Kat held her breath as the cop's hands reached Mad Dog's boots, but the man quickly stood upright and waved Mad Dog on.

That the next cop searching Kat put his hand on the side of her breast did not go unnoticed by her, but she maintained her bored expression and otherwise didn't react.

When he finished, the cop took in a deep breath through his nose, stealing a whiff of her perfume, then cocked a thumb over his shoulder and smiled like a shark.

She pursed her lips and nodded politely.

Their tickets placed them in carriage number four, but they needed to make a pass through carriage seven in an attempt to spot Bibby.

"We're lost," said Mad Dog.

"Yes," she said, understanding what he meant immediately. "Where the hell is our carriage?"

Kat noted the two provodniks standing outside of carriage number six. They were directing passengers on the platform and guarding the entrance. That carriage, along with two others, had broad doors along its sides to load cargo.

They passed the provodniks and reached the entrance to carriage seven, where they were immediately accosted by a young, dark-haired provodnik who asked to see their tickets.

"Oh, honey, don't you have them?" asked Kat in English, as Mad Dog pretended to search his coat pockets.

"Yes, they're here somewhere," he said.

"You're Americans?" asked the provodnik in broken in English.

"Yeah, we're here on our honeymoon," said Kat. "We're in carriage number seven, I think."

"Not possible. This carriage is full, booked all the way to Vladivostok."

"Really, because I'm almost positive our tickets say—"

"Here they are," said Mad Dog, widening his eyes on Kat.

"Ah, yes," said the provodnik. "Carriage four, *not* seven." He pointed up the line.

"Oh, all right," said Kat. "But can't we just board here and walk through?"

The provodnik grew uncomfortable. "Uh, no, not possible. Police are still inside, searching. Sorry."

"What happened?" asked Kat. "Was someone really shot on board the train?"

The provodnik frowned. "I'm sorry, my English is not so good."

Kat knew he understood her. "Oh, uh, okay."

"Thanks," said Mad Dog, tipping his head. Kat joined him as they hurried forward. "He knows something," he added.

"And he's a terrible liar. How're we going to get back in there?"

"Let's find our room, lay low until the train departs, then we'll figure it out."

"Okay. But you know we've come so far, and we're this close . . . I don't want to blow it. I just have to know about Bibby."

"Me, too, but if he's alive and we rush in there without a plan—"

"Whoa, Marine. It's my understanding that even the best plans rarely survive the first enemy contact."

Mad Dog smiled knowingly. "Yeah, if Plan A sucks, you go to B. Then C, D, E, and after that you kill everyone and let God sort 'em out."

"Lovely."

Mad Dog's satellite phone began to ring, and he snorted at the intrusion.

"You want me to get that?" asked Kat.

He shook his head, slipped the phone out and listened for a moment. "Wolfgang," he told Kat.

"With good news," she said, trying to confirm it through her tone. It was time to muster some positive energy.

"Wolfgang, I'm a little busy right now trying to get on board another train. Give me ten minutes, call me back." Mad Dog hung up.

"Good news, right?"

Mad Dog snickered. "He didn't sound too happy. Come on."

They found carriage number four, showed their tickets to the provodnik, a lean old woman with a crow's beak for a nose, then passed into the narrow aisle and found their room.

Kat dropped onto the bunk while Mad Dog closed the door. She immediately removed her boot and withdrew her pistol. The goddamned thing was killing her. She stuffed it under her mattress.

Mad Dog narrowed his gaze in thought. "We need to recon that carriage."

"That kid's probably well paid. He won't let anybody get by him."

"Maybe he can be bought."

"We blow our cover if we try."

Mad Dog threw up his hands. "I'm fucking tired of this shit. You know I'm almost wishing that—"

Kat pointed an index finger at him. "Don't say it. He's still alive."

Mad Dog's satellite phone began to ring. He rolled his eyes. "Fucker can't tell time."

"Let me get it."

"Be my guest."

She took his sat phone, answered. "You call that ten minutes?"

"Kat?"

"Come on, asshole, talk to us. I'll put you on speaker."

"All right. Moody's right here in my hotel room. We've been working on a lot of shit. First off, where the hell are you?"

"Skovorodino Station, about thirty-six hours away from you guys."

"Okay. Listen to me. Moody's got the name of a Russian crime family: Svetlanov. We already ID'd the father here in Vladivostok. They've been casing this place for days. The son, Sergei, may very well be on board your train, and his organization might've stolen the diamonds."

"Wonderful. That all you fucking got?"

"Hey, asshole," called Moody in the background. "I'm busting my ass for you for free!"

"No, you're not. You'll have your hand out when this is over."

"Just listen up!" cried Wolfgang into the phone. "One of Moody's informants picked up some intel about a nuclear warhead exchange happening somewhere in Russia. Two tactical nukes for twenty million in diamonds. The informant says the warheads are supposed to be delivered to Hezbollah agents in Fushiki, Japan."

"I'm straining to make a connection here, guys."

"Give me that fucking phone," said Moody, then his voice grew suddenly louder. "Hertzog, I think we got two Russian nukes on that train. They're being shipped to Vladivostok. From there they'll be ferried over to Japan, sold to Hezbollah, then sold to Iran, who's going to use them to nuke the Israelis and blame it on terrorists. Your boy Bibby is right in the middle of it all."

"There're nukes on this train?" asked Mad Dog. "Jesus, this just keeps getting better and better. Is Bibby involved in the sale of these nukes?"

"Don't know, but I think the nukes were loaded in Irkutsk. The colonel gave you misinformation, sent you up to Khabarovsk to keep you out of the way. But there was some shooting at the Irkutsk station, a small incident. And we've managed to hack into the railway's data base, got the manifest, noting two large crates of agricultural machinery loaded in Irkutsk. The crates belong to a company that is a subsidiary of an air freight firm owned by the Svetlanov family."

"So you're saying these Russian mafia idiots have two nukes and loaded them on this train back in Irkutsk?"

"That's the theory. You're there. You can prove it."

"Well, Mr. Wizard, how the fuck did they get the warheads in the first place?"

"That's where your buddy Colonel Sinitsyna comes in. We're still working on this part of it, but there's little doubt that he's well-connected within the Russian military. He made a lot of friends during the time he spent fighting in Afghanistan."

"But Jimmy boy, we're talking about nukes, not drinking buddies. How does some NKVD colonel assigned to the London embassy come up with nukes?"

"About eighteen months ago there was a big ammo fire at a weapons depot not far from Irkutsk. The Russkies claim to have lost a lot of warheads in that fire. But maybe they didn't. Maybe those warheads wound up on the black market. Come on, Hertzog, you know this shit happens all the time. The guys who stole the nukes used the colonel and his contacts to move them."

"All right. So you think the colonel arranged some kind of deal with the mafia?"

"Maybe."

"But what about Bibby? What's he doing here? Was that woman really his wife?"

"Listen to me carefully now. I might be helping your little merry band, but you're right—we're talking about nukes, about attacking an ally of the United States. So you need to do what I tell you."

"So you aren't just helping my merry band, you've decided you're going to run the fucking show? No dice, asshole!"

"Who asked for my help? Uh, let me see—you, ass-hole!"

"I run the show. You give me advice, not orders. Last time I checked, I wasn't a fucking spook."

"Okay, here's some fucking advice. If Bibby's on the train with you, you need to get him and find out what's going on. Maybe it's even worse than I think. And if it's the son, Sergei, who's holding him, then we need him alive."

"Why?"

"I'll lay it all out for you, but I won't waste my time till you call me back and tell me you got him."

"And Bibby."

"Yeah, and Bibby, if he's alive."

"Okay."

"Don't let me down, Hertzog."

"Let you down? It's my fucking money we're after."

"Buddy, time to refocus. It's all about stopping those nukes from reaching Japan. Do you read me?"

Mad Dog closed his eyes.

"He reads you, Moody," said Kat. "We'll keep in touch. You come up with anything else, call us back."

"Roger that. Talk to you soon."

Mad Dog crossed to the bunk, took a seat. "If Bibby's alive, I'm going to kill him. That's it."

Someone knocked at their door. Kat rose, slid it open. It was their provodnik, a middle-aged man with a thin moustache and long, thick sideburns, who said, "Hello, you are Americans, no?"

"Yes."

"Okay, so sorry about the delay. They say we will be leaving station in no more than thirty minutes."

"Okay, thanks."

"My name is Elvis Presley. Let me know if you need anything."

Kat grinned. "Elvis?"

"My nickname. Always makes people smile."

"Okay, Elvis, we will."

Kat slid the door closed, then suddenly opened it. "Oh, Elvis? Yes, you can help me." She stepped out into the aisle and got close to the man, gazing salaciously. "We came through a few of the carriages. I think we were in number seven and I felt something strange. When we got back here I realized my necklace must've broken and fallen off there. Would you mind coming with me? Maybe while we're waiting we can take a look for it?"

Elvis frowned. He didn't quite understand her. So she gestured with her fingers around her neck, said, "I lost my necklace in number seven."

"Oh, okay, jewelry, necklace, you lost it. Come on. Let's go. I take you."

"No patience," said Mad Dog, rising from his bunk.

She made a motion for him to stay put, and he mouthed a question: *Are you sure?*

Yes! she mouthed back.

They shuffled quickly through carriage four, then five, and into six, with Kat checking the floor, putting on a great act, even spotting some lost change.

She had to give herself a little credit for making up a good story on the spot and using her assets to get Elvis to help.

As he opened the door, allowing her to pass into carriage seven, a tall, well-dressed man with jet black hair glazed with mousse and a twinkle in his dark brown eyes confronted her. He wasn't a provodnik, and in Russian, he asked, "Can I help you? This is a private carriage."

Elvis quickly said, "She's lost her necklace."

Before the man could respond, Kat pushed past him, her gaze divided between the floor, pretending to search, and tossing quick glimpses through the open doors of some rooms. The carriage had nine compartments, and she counted only four of the nine doors open.

As the tall man called after her, she reached the end of the aisle, realizing that if Bibby were in the carriage, he was behind one of the closed doors—

Just like a frigging game show.

And behind door number one we have a thief and traitor—

Or a man with complex problems who needed to explain himself.

It all depended on your point of view.

Interestingly, the tall man, shouting now, drew the attention of some of the occupants inside those compartments, and a few doors began to slide open, a few heads appearing in the aisle.

Kat waved her hand and cried, "So sorry! I really thought I lost it in here."

As she moved past a compartment whose door was marked 4 in Cyrillic, she stole a peak inside, saw Bibby, whose gaze caught hers for a nanosecond before she passed by.

A word echoed loudly in her head: *Yes!*

She rushed back to the tall man. "I apologize! I didn't mean to intrude."

"It's okay. Maybe I can you buy you drink later?" He wriggled his brows.

Though she wasn't sure she could, Kat tried to blush. "Uh, I'm sorry. Perhaps some other time."

"Okay."

"I'm sorry you didn't find your necklace," said Elvis. "Maybe it is on the platform?"

"Maybe. Thank you."

Kat followed Elvis back to their carriage, thanked him again, then slipped into their compartment.

She grabbed Mad Dog by the shoulders, hugged him, and gasped, "He's there. I saw him. He's alive, he's there, he looks okay."

"Not for long."

"Come on, Michael. He asked for our help. He wouldn't do that if he was trying to steal from us."

"What do you mean trying? He did. And maybe his plan went south, and now we're all he's got. He's desperate. So we'll help him, just so I can get my hands around his neck. Now get out your train map. I have an idea."

Bibby glanced over at Hannah, who stared back at him, her expression softening. "I'm scared."

"It's okay. We'll be all right."

"How do you know?"

Bibby glanced up at Svetlanov, who was speaking quietly on his cell phone. "I know."

"Daddy? I'm sorry."

"Hannah, if only we could've talked."

"How? On the phone? As usual? You halfway around the world, and me trying to believe you care?"

Bibby closed his eyes.

"Hey, wake up," said Svetlanov.

When Bibby opened his eyes, he found the mafia punk's face in his, the kid's breath foul, his cologne much too heavily applied. "That was my father on the phone. Do you know what he told me? He said I was a coward. He said if you know where the diamonds are, I should torture your daughter in front of you."

"But you won't," said Bibby. "Because you love her."

"No, he doesn't," Hannah snapped. "He loves money."

"I'll tell you what we're going to do. You two are going to sit here and think about it. And then, when we reach Vladivostok, if you don't tell me where the diamonds are, I will kill her. I promise you that."

"Fuck you, Sergei," said Hannah, choking up. "Fuck you."

Svetlanov moved toward Hannah, and Bibby fought against his fresh bonds, the wire once more digging into his wrists.

Svetlanov grabbed Hannah by the throat with one hand and began choking her. "You turned out to be a whore, didn't you?"

"You hurt her, and I'll die with the diamonds just to spite you. Don't test my resolve."

Svetlanov released Hannah, shoved her back, then moved to the door, slid it open, and left as Ustin came into the room. He was portly, with bushy brows, and wore a smirk.

"No one looks happy," he said in broken English.

Rossiya Train Number 2
Trans-Siberian Express
Ussuriysk Station
34 Hours Later
0105 Hours Local Time

Ussuriysk Station was the very last stop on the train's route before reaching Vladivostok, just three and half hours away now. The train was just pulling up to the platform and rumbling to a stop.

It seemed to Kat that laying low for nearly a day and a half had just about killed her, but she'd kept her cool, ate her meals with Mad Dog in the restaurant car—God, did the food suck—and done the best she could at reconnoitering from afar the train's cargo carriages during their stops at every station. The most heavily guarded carriage was number six, right behind seven, where Bibby was being held, so it seemed likely that the warheads were stored there.

While they couldn't be sure how many men were holding Bibby, she had already counted at least four who she suspected were involved, but there could be even more—and that was where their plan could fall apart: unaccounted for enemy help.

She could only presume that many passengers on the train were asleep and wouldn't bother getting off at one in the morning, since they would reach their last stop of the journey just three hours later. So there wouldn't be much interference.

"You ready?" asked Mad Dog, shoving a backpack toward her.

"You?"

He nodded. "Looks like it's snowing again."

"Yeah. And it's getting colder." She looked at him, and then she knew. "You're nervous."

"About you."

"You should be. I'm risking my ass for your money."

"No, you're not. For your friend."

"He's you're friend, too."

He took in a long breath and didn't answer.

They left their room, headed down the aisle, and reached the door at the end of the carriage, where Elvis was waiting for them just outside. "Ten minutes!" he cried. "Only ten minutes here!"

"Okay," Kat said, smiling. She hustled off, not looking back, knowing Mad Dog was right behind.

She strode gingerly along the platform, passing loose knots of passengers lighting up cigarettes and glancing up into the night sky. There were only a few vendors who had set up shop on the platform; it seemed most had gone home for the evening. The snow fell with a hiss.

Her pulse increased as she passed carriage seven, moved along it and toward the single guard standing outside carriage six. The platform was dark, the others out of earshot, just as they had expected. The guard, who wore a trench coat and had a rifle slung over his shoulder, moved away from the door as she approached. He called out for her to stop.

And that's when she slipped. Went right down on the icy concrete, her backpack falling from her grip.

The guard came over to her, leaned down.

She sprang up, draped the wire behind his head even as she came around him—

And suddenly pulled it tight, slicing into his carotid artery, the blood squirting as he fought against her grip.

But she dragged him back down to the ground, underestimating her force, and both of them rolled back and off the platform, thumping a meter down to the tracks below.

She'd never lost grip on the wire. In fact, the force had pulled it even tighter around the man's neck, and he summarily passed out by the time she rolled over.

Sometime during the struggle he probably realized that she'd intentionally slipped and that his reflexive reaction to help her was about to cost him his life.

"Who are you?" she muttered, searching his pockets for a wallet. All he had was a money clip, a set of keys, and several train receipts. No identification. That was probably intentional.

She composed herself, climbed back onto the platform, then grabbed her pack and went up the stairs to the cargo carriage's door. She tried two keys. The third opened the door.

Her cell phone vibrated. She answered. "I'm in."

Mad Dog slipped his phone back into his pocket and checked his watch. *Shit, shit, shit, she'd better hurry up.*

He positioned himself on the platform outside carriage number seven and pretended to stretch his legs in front of the young provodnik who stood near the door. As he leaned down, he felt the pistol tucked into his waistband dig in, and the pain was actually comforting at that moment. He thought about how close he was to shoving that gun into Bibby's face.

"Almost time to go," said the provodnik. "Better go back to your carriage."

Mad Dog forced a grin and nodded.

Inside the cargo carriage, Kat found the two large crates labeled AGRICULTURAL MACHINERY, crates clearly large enough to accommodate a tactical nuclear warhead.

But the sons of bitches were sealed up tight, and it wasn't as though she kept a crowbar in her back pocket. She did, however, find a seam between planks and was able to pry them apart with a pen from her pack. She shone her penlight into the hole and squinted.

"Holy shit."

All her years spent protecting VIPs could not have prepared her for that moment.

She was staring at the smooth nose cone of a warhead, a nuclear bomb, and could almost feel its power course through her, almost smell the radiation.

And then she remembered to breathe.

Come on, Kat. You still have a lot to do.

Svetlanov had fallen asleep with his pistol lying on his chest, and as he dug his head deeper into his pillow, he realized the gun now lay on the mattress beside him, so he reached out for it in the dark.

It was gone.

His eyes snapped open and he sat up.

There was Ustin in the chair, wide-awake, his pistol trained on Bibby and Hannah, who were sleeping quietly, Hannah on the bed, Bibby on the floor.

"Are you okay?" Ustin asked.

"Yes, I just . . . " Svetlanov spotted the gun beside his pillow. "Maybe I had a dream."

"You've been restless. We're almost there. Sleep a little more."

Svetlanov nodded, eased back down on the mattress.

Just as an alarm blared through the carriage.

Chapter 13

....

After sounding the alarm, the provodnik had gone running off, toward the fire burning on the platform just outside carriage number six and the smoke coming from that carriage's open door.

The flames only rose about a meter or so from the platform, but they were enough to garner the attention of even the sleepy-eyed train personnel inside the station, some of whom came rushing out from the building. Despite the gloom and flurries, a sizable column of smoke grew from the carriage, fanned by the breeze.

Mad Dog watched an old man who might have been station security brandish a fire extinguisher, stop in the middle of the platform and struggle to free the hose from the tank. They obviously didn't get too many fires around here.

When the provodnik took the bait, he rushed up and into carriage seven. He turned left, slipping into the washroom at the end of the aisle, then peered out, toward compartment four, where Bibby was being held.

A lean man in a heavy black sweater and trousers came forward. The guy was young, perhaps the mafia son that Moody had mentioned.

One way to find out . . .

As the man drew closer, Mad Dog yelled, "Svetlanov!"

The guy's eyes widened and he reached toward the back of his pants.

After tearing off pieces of fabric that lined the compartment bulkheads of the cargo carriage, and gathering up some empty cardboard boxes and small pieces of wood that had broken off from some of the shipping crates jammed into the tight confines of the carriage, she had started a couple of pretty nice fires—despite being an amateur arsonist.

Hopefully, her work wouldn't be so good that the warheads would be damaged. She doubted that. But could you rely upon the fire suppression skills of a tired train crew and the staff of small Russian station, especially at one in the morning?

Too late to ask now.

Once the flames had started, Kat doused her hair with a water bottle from her pack, removed her sweater, then wrapped a towel around her waist.

She now ran bare-breasted along the platform, hair wet, screaming, "Fire!" in Russian, making all the provodniks and passengers believe she had been caught washing up or changing and spotted the blaze.

And if the fires didn't create a large enough diversion, she figured a nice pair of tits bouncing in the cold would.

Call her insane.

The young provodnik who worked carriage seven came right up to her, his eyes hardly leaving her erect

nipples as she spoke rapidly about the fire and that someone had better do something and that the carriage was
beginning to burn.

He nodded, began to remove his jacket—

When she glanced furtively to her left and right, then
dropped her towel, revealing her panties and the gun
tucked into them, threatening to fall out.

He frowned, understood, opened his mouth.

His arms were caught in the jacket.

She tugged out the silenced pistol and in one liquid
motion shot him in the heart.

And all the while told herself that killing in cold blood
was the only way to save Bibby. *Don't feel anything*, she
ordered herself.

But he was so young. So very, very young.

Beneath his jacket, he wore a nametag: ALEK.

She let the provodnik fall toward her, then dragged
him to the edge of the platform, rolled him over the side,
again checking to be sure no one had seen her. She
tucked his body out of sight beside a few of the girders
holding up the platform, where he wouldn't be found until daybreak. The guard she had finished with the wire
would be found dead inside the burning carriage, hopefully all traces of his murder scorched away.

With that task completed, she donned her pants and
sweater, realizing with a curse that she'd left her jacket
back in the burning carriage.

Mad Dog's pistol was already pointed at Svetlanov's head,
even as the young man reached for his own weapon.

"You speak English?" Mad Dog asked.

"Fuck you, asshole! Who are you?"

"Very good, I see you've learned all the most important words . . . " He quickly moved up beside Svetlanov
and disarmed him. "Turn around. Back to your room."

"They sounded the fire alarm!"

"Yeah, and you know where the fire is? Cargo carriage. Your precious nukes."

"Who the fuck are you?" cried the Russian.

As they pushed into Svetlanov's compartment, a fat guy with a unibrow glanced up, saw Svetlanov with his hands raised and immediately trained his weapon on Mad Dog.

But Mad Dog wasn't paying much attention to him. He was staring down at Bibby, who was seated on the floor, looking as groggy and guilt-stricken as ever. His glasses had slid down the bridge of his nose and his hands were bound behind his back. He glanced to the bed, to a young woman who glared at him.

"What's going on?" she cried.

From the corner of his eye Mad Dog detected movement and reflexively squeezed his trigger.

Thump!

The unibrow man's head snapped back as a bloody third eye appeared on his forehead. He hit the wall, then fell forward, just as Mad Dog swung around and jabbed his pistol into Svetlanov's ribs. "Sit down."

The Russian moved to the bed and slowly sat, eyes still burning on Mad Dog.

"Hello, Mr. Hertzog," said Bibby.

"And you motherfucker, you shut up for now!" cried Mad Dog. "I got a bullet with your name on it!"

"Please, we have to talk."

"Oh, yeah, we do!"

"Daddy, who is this guy?" the girl asked Bibby.

Daddy? Mad Dog glanced to the girl.

And oh my God, she had Bibby's face.

As Kat ran along the platform, men rushing up to the burning carriage behind her, she passed an old babushka wearing a woolen shawl, a *pashmina*. The woman sat on a bench, near a table of smoked fish, and Kat rushed up to her and said in Russian, "Give me your shawl."

She was still wet and freezing her ass off.

And hell, a coat was a coat!

The old woman scowled at her. "No!"

Perhaps the cold was affecting her reasoning as she withdrew her pistol and pointed it at the old woman's head.

"Your *pashmina*! Now, bitch!"

"Hannah, please," said Bibby.

Mad Dog's frown deepened. "Is she really—"

"Yes, she is," the Brit finished.

"And is *she* why you're here?"

"You've no idea . . ."

Svetlanov glared at Mad Dog. "Who the fuck are you?"

Mad Dog leaned over and pointed his pistol between his eyes. "Listen, Boris, if I want to hear anything come out of your fucking hole, I'll ask. Shut the fuck up."

"No, you listen to me, American asshole. I have men on board this train. You have no chance."

"He's full of shit," said Hannah. "Don't listen to him."

"Hannah, untie your father," Mad Dog ordered.

"I'll try. Who are you?"

Mad Dog grinned crookedly. "Just a fucking idiot who wound up in the wrong place at the wrong time."

Damn. His cell phone rang as he scooped up the unibrow's pistol and tucked it into his waistband. He answered, "Yeah?"

"On my way," said Kat.

"Good. We're all here waiting for you."

"Excellent." She began to ask him another question,

but he accidentally hung up on her. Didn't matter. She'd arrive soon enough.

"The fire will delay this train," said Svetlanov. "And they'll search the carriages again."

He went up to the Russian, grabbed him by the neck and jammed his pistol into the little fucker's eye. "Shhh. Okay?"

"Okay."

Now the sat phone began ringing, and Mad Dog slowly released Svetlanov and answered the call, his gaze locked on the Russian. "You got Bibby yet? And the Russian?" asked Moody.

"Yeah."

"Don't harm the Russian. Kat's his new girlfriend, stays close with him, get it?"

"Then what?"

"Let 'em offload the nukes. I got it covered from there."

Mad Dog snorted. "Oh, really?"

"Believe it."

"You don't sound too convincing."

"You find out how Bibby's involved in all of this?"

"I was going to, until you called, asshole."

"Then I'll let you get back to work."

"Gee, thanks. I'll call you back."

"There," said Hannah, tugging free the last wire binding her father's wrists.

Bibby bolted to his feet, rubbing his wrists and lifting his chin to Mad Dog, who withdrew the unibrow's pistol and aimed it at the Brit. Now he covered both men, his gaze divided between them.

"I was going to ask for that pistol," said Bibby.

"You stole my necklace, you stole my money, and I've been humping halfway 'round the globe trying to find you. I've been shot at, crashed in a car, and watched one of our friends die. Give *you* the pistol? Fuck off, Alastair. Fuck off."

"Who died?"

"Yury. And do you know about Waffa?"

"Oh my God . . . "

Mad Dog bared his teeth. "Yes, they're both dead, so you can what? Help these assholes move the nukes?"

Abruptly, the door slid open and Kat rushed inside, hair wet, cheeks rosy. She wore an old shawl. "Local cops are going to make everyone get off the train."

She had barely finished that sentence when another man appeared behind her. Mad Dog assumed it was one of Svetlanov's men, since he jabbed a pistol into the back of Kat's head and uttered something in Russian that escaped him.

"He'll shoot her if you don't lower your weapons," said Bibby.

"You see, American asshole?" asked Svetlanov. "I wasn't lying. Now I'll have some fun with you."

**Train Station
Vladivostok
0135 Hours Local Time**

CIA agent James Moody had rented a car and found a perfect parking place in the lot adjacent to the station, but the goddamned piece of shit car had a heater that barely worked, so he sat there, fidgeting with the control while surveying the platform with a pair of night vision goggles.

The two mafia meatheads he and Wolfgang had identified earlier had come and gone about an hour before, and then, just moments ago, a deuce and a half truck probably once used in the Russian army but now bearing civilian markings had arrived on the cargo platform, its tarpaulin bed cover rolled back for easy access to the bed.

The driver had climbed out, lit up a cigarette, and stood there, leaning on the bumper and smoking, while a pair of station security personnel inspected the vehicle and a set of papers he handed to them.

Earlier in the evening, Moody had gone up to the third floor of the ferry terminal, located behind the station, to purchase tickets for everyone, and the ferry to Fushiki was running on time.

Now if he could just get that asshole Hertzog to buy into the rest of the plan, they would intercept this transfer, save the day, pin medals to their asses, and go home.

His sat phone rang, and the number made him grin. His poker buddies from Langley had come through . . . big-time.

As he reached for the phone, another truck arrived beside the first, this one with a crane attached for loading and unloading heavy cargo.

Rossiya Train Number 2
Trans-Siberian Express
Ussuriysk Station
0136 Hours Local Time

Kat looked at Mad Dog, wondering if he would take the shot. The guy behind her applied a bit more pressure to the pistol, forcing her head down.

"Better listen to him," said Svetlanov, gesturing to his man. "He'll shoot, trust me."

"Don't do it, Michael," Kat said.

But how could he not? He loved her, and she just knew he'd cave.

"Hold your fire," he said, lowering his pistols.

Kat sighed. "Fuck."

But then a thump came from behind her, and even as she whirled, the thug who had held her at gunpoint dropped to the floor.

Wolfgang appeared behind him, trailed by a familiar young man wearing a provodnik's uniform, both his ears pierced—

It was Viktor, Yury's son, who had saved them back in Khabarovsk.

"Late as usual," said Kat.

"Blame him," said Wolfgang, eyeing Viktor. "Told me he knew a shortcut to get here. Road was shit."

"Viktor, why?"

"I called Wolfgang, told him I wanted to help. For my father."

Kat's voice cracked. "I understand. Thank you."

"Wolfgang, you and Viktor secure the rest of this carriage. And does he got ID?"

Wolfgang gave Mad Dog a thumbs-up. "And the carriage is already secure, but I'll double check."

"Good work. What about the police outside?"

"They're making everyone get off the train, but not us. We've taken care of that, too." Wolfgang rubbed his fingers, indicating the cops had been sufficiently bribed.

"Do not shit me," said Mad Dog.

"Don't worry, boss. We were generous. And they're understaffed."

"He's right," said Viktor. "They won't bother us."

Mad Dog nodded as the two men turned and left.

Kat leaned down and dragged the body of the man Wolfgang had shot farther into the compartment. "You mind if we take this party somewhere else?" she asked. "I see dead people, and I'm not happy."

"Bibby, you stay here," said Mad Dog. "Kat, you take this girl and Svetlanov next door, so Bibby and I can chat."

She shook her head. "I'm not leaving you alone with him."

"Daddy, who is she?" the girl asked Bibby.

Kat set down the body and looked up. "Oh my God, Alastair, is she—"

"Please," he said, raising a palm. "I'm happy to explain everything—if you'll only give me the chance."

Wolfgang liked this kid a lot. His father had taught him everything there was to know about the weapons their family bought and sold, and the kid could hold his own. A fascination for the deadly arts bridged all cultural and generational barriers, thus he and the kid had a lot in common.

When they had boarded the carriage, the kid had expertly assisted him in searching each of the compartments and had shot the remaining two men who were part of Svetlanov's group. Better still, Viktor had taken out those guys with quiet proficiency and not an ounce of bravado. "I got two," he'd simply said.

So according to Wolfgang's best intelligence, the ring leader punk was the only guy left.

But he couldn't be sure, since the fire had probably drawn some of them out. He posted Viktor at the entrance to the carriage, then double-checked each of the rooms. Through one of the windows he spotted groups of sleepy passengers heading back toward their carriages. Maybe the search was over and they were getting under way.

Viktor came back into the carriage and shouted confirmation of that, so Wolfgang rushed through the aisle and arrived to tell the boss, who nodded and said, "Take Hannah, here, and Svetlanov to the next room and hold 'em."

"You got it."

*   *   *

Once Kat, Mad Dog, and Bibby were alone, Mad Dog motioned for Bibby to sit on the bunk, and, still holding him at gunpoint, said, "Spill your guts . . . before I do."

"Michael, that's not necessary," said Kat.

"She's correct," said Bibby. "God, I didn't mean for any of this to happen."

"You brought your daughter along to make an arm's deal?"

Bibby shook his head, seemed to stare off into space.

"Alastair," said Kat, "we already know about Simone."

For a moment Bibby massaged his temples, bit his lip, then raised his voice. "They killed my wife!"

"You here for revenge?" said Mad Dog. "And you stole my money to make it happen?"

"It's strange how fate works, Mr. Hertzog, how karma works, how we must all pay for our sins at one time or another."

"Alastair, please," said Kat. "Talk to us. We're your friends, maybe your only friends. You have to trust us."

Hannah sat down in the chair, while Sergei stood by the window. She was surprised that she actually felt guilty about what was happening to him, wanted to comfort him, then she told herself he was a thug, a criminal involved in something so terrible she could hardly imagine it.

"Ever see one of these?" asked the man called Wolfgang. He held up a long, thin piece of plastic. "Zipper cuffs." He waved his pistol. "Turn around."

"You won't need them. I won't give you any trouble. The rest of my men will."

"Your men are gone, dude. Turn around." Wolfgang moved up to Sergei and roughly applied the cuffs.

"I will kill you personally."

"That makes me feel special. Now shut the fuck up.

And by the way, anyone ever tell you that you look like a scrawny John Travolta look-alike from the seventies?"

Hannah rose, went up to the man. "Are you a friend of my father's?"

"Ain't it obvious?"

"Then I'm disappointed that he hangs out with assholes like you, good looking or not."

"Wait a second. Did I miss something. Your father . . . who's your father? The boss?"

"No, my father is Alastair Bibby."

"What the fuck . . . well, maybe, ah, maybe it makes sense."

"What does?"

"This. Everything."

"Wolfgang, listen to me," began Sergei. "When this train reaches Vladivostok, you're fucked. But if we negotiate now, I will let you live."

"You just said you would kill me personally."

"Let's discuss it."

"Your name's Svetlanov, right?" asked Wolfgang.

"Mr. Svetlanov."

"And your father is like the big don of a Russian crime family, right?"

"We're not criminals. We're businessmen."

"Yeah, whatever, so you want me to make a deal with you, so that you'll let me live, when I know that you're a fucking scumbag, greaseball, motherfucking Russian mafia motherfucking drug dealer trying to sell nukes to motherfucking terrorists, and you want me to forget about that, look the other way, you know, just say to myself, 'Wolfgang, this motherfucker doesn't look so mean, and maybe I should be scared because he could be right, and I'll be fucked once we reach the end of the line, so maybe I should hear this guy out and think about it, and maybe try to work out a little deal on the side for myself, because in the end, really, you know, we're born alone, we die alone, so what the fuck?' I should consider all possibilities for taking care of my own ass, even it means listening to the utter bullshit coming out of the mouth of a fucking slimy worm sitting in front me trying to smooth-talk his way out of me fucking him upside the head, right?"

"Right."

Wolfgang grabbed Svetlanov's chin and squeezed his cheeks. "You fucking dummy." Then he smacked him across the face. "I didn't punch you," he told him, "because we need you. You're going to be our bitch, and bitch slapping is what you get. And so, now, the negotiations have concluded."

Hannah swallowed and repressed a chill. "You're crazy. My father hangs out with a crazy man."

Wolfgang howled like a werewolf.

Bibby took in a long breath as the train lurched forward, then started away from the station. "Mr. Hertzog. You don't have children. You would never understand."

"Try me."

"I've spent a lifetime trying to protect them. And for what? I even stole from you."

"Why, Alastair? Why didn't you come to us?"

"Because no one should know. Because that puts you and them at risk."

"Spell it out for me, buddy, before I fucking strangle you," said Mad Dog.

Bibby looked at Michael Hertzog, and he fully understood the man's frustration, the man's hatred for him. "I'm sorry."

"Did you bring Hannah along, or was she in trouble? Did they kidnap her?" asked Kat. "We just want to understand."

"I would've felt better if he had, in fact, kidnapped

her, but she became involved with him, and my wife went to Waffa and learned who he was. And then Waffa told me what Svetlanov's plans were, and I realized that through fate or happenstance or as penance, my own daughter was involved. I'm not here to sell arms. I came only for her, but I realized I could stop this transaction if I could get to Zakarova first."

He went on to explain who Zakarova was and how the deal had gone down in Irkutsk.

"So you still have the diamonds?" asked Mad Dog.

"Not on my person. I hid them before we stopped in Irkutsk."

"Where?"

"I'll tell you."

"But not now," said Mad Dog. "You need to hold out a carrot, so we don't kill you."

"Listen to me, my daughter's life was at stake."

"You should have come to me."

Bibby bolted to his feet. *"They killed my wife! And he would've killed my daughter!"*

"I want my fucking money!" cried Mad Dog, rising to meet Bibby's gaze. *"You stole from me, you fuck! You were my friend! I would've died for you!"*

Kat forced herself between them. "Enough! You either talk or I'm going to tie and gag both you."

"Where is my money?" asked Mad Dog. "Did you already blow it all? You said you didn't have time to cut the deal with Zakarova."

"That's right. When I took IPG's money, I transferred the funds into my Swiss accounts, but after Zakarova's death, I realized I wouldn't need the money anymore. It was too late to outbid the mafia."

"So where is it?"

"Where else, but back in IPG's accounts. Kat, you can

verify that. It's obvious you haven't checked those accounts in some time."

"Why would we?" she asked. "We assumed you weren't giving the money back."

"But what if you died with the money still in your accounts?" said Mad Dog. "Then your daughter would get it all?"

"No, I made provisions that if I didn't, or couldn't, sign in every twelve hours, an e-mail would automatically be transmitted to you disclosing where the money was, along with a password question needed to reclaim the funds. Svetlanov confiscated my BlackBerry more than twelve hours ago, so I imagine you'll find my e-mail waiting for you."

Kat had already dug out her laptop from her pack and was firing it up, making an Internet connection via her sat phone.

Bibby went on: "I needed the major and Svetlanov to believe I was a rogue, acting independently, and it would be more convincing if the world could see IPG was after me, too. I knew you and Kat would hunt me down anywhere in the world if I took your money. You were my involuntary backup, I'm afraid."

"And the necklace?" asked Mad Dog. "I know you gave it to the colonel, and he's managed to escape from London."

"Well, that's not entirely unexpected."

"Are you kidding me?"

"The colonel was well-connected. I thought an escape attempt might be planned, which is why I put a GPS transponder microchip inside the diamond clasp. If you read to the bottom of my e-mail message, you'll find the code to ping the chip for its location. It's accurate to within three meters."

"He's telling the truth," said Kat. "The funds are back in our accounts, and his e-mail is right here."

Mad Dog read Bibby's e-mail over Kat's shoulder and the corners of his mouth lifted briefly when he read the password question: "Define a rare disease?"

"You see," said Bibby. "God help me, I didn't want to do this. I had to."

"I have the code to ping the chip. Sending now," said Kat.

The double round trip to and from the satellite would take about six seconds, Bibby knew.

Kat glanced at him and nodded, looking somewhat relieved. He could see that she probably hadn't wanted to believe that he'd gone rogue on them, and this was perhaps a divine moment for her. He mouthed an *I'm sorry* once more, and she nodded.

Mad Dog stared at the laptop in awe. "Zooming in on the location. Holy shit. The necklace is in Vladivostok."

"Again, not entirely unexpected. The colonel must be there to supervise the transfer."

"Who's he working for?"

"I'm not sure. Could be Hezbollah, the Iranians . . . "

"Well, if he can recognize us . . . " said Mad Dog.

"But not me," said Kat.

"Give Moody a call. He's been playing this out. He needs a heads-up on this."

"Right now," said Kat.

Mad Dog stood and pointed his weapon at Bibby's head. "Location of the diamonds?"

"Michael, what the hell are you doing?" asked Kat.

"I'm posing a question in an aggressive manner."

"It's okay," said Bibby. "I'll tell you."

Chapter 14

....

"We'll reach the station in about thirty minutes," Kat said, checking her watch. She could barely keep her eyes open, the need for sleep tugging on her shoulders and turning her spine into mush.

"I won't cooperate," said Svetlanov, slurring his words. "Unless you tell me where, uh . . . what was I saying?"

Mad Dog took a deep breath. "I'm telling you, this guy's a waste, and Moody's plan is fucked."

"Moody knows what he's doing," she insisted. "And our friend here is drunk enough. We'll be okay. Stop bitching."

"Whoa."

"I'm just tired. Cranky. Missing my own bed."

"Me, too."

"What about me?" asked Svetlanov. "I'm going to shoot both of you and dump the bodies—wait, where is my bottle?"

During the past two hours, Kat had force-fed Svetlanov enough vodka to topple an elephant, but the son of a bitch had a strong tolerance. Finally, though, he'd begun to succumb. They wanted him nice and docile once they reached the station, so that most of what he said could be blamed on the vodka.

Oh, he's so paranoid, she could say. *Talking about secret plans and American mercenaries all night! He was the life of the party!*

It was, after all, three in the morning, and she would play up the train party story as much as possible.

Bibby, still wearing a provodnik's uniform, had gone off with Wolfgang to fetch the diamonds, which he said he'd hidden just beneath the cargo carriage's forward wheels. He and Wolfgang returned with the two bars of soap, and Kat and Mad Dog nearly fainted at the sight of all those gems.

"We split 'em up," Mad Dog had said, dividing the stones between himself, Wolfgang, and Kat. "Don't lose 'em."

"I don't know if I want this much responsibility," Wolfgang told him. "Unless I get to keep them."

Kat smiled over the thought and patted her own pocket. Yes, they were some very nice stones.

She and the others had also learned from Wolfgang and Bibby that her fire had only caused minor damage to the carriage, which was fortunate since Bibby had been unaware that she started it so close to where he'd hidden the gems.

Had those bars of soap melted and the bag been burned off from where he tied it, they'd be forced to retrace the tracks all the way to Ussuriysk, searching for the gems while a snowstorm threatened to bury them.

Now she, Mad Dog, and Svetlanov sat in the latter's

compartment, just waiting for the train to pull into Vladivostok Station.

As their luck would have it, more snow had kicked up, and she assumed that by the time they reached the station, they'd be caught in another storm; however, poor weather would inspire a quick weapons transfer.

She lifted her chin to Mad Dog, who was beginning to drift off. "Hey . . . "

"I'm good."

"Almost time to call Moody."

He checked his watch. "Yeah."

Train Station
Vladivostok
0314 Hours Local Time

Well, the car's heater, which he thought for sure he had fixed by jiggling the switch a certain way, finally died and wouldn't come back on.

Moody cursed it, checked his watch. Hertzog and his pups should be checking in about now.

On the seat beside him sat his computer, and glowing on the screen was a passenger list of the ferry bound for Fushiki. At least two of the names had already commanded his attention: Vladimir Svetlanov and Sergei Svetlanov, father and son. Were they just being sloppy by traveling under their own names, or did they have a larger plan to erase themselves from existence following the deal?

The two trucks were still parked near the platform, the drivers returning to the cabs to stay warm. Somewhere inside the terminal was Papa Svetlanov and his cronies. Moody had gone inside to recon their numbers. He had also searched for Colonel Boris Sinitsyna, based on the coordinates given to him by Kat, but the man must have moved or was waiting in a nearby car or bus. He'd had better luck with the new Russians, and spotted four accompanying Papa Svetlanov, but he guessed there were more posted throughout the terminal.

But it didn't matter how many were there. Those mafia meatheads wanted the same thing he did.

Only difference was, his ultimate destination for the warheads was slightly different.

U.S. nuclear weapons were manufactured and assembled at Sandia National Laboratories in New Mexico and California. Moody's bosses wanted the two warheads sent there for disassembly and study, and they always got what they wanted.

Consequently, he was spearheading an operation so significant, so incredibly fucking cool, that this would be the magnum opus of his entire career, the ultimate operation to thwart nuclear weapons from falling into the hands of a terrorist nation.

His name would be echoing off the walls of CIA headquarters for decades to come.

They would do case studies on him, teach his tactics to new agents, write scholarly articles, even as he published his own memoir to the tune of millions.

When you Googled him, you'd get hits up the ying yang, and his Wikipedia page would be a mile long.

Shit. Moody started to chuckle, realizing that it all rested upon the shoulders of a half-assed Marine who had once ripped him off, a half-assed Marine who didn't trust him, who might screw the pooch and embarrass him into suicide.

All right, so he was being a little harsh. Hertzog had pulled off some pretty impressive shit in his day, but that op in Uzbekistan had gone seriously south, and the wounds were still fresh, Moody knew.

And maybe the Brit wasn't being entirely truthful, either. His confidence in Hertzog had to have waned after losing half of their team, and maybe he did have secret plans to embezzle or rob from the kitty—or the dog, as it were.

So these were the folks he trusted with his legacy.

Aw, shit. All these delusions of grandeur were inspired by lack of sleep, no doubt.

The operation was significant, to be sure, but the Agency would probably deny its involvement and his very existence. He could save the whole fucking world and wouldn't see an extra nickel on his pay stub. The government this year was too busy analyzing unreconciled transactions, just a measly $24 billion that they'd somehow "lost."

The sat phone rang. "I wonder who," he muttered sarcastically as he picked it up.

"Still awake, asshole?" asked Mad Dog.

"Hello, who is this?"

"It's me, the guy who thinks your plan sucks."

"Listen to me, numb nuts, when that train pulls into the station, the place'll be crawling with Svetlanov's boys. Daddy is in there, with a couple more. I uploaded some pics to Kat. Tell her to look for them, so you can ID these bastards."

"I'm sure the kid'll do that for us."

"You get him drunk?"

"Yeah, but he's going to blow it, so I think he shouldn't show up. We'll have Bibby meet the father and go from there."

"No. He's expecting the son. If he's not sure, he won't put those nukes on board the ferry. He'll drive off with them. Trust me. We have to make him feel comfortable."

"You spot the colonel yet?"

"No, which is really pissing me off. Send his latest coordinates."

"I told you, he's right fucking there. I can't believe you haven't seen him."

"Maybe he put the necklace in a locker. Or he might already be on the ferry."

"Or he's sitting in your backseat."

"I'm going to assume those are your nerves talking because you're scared shitless."

"Look, we're good to go. I hope you are. Last call when we pull in."

He hung up, and Moody rolled his eyes. He checked his computer for the colonel, received the data from Bibby's GPS chip, then pinpointed it on his map.

Accurate to within three meters? Bullshit. He'd already scoured the station's waiting area. Colonel Boris Sinitsyna was not there.

But what the hell, he'd make one more pass through. He grunted, shut off the car, and moaned his way out. He was bundled up in a heavy woolen coat, his bald pate covered by an *ushanka* made of beaver fur, the flaps pulled down tight over his ears. He could pass for a local—until he opened his mouth.

He slipped through the parking lot, his breath trailing behind him, the station's lights reaching out into the snow and mist. It was only slightly warmer inside the station.

The harsh light inside left him squinting. He moved down a long row of lockers, then turned toward the rest rooms.

A sharp pressure awoke just beneath his left shoulder blade, a gun, and then a few words in Russian muttered into his ear: "Keep walking. Keep your hands in your pockets. I am with you. Go to the lavatory."

After sighing through a curse, Moody answered, "Okay."

Rossiya Train Number 2
Trans-Siberian Express
Nearing Vladivostok
0317 Hours Local Time

Bibby put his hand on Hannah's shoulder, and her eyes suddenly snapped open. "Oh my God."

"What? Are you all right?"

"I had a dream. You were trying to call Mom, but she wouldn't pick up."

"It was just a dream."

"Then call her right now. You have your phone. Your BlackBerry. Send her a text."

"Hannah . . ."

She bit her lip, began to tremble. "She's not okay, is she . . . and it's your fault, isn't it?"

Yes, he'd told himself to lie, but she needed to know, and he needed to phrase it in such a way that she didn't blame herself, because when it came right down to it, if she hadn't run off with fucking Svetlanov . . . too late to fix that. It was okay if she hated him, decided that her life had been ruined because of him. He had wanted both worlds, thought he could beat the system, thought he was clever enough to have it all.

He had lost Simone. And now he might lose Hannah. Lose it all.

Those bloody bastards had been right. Try as you may, your family would always suffer.

"Hannah, I'm afraid your mother—"

"Don't say it." She rose, started for the door. "They found her, didn't they? They wanted information from her, and she wouldn't give it, so they killed her. You think I'm stupid. You think I don't know about you. But I know a lot more than you think. And so did she, and that . . . " she trailed off.

"Where are you going? You can't leave. We're almost at the station, and you have to do what I've asked."

"I don't have to do anything."

She slid open the door, to find Viktor standing in her way. "Is there a problem?" he asked.

Hannah glared back at him.

"When we get to the station," Bibby began slowly, carefully, "you're getting in a taxi with Viktor, and he's going to take you to the airport. And you're going to buy a ticket and fly back home. And I'm going to meet you there soon. That's exactly what you're going to do. And then, after that, if you don't want to talk to me . . . if you don't want to see me . . . then okay. I understand. But for right now, you're going to listen to your father. This isn't a game. You could die."

"And that would what? Make you feel more guilty?"

"I won't argue."

"You never do."

"Don't worry," Viktor said, struggling with his English. "I'll make sure she gets to plane okay."

Hannah moved back to the bed, dropped in a huff, then slammed onto her back and draped an arm over her eyes. "I might die? Well, that sounds pretty good. Mom and I can be together, waiting for you, as always. And you'll never come home. Bastard."

Train Station
Vladivostok
0320 Hours Local Time

Moody reached the rest-room door. His hands were still in his coat pockets, and he had discreetly hit the Redial button on his sat phone, opening a call to Kat. His failure to answer would set off the alarms on their end, he hoped.

"Open it," the man said.

This was the part where his unseen attacker shoved him into the bathroom, where he would murder him and leave the body inside one of the stalls.

Or this might be the part where the old but still fit CIA agent decided to take a chance, whirl around and wrestle the man for his gun.

But the threat of being shot seemed too great. There was no fucking way in hell that his hands would reach the weapon before the asshole pulled the trigger.

Is this where you want to die, old Jimmy boy? In a fucking bathroom in Russia?

Better find your balls and make your move.

Moody opened the door and slowly entered.

Just as the door closed behind them—

He dropped suddenly, hooking his leg around the man's, and both of them went down onto the cold, slick floor while he reached for the man's gun, a Berretta with a long silencer attached to the barrel. Moody got a hand around the silencer as the gun went off, blasting tile behind them.

With his other hand, Moody reached into his coat pocket to withdraw his own pistol, but his assailant, one of Papa Svetlanov's four mafia thugs he had observed earlier, did the same goddamned thing.

And so they lay there, each with a pistol pointed at the other's head.

"Why are you watching us?" cried the Russian.

It took a moment for Moody to translate. His Russian wasn't bad, but he was damned rusty. Then it took another moment for him to consider his reply: *"Passossee mayee yaitsa."*

Okay, so he'd told the guy to suck his balls. Bravado had nothing to do with that. He was insulted that this asshole showed no fear, absolutely no fear at all.

Hello, you fucking monkey, I have a gun to your head?

The guy told Moody to suck *his* balls.

"Now we're getting somewhere," said Moody. "Communicating."

Bang!

Oh, shit. He had reflexively pulled his trigger, out of nowhere, that fast—so fast, in fact, that he'd surprised even himself.

No silencer on his pistol, shit. And he had just splattered the guy's brains across the bathroom floor.

"Fuck, fuck, fuck," Moody muttered as he dragged himself to his feet. He collected the weapons, then dragged the guy toward the nearest stall, propped him up on the toilet and shut the door, which wanted to hang open, God damn it.

Then he checked a door in the back of the lavatory, a storage closet, and found cleaning supplies for the porters. He got out the mop and bucket, turned on the water, shoved the mop into the sink, got it wet, and began to clean the mess just as a man entered the room.

"Please," Moody said in Russian, holding up his hand. "I'm not finished cleaning this one."

"Okay," said the man with familiar eyes. "I'll use the other."

As the door closed, Moody thought a moment, then it hit him. The man, bundled up tightly, his face half cast in shadow, was Colonel Boris Sinitsyna.

He wanted to call Mad Dog and tell him he'd finally found the old bastard, but he had a mess to clean up, a mess much bigger than blood and brain matter on the floor:

Papa Svetlanov would now know something was wrong. One of his men would go missing.

Moody finished with the floor, then went back to the stall, fished out the man's cell phone. He hit Redial, and a gruff voice answered. Shit, Papa Svetlanov himself. "What do you want, Mikhail?"

Moody coughed loudly, then, through the coughing said, "I'm not feeling well. Something I ate. I'm sorry, I won't make the ferry. So sorry . . . "

"I can barely understand you!"

From outside came the muffled thunder of the approaching train, and Moody was about to hang up when Papa Svetlanov launched into a fit of screaming.

After listening for a few seconds and getting a decent charge out of pissing off the Russian fucker, he coughed again, then hung up.

Well, that was a Band-Aid at best.

Still, he'd picked up a nice pistol and proved that he was still a quick shot. He called Kat back, told her what had happened, told her he'd be in position.

"All right," she said. "We're here."

Kat watched as Mad Dog buttoned up his coat, checked his pistol, then pocketed it.

Because he and Bibby could be identified by the old colonel, they both needed to leave the train and immediately board the ferry.

While Viktor and Wolfgang watched over Svetlanov for a moment, Kat gave Mad Dog a bear hug, then held his head in her hands. "Planes, trains, automobiles, and now fucking boats . . . "

"Yeah," he said. "Fucking boats."

"See you there."

"I'll be watching. You give me the signal if it goes south, and we'll be right on them. Don't push it, all right?"

"All right."

He grabbed her hands. "You're trembling."

"You're so handsome, you do that to me."

"You must be half blind." He pursed his lips. "Kat, it's not too late to change your mind."

She squeezed his hands. "Go." Then she stole a quick kiss and shoved him toward the door. "And watch your step out there. Snow's coming down real hard now."

God, she sounded like his mother.

He nodded and pushed past Viktor and Wolfgang. Viktor would take Hannah off to the airport. Wolfgang would shadow Kat and Svetlanov, ready to engage should it all go to hell.

Kat went over to Svetlanov, who was sitting in the chair, his head lolling back. Oh, yes, he was their puppet now.

She figured before getting out there, she'd practice a little, just to be sure. She grabbed him, kissed him hard, and he suddenly responded, opening his mouth, thrusting his tongue into hers as she pulled away.

"Oh, you're hot," he said.

"I know. Let's go outside and show Daddy."

"Okay . . ."

"But first, another drink." She shoved the vodka bottle into his mouth, and he downed some more.

He could barely stand, and it was all she could do to lift him out of the chair.

Mad Dog went to the next compartment, where Bibby was waiting. "Ready?"

"I don't think I can."

"What?"

Bibby tipped his head toward Hannah. "I need to get her on a plane."

"Viktor's got us covered."

"I need to be sure. And I can't leave her alone right now."

"Jesus Christ . . . you got me into this fucking bullshit, and sure as shit I'm not letting you off the hook. You're not going to the airport with her."

"You have the diamonds. To hell with Moody. To hell with the warheads. Let somebody else do it."

"So you can make sure your daughter is safe."

"Michael, I don't care anymore. I'm done. This is it for me. I ruined my life."

Mad Dog closed his eyes and sighed. "I need help right now. And you owe me."

"I'm sorry."

"So am I." He'd said that for what he was about to do:

Mad Dog walked over to Hannah, looked at her, looked at Bibby, then reached into his pocket and withdrew his second pistol, one Wolfgang and Viktor had confiscated from Svetlanov's men. He handed it to her.

She gazed at him curiously.

"What are you doing?" asked Bibby.

"Hannah, we're going on a little boat ride. Want to come?"

"Yeah," she said, then expertly gripped the pistol, released the safety, and aimed it at her father.

"Whoa!" cried Mad Dog.

Bibby's face twisted in shock. "Hannah!"

"I'm not going to shoot you," she said darkly. "Although I could. I know how to shoot. I'm pretty fucking good."

"Really," said Mad Dog.

Hannah faced Bibby, her eyes burning. "My mother taught me. She was an expert marksman. She said we needed to know how to protect ourselves."

"Your mother didn't know how to shoot," said Bibby.

Hannah snorted. "That's what you think. She knew that one day your job would come to haunt us."

Mad Dog started for the door. "She can hold her own. Let's go."

Bibby rose. "I won't allow this."

"Then you can stay here," said Hannah. "Because I'm going on the boat to help your friends."

"Why?"

"Because that's what Mom would do."

Mad Dog gave the young woman a quick wink, then waved her into the aisle. He told Viktor, who was waiting there, to join Wolfgang.

Through clenched teeth, Bibby said, "If anything happens to her—"

"She'll be sitting in a cabin," snapped Mad Dog. "We're late. Come on."

Wolfgang walked across the snow-covered platform, heading toward the ferry terminal, which loomed to the east, the harbor beyond invisible in all the gloom. He and Viktor were supposed to remain in position outside the terminal's main doors, waiting for Kat and Svetlanov to meet up with the old man who Moody called Papa.

Talk about half-assed operations, Wolfgang thought. He wasn't used to this shit. Damn, they were only packing pistols, and his car full of explosives was sitting useless in the lot. He'd wanted to take a few toys on board the ferry, and managed to sneak a little C4 and a couple of detonators into his jacket, but Mad Dog had ordered him to leave the rest of the fireworks alone. All they needed to do was make sure the nukes got loaded onto the truck and that the truck got driven onto the ferry. Moody had plans from there, and apparently even the boss didn't know what they were.

And therein was the problem with this whole little ploy: piss poor communications, and even when they did talk it was with fucking sat and cell phones. Come on. He was used to his radio, the boom mike at his lips, channels always open, Blackhound to Blackhound, just like the good old days.

Now he'd have to keep a line open to feed the boss his play-by-play, and that meant he'd be distracted. One hand on the phone, the other on a pair of night vision goggles, shit. He'd have to rely on Viktor to get off a first shot if it came down to that. Kid was good, but he was better.

"Don't look back," Wolfgang told Viktor, who was doing just that.

"Okay, but she's having hard time with him. Fucking drunk motherfucker. I want to shoot this fuck."

"He didn't kill your dad. I'll tell you who I think did."

Viktor shifted closer to him, increasing his pace to keep up, since Wolfgang was on a mission to reach the end of the platform within a minute. "The boss got bad intel from a Russian colonel, guy named Sinitsyna. We think he's here. Now, he's the guy who set up the boss and probably hired those guys to make a hit. Your old man just got in the way. So if you want to point fingers . . ."

"You say this colonel is here?"

"We're tracking him. He's got something to do with all this. Boss might know more than me. I just came here to shoot people, you know?"

"Yes, I know."

"Maybe you'll get your chance for a little payback."

"I hope so."

Wolfgang didn't care if he'd just thrown gas in the fire. He'd rather have a guy bent on revenge at his side. He tugged out his phone, called Mad Dog. "Hey, boss. We're good to go here."

"I can see you."

"Where are you? Heading onto the ferry?"

"Right now."

"Okay, boss. Hold your breath. Because Kat's about to make contact with Papa Svetlanov. The old man and three guys are walking up to them." Wolfgang lowered the phone, widened his eyes on Viktor. "Dude, get ready."

Chapter 15

....

James Moody had crawled beneath the maintenance truck, and now he felt like a vodka-soaked sardine.

But it was all for duty, honor, and country.

Especially the vodka part, even though that would come later.

The truck was parked beside a storage garage about twenty meters adjacent to the cargo platform. Moody pushed up on his elbows and raised the night vision goggles.

Lo and behold, the transfer was already in progress. The crane affixed to one of Svetlanov's trucks had moved up to the cargo carriage, and the first crate was gliding through the snow-filled air, bound for the second truck's flatbed, on which sat another pallet. Since Mad Dog kept an open phone line with Wolfgang, Moody fed his intel to Bibby: "You there?"

"Still here, Mr. Moody. Report?"

"The transfer's happening as we speak. Looks like they got a driver, crane operator, and two schmucks guarding."

"Very well. Call us back if there are any problems. We'll meet you here."

"No doubt. That's one boat I'm not missing."

"I hope once you're on board you'll let us know what you plan to do."

"I might talk. We'll see."

"It's never easy with you. Good-bye."

"Bibby, wait. I just want to ask you—"

Damn it, the Brit had hung up.

"I just wanted to ask you if you were full of shit," muttered Moody. "If you're still lying to us and thinking we'll play into your hand."

He lowered the goggles. "Because I got a real surprise waiting for you, old chap."

Back on the platform, Kat dragged Svetlanov toward the four men. The mafia's prodigal son could barely stand, pressing nearly his full weight on her shoulder. She giggled, pretended she was nearly as drunk as he was. She even nibbled on his earlobe, trying to arouse him as the old man, assumedly Svetlanov's father, cleared his throat.

"Sergei! What are you doing?" he demanded in Russian.

Svetlanov glanced lazily at his father. "We got a lot of trouble!"

"Yes, we do, you fool! What have you been doing on board that train? Nothing but drinking? Where are your men?"

"They're dead! All dead," he cried, breaking into laughter.

"Don't lie to your father," said Kat. "He fired them all,

told them to go home. He was . . . crazy!" Kat began laughing herself, then grabbed Svetlanov's ass.

He wriggled and said, "Not now! I need to sleep! But she is not—"

"She's your whore!" cried Papa Svetlanov.

"Let me take care of him," said Kat. "I will get him on the ferry, okay?" She widened her eyes, and the old man's hard gaze began to soften.

"Are you Hannah, the one he spoke about?"

"Yes."

"He told me you were a brunette. He told me you were much younger, going to college."

Kat opened her mouth, racing through replies.

"I don't know, boss," said Wolfgang, observing Kat through his binoculars. "She could be shitting a pickle."

"Just hang tight."

"Moody call you?"

"Yep, they're loading the second missile now. Bibby's saying they'll probably load that truck first, so they're first off in Japan. Pope's been doing some good work from home, and I just heard back from him. He says that once the warheads are in Japan, they'll be loaded on board the MV *Osaka Maru* for shipment to Lebanon, according to our ferry's manifest. We expect Papa Svetlanov to collect payment in Japan before that happens."

"Makes sense."

"What's happening with Kat now?"

"Not much. They're still talking."

Kat shifted closer to Papa Svetlanov, slapped a gloved hand on his shoulder. "So that's what happened."

The old man frowned. "So you're *not* Hannah?"

"No."

"And he wanted you to lie?"

"Because he didn't want you to know that he was with me—isn't that right?" Kat shoved Svetlanov, and his eyes opened. "Isn't that right?"

"Yes, yes, yes . . . I'm not with you."

"Then what happened to his precious girlfriend?"

"She left him. Got off the train. I watched."

"My son can't do anything right. He has failed our family, failed himself."

"I will take him to the ferry."

"You do that."

"I'm sorry."

Papa Svetlanov shifted up to her, opening his mouth slightly. "After you put him to bed, you will come see me. Understood? I will call you on his phone."

Kat nodded. She imagined she looked scared. Summoning up the look didn't take much, only one mind picture of the old man naked and coming at her.

The tarpaulin flaps on the old truck were pulled taut and sealed by the crane operator, then the driver climbed inside.

That was his cue to haul his overgrown and half-frozen ass out from beneath cover. Moody rose slowly in the darkness, the wind buffeting him, snow swirling as though inside a water-filled globe.

He kept tight to the truck until Svetlanov's vehicle moved off, heading toward the docks. Then he started across the platform, swallowed by the storm, and made his way around the station and terminal, both of which were mostly deserted now, with travelers either inside or in the parking lot, getting taxis.

He came around the terminal building and saw the 13,000-ton ferry floating quietly in the distance. Her white hull shimmered faintly in the harsh dock lights, and vehicles and passengers were already moving up gangways and into the hold or main deck, respectively. She had 114 cabins to service about four hundred passengers and crew, and really, she wasn't a bad ship at all, with phones and air conditioners in every cabin. Moody had heard that the restaurants and entertainment were pretty good, too, although he'd spend any down time at the veranda casino. He checked his coat pocket for his ticket.

When he reached the boarding line, he noted that the security officers were patting down each passenger. His pistol was already shoved into his boot, like Mad Dog had told him—though he didn't need the jarhead to remind him of that—and he moved onto the ship after a perfunctory inspection.

Ferry MV *Rus*
Bound for Fushiki, Japan
0440 Hours Local Time

They had booked cabins 4451 and 4453 on the main deck. Kat had rummaged through Svetlanov's belongings, discovering he'd booked cabin 4456 on the starboard bow of the ferry, and that's where she took him. She was about to call Mad Dog when someone knocked.

She called out in Russian, "Who is it?"

"Me."

She cracked open the door, her eyes burning a little, then opened it fully to admit Moody.

"You all right?" he asked.

"We're good here. He's passed out." She lifted her head toward Svetlanov, draped over the bed. "How the fuck are we supposed to do this? It'll take forty hours to get to Japan. I can't keep him drunk for that long. We need to drug him or something. Keep him unconscious. We can tell his father he overdosed or something."

"I like it. Maybe we can load him up with Dramamine."

"Get somebody to get us that. I'll be here. The father wants me to fuck him, and I might need some interference."

"Yeah, I'm sure Hertzog would have a problem with you fucking on company time."

"Get out of here."

"Hey, I know I can be a wiseass sometimes, but—"

"Yeah, you sure can."

He opened the door, stepped out, and she slammed it after him. She figured he'd wear his crooked grin all the way to Mad Dog's cabin.

Bibby was at the portside rail near the stern, watching the last of the cars roll onto the ferry. Their precious truck with its even more precious cargo had, indeed, been first on board, making it first off once they reached Japan. He removed his gloved hands from the railing as the loading was completed.

A crewman approached, suggested that he go below for a cocktail to warm him up. He also said they were in for a rough ride, with the storm blowing through. Bibby nodded and started away, reaching into his pocket for his phone. He called Mad Dog. "They're on board, and we're leaving."

"Good, now get the hell down here. Moody's here, and we need to talk."

Wolfgang and Viktor prowled one of the long corridors, threading through guests still trying to find their cabins. A wet-carpet stench hung in the air, along with the usual salty tang of the sea, odors that seemed to draw the life out of many of the passengers. Wolfgang could barely raise a smile from two Japanese women who passed them, both young and hot.

The boss had confirmed that Colonel Boris Sinitsyna was on the ferry, traveling under an unknown alias, and it was his job to find and apprehend him. They thought to use the chip in the necklace the colonel was said to have on him, but they'd already tracked the chip's signal to one of the safe deposit boxes located in the purser's office.

"Shit," had been Wolfgang's response.

He now had about forty hours to complete his mission.

"And if you can't find one fucking guy on board a ship at sea, then I want your resignation when we reach Japan," Mad Dog told him.

So the pressure was on. But it wasn't enough to calm his libido.

"Those Japanese girls were hot," Wolfgang muttered.

"I think the British girl is hot," said Viktor as they walked a little more slowly, eyeing each passerby, their legs wobbly as the ship began to depart and was struck by six to ten foot swells.

"You mean Bibby's daughter Hannah?" asked Wolfgang.

"Yes."

"Oh, shit, dude, don't touch that."

"I saw you looking at her, too."

"Just reading the menu, buddy. You order that shit, and you'll see one crazy Englishman."

"You came to Russia because of him, my father said. It is his fault. He stole your money, right?"

"Not mine. The company's. But he gave it back."

"I don't understand."

"Neither do I. But we take it out on him by flirting with his daughter? Shit, she's all fucked up now. Found out her boyfriend likes to sell nukes. I don't need that. I like women with big boobs who never talk."

"Oh, yes. Me, too."

Wolfgang's sat phone rang. "Yeah?"

"I need you to find the duty free shop. Buy all the fucking Dramamine they got, and any other painkillers you can find, muscle relaxants, whatever they have to keep Svetlanov knocked out. You read me?"

"Got it, boss, but if I clean 'em out, that's going to raise a few eyebrows."

"You deal with that. When you get the shit, bring it to Kat's room."

"On our way."

After Wolfgang explained to young Viktor what they needed to do, the Russian just shook his head and said, "Why don't we just kill him?"

"I like your style, buddy, but the boss has his reasons. Keep looking for the colonel, okay?"

"Oh, his is a face I will not forget."

"Just remember, we take him alive back to the boss, and we get a bonus. We bring in a body, and the boss might kill *us*."

"I understand. But I don't agree."

"Yeah, I know, but they want to interrogate him. The boss was emphatic about that. I think this colonel is linked to some big-time players. Everybody wants a piece of him."

"But I get to kill him later."

"Hey, Viktor, if you get your chance, maybe you'll take it. But you know what? It's just never enough."

"What do you mean? You said he hired the men who killed my father. He dies. That's all."

"What I'm trying to tell you is that I've been there, and let's say you get your chance, but—"

"But what? You have regrets?"

Wolfgang shrugged. "I'm just saying . . . I don't know what I'm saying. Let's go."

*   *   *

Colonel Boris Sinitsyna opened his cabin door to find two men already inside.

"What the fuck is this?" he asked in Russian.

"Speak English," said the taller of the two, a dark-skinned man with several pens in the pocket of his ivory-colored suit shirt, the sleeves stained around the edges. "I am Yassir. This is Kassam. We are the engineers." He nervously stroked his thin, graying beard.

"Are you armed?"

"No."

The colonel chuckled.

"What is so amusing?" asked Kassam, the slightly shorter, slightly heavier man, his quilt-thick beard reaching toward his shirt pockets.

"They tell me they are sending Hezbollah, and what do I find? As the Americans would say, two fucking nerds."

Kassam frowned at Yassir, then said, "I don't know what he said."

Yassir spoke quickly in Arabic, then Kassam nodded and glared at the colonel. "Like the Americans say, fuck you."

"Well, okay then, boys. Now that we have met, you can get the fuck out of my cabin."

"We are sharing this one."

"There are only two beds," cried the colonel.

Kassam rolled his eyes. "I will sleep with him."

"You'll sleep with each other!" The colonel set down his briefcase, then ordered both men to sit on the lower bed. "If you're not going to shoot, then the least you can do is provide me with intelligence. I'm going to show you the photographs of several Americans and one Brit who might be on board this ferry."

"You want us to confirm that?" asked Yassir.

"Yes, because if we don't, then you won't get a chance to play with your little calculator, understand?"

Both men nodded.

"Now then, let's begin." The colonel reached for his case, opened it, dug out a file folder.

Mad Dog knew that if he closed his eyes for even a minute, he would be dead to the world for at least ten hours, maybe twelve. He leaned back on the bottom bunk, glancing across the room at Moody, who was on his little laptop, banging away.

"You know what I was thinking?" asked Mad Dog.

"That you didn't want to talk right now, because I'm busy updating our situation with Langley?"

"No. I was thinking that since Bibby gave me back the money, and all I'm trying to recover here is my necklace—"

"The one you stole from the colonel's daughter."

"Yeah, the one I took for my trouble, the trouble that involved losing good men because the bitch set me up."

"Hey, asshole, you don't have to preach it to me. I was fucking there, remember?"

"Anyway, I'm just here for that, and anything I do for you is gratis. But it's just like working for the CIA. Again."

"No, you're just assisting us as a good American citizen. One hand washes the other, right? Yeah, I know you might walk out of here actually losing money, but that's the way it goes."

Moody didn't know about the diamonds, and Mad Dog had every intention of keeping it that way. He'd told the agent that Hannah had stolen the diamonds, but then they were lifted from her by two agents on board the train who had vanished. And he'd left it at that.

A knock came at the door: Bibby. Mad Dog let him in,

and the Brit took off his coat and gloves. Suddenly, the ferry listed to port, then came back. "I think we're all going to need some meds after this ride," said Mad Dog.

"Indeed. Where is Hannah?" asked Bibby. "Still in the room next door?"

"Last I checked."

"All right, gentlemen, let's get down to business," said Moody. "First thing we need to do is eliminate the threat, then take control of the warheads."

Mad Dog cracked a smiled at Bibby. "Thank God we have an expert from the CIA here."

Moody snorted. "This from the same asshole who wants to hire me."

"All right, come on," said Mad Dog impatiently. "What do you have in mind?"

"First, I'm telling you right now—this plan unfolds on a need-to-know basis. You fucks don't even trust each other, so there's no way in hell I'm trusting you—not when I got a couple of nukes sitting on this boat."

"Hey, buddy, we could've all walked away back there."

"He's right," said Bibby. "We're here to help"

"You are, huh? Let me ask you something, *Mr. Bibby*. If you could've bought the nukes from Zakarova, what would you have done with them?"

"Returned them to the Russian army, their rightful owners."

"Bullshit."

"What do you think I would've done? Brought them back to the queen for her inspection?"

"Maybe. Or maybe you and our boy Waffa would've set up something very lucrative."

"You don't know me at all, Mr. Moody."

"No, I don't."

"And what you also don't realize is that when I spoke

to Zakarova, he mentioned he was transporting two of his warheads. That's exactly the way he put it—a little slip of the tongue, as it were. *Two* of his warheads."

Moody sighed deeply. "Jesus Christ."

"Who knows how many more there are?" said Bibby. "But I argue there is at least one other man who can confirm that and might even know the location of the other warheads."

"Colonel Boris Sinitsyna," said Moody.

"Exactly."

This was old news to Mad Dog; he and Bibby had already discussed it, and now the bigger picture was becoming more distinct.

"So we need to take him alive," said Moody. "Interrogate him. Make sure those remaining nukes don't get jacked by some other assholes."

"More hero work for our friendly neighborhood spook," said Mad Dog. "Can you handle it?"

"Shut up, I'm thinking. I'll see if I can get eyes in the sky to sweep the entire area around Irkutsk and mark potential cache sites."

"Listen to me, Jimmy boy. We'll make you look good when this is all over," said Mad Dog. "But you gotta play it our way. This need-to-know bullshit is just that. If you have a plan, I need to know every fucking detail . . . right . . . now . . . "

Kat rose from the chair to answer the door. It was Wolfgang, who handed her a bag full of Dramamine and other over-the-counter drugs. "This should help," he said. "And are you okay? You don't look so good."

"Never say that to a lady."

He shrugged. "You look hot, and I want to bang you?"

"That's better."

Svetlanov's phone began to ring. Kat glared at it, muttered, "And speaking of banging . . . " She picked it up as Wolfgang left. "Yes?"

"How is my son?"

"Passed out."

"Good. Come to my cabin, 4424 on the port side."

"Okay." Kat hung up, grabbed her own phone and called Mad Dog. "Time to move."

"On our way."

She hung up, glanced over at Svetlanov, snoring loudly now. She'd placed a bottle of water near the bed, one in which she dissolved some Dramamine. A whole lot of Dramamine. If he awoke, he would certainly reach for the drink—being drunk and dehydrated. And once more he would pass out.

After tucking her pistol into her purse, she quickly left, heading down the hall to meet up with Mad Dog and Bibby.

Wolfgang and Viktor were in one of the many service areas, speaking to a member of the cleaning staff, a lean old man in a pale blue ship's uniform that would fit Viktor just right.

They ordered him toward the back of the room, behind stacks of unwashed bedding, and there, at gunpoint, relieved him of his uniform. The old man got all dramatic and wanted Viktor to shoot him because he had never been so humiliated in his entire life. The indignity of taking off his clothes!

"No, old man. No bullet for you. You're going for a swim."

Wrong place, wrong time. That's all it was. That's what fate had dealt the old dude. And there was nothing they could do about it. They couldn't trust him. They couldn't leave him tied up somewhere, unless they brought him back to the boss's room. Nah. Wouldn't work.

So they had him change into Viktor's clothes and escorted him quietly up to the main deck.

No one was outside. The wind howled. The ferry rose up the swells, settled down, rose again in an unceasing rhythm.

Wolfgang nodded and turned away, listening to the old man's faint cry.

"I didn't even force him to jump," said Viktor. "He just climbed over the railing, looked at me, then let go."

"Yeah . . . " Wolfgang's gut churned at the thought.

"So I have the uniform. Now what?"

"You knock on every door until you find him."

"Are you crazy?"

"I'll patrol the restaurants and casino, and that saloon and the bar. I'll swing by the open games area and the disco, too. You hit the doors, I roam. We stay in touch."

"While you're looking for some Japanese whore to bang! I know what you'll do!"

"Look, it's the only way. If the colonel stays holed up in his room, we'll never find him. You have to start knocking and checking. Just ask the people how they are and if they need anything. If he answers, you hold him there and call me, got it? Don't do anything else!"

"You know how long this will take?"

"That's like a hundred and forty rooms or so? Shit, a minute at each? Two, three hours maybe. And, oh, yeah, use the master key on the doors that aren't answered."

"Okay."

"And Viktor, when this is all over, I'm going to take you to the Philippines, to Cebu, show you around. You're going to love it there. I'm going to invite your whole family."

"Thank you."

The kid took off.

Before Wolfgang headed back inside to recon the casino, he hustled down to the hold, where all the cars were lined up. He pulled out a small pair of night vision goggles and studied the truck. Two men sat inside the cab. "Son of a bitch," he muttered. "They ain't fucking around." He called the boss. "Looks like Papa left two with the truck."

"Got it," said Mad Dog. "Let me call you back. We're moving in on the old man's room."

Hirbod knew that the American mercenary did not see him, and as he lowered the binoculars and hurried off, he nodded slowly to himself. He was thirty-five, an experienced agent, not as reckless or careless as these Americans, and not as egotistical or arrogant as Colonel Boris Sinitsyna, who had been hired merely to keep the engineers company.

He and his three men were the true guardians of the warheads. They were Iranian Islamic Revolutionary Guard Corps agents, commonly known as Seppah-e Pasdaran, or just Seppah agents, and their job was to physically witness and report that the nukes were on board the ferry, follow them to Japan, witness the deal between the agents and Svetlanov, then kill all involved before the boat left for Lebanon. They would turn over the nukes to their superiors once the boat docked in Lebanon. Failure was punishable by death.

Hirbod rose from behind the small pickup truck, tugged his collar tighter about his neck, then started up a small staircase to head inside.

On this cold, miserable night, in the middle of a snowstorm aboard a ferry cutting through rough seas, he felt warm with the knowledge that the final jihad would soon come.

Allahu Akbar!

Chapter 16

· ·

K at knocked on Papa Svetlanov's cabin door and said, "Mr. Svetlanov? It's me."

Within the next pair of nerve-racking seconds, she contemplated her own death:

A quick bullet to the heart—

A last look from the man she loved—

The ceiling, then light, the beautiful light . . .

Or eternal darkness.

With a shudder, she rolled away from the door as it creaked open.

Mad Dog kicked the door in, knocking Papa Svetlanov onto his back. Carried by his own momentum, he charged into the room, Kat right behind him. He swept left and she right, where she leveled her silenced pistol on one of Svetlanov's men.

His eyes bugged. He looked for his pistol, lying on the bed.

She put a bullet in his head before he could blink again.

A second man stepped out of the bathroom, reaching for the pistol holstered beneath his arm, and Mad Dog fired one round from his silenced Beretta. A sudden rose bloomed across the man's white shirt as he dropped.

Meanwhile, Bibby, who'd come in last, literally leapt on top of the old Svetlanov, pinning him to the floor, though a pistol was still clenched in the Russian's right hand.

Kat was there in a heartbeat, prying the weapon free even as Mad Dog shoved his pistol into the old man's head.

"Okay, okay," said Svetlanov in Russian. "No need for further violence."

"Let him up," said Mad Dog.

Bibby slowly released his grip on Papa's arms, then rose and climbed off the man.

Papa sat up, blinked, rubbed the nape of his neck, then smiled at Kat. "If you told me you wanted to play with other boys, I would've said okay. Is this part of your fantasy?"

She snorted. "You wish."

"How many did you bring on board?" demanded Bibby. "You've got two down with the truck. Two here. And your son."

Papa Svetlanov grinned. "You're Mr. Bibby, aren't you? My son spoke at length about you."

"Answer the question."

Bibby's Russian was good, very good, and Kat could see that Mad Dog was having a hard time following, so she moved to him, whispered what was happening in his ear.

"I have two men left at the truck. And my son. That's it," the old man answered.

"And you're going to believe him?" asked Mad Dog, after Kat had translated.

"Why would I lie?" asked Papa in English. "You have me. You won't kill me. I can be a friend. We're all in this for money. We understand that, don't we?"

Bibby glanced to a small dresser, spotted a cell phone, grabbed and tossed it to Svetlanov. "Call your to men at the truck. Ask them how they're doing. Tell them you're sending down something to eat. That's all."

"Clever boy." The Russian smiled. "I suppose *you* will be delivering the pizza?"

Bibby nodded. "With anchovies."

Viktor approached the next door and rapped on it with sore knuckles.

The bearded man who answered looked angry and tired. "What is it?"

"Just making sure you have enough linens and towels, sir," he said, pushing himself into the cabin. "And if there's anything else you need?"

"We're fine!" cried another bearded man, shorter and even angrier. "Please leave! We want to get some sleep!"

Viktor nodded and quickly left the cabin.

It wasn't until three doors later that he realized someone had been sleeping in the top bunk in that room, someone whose face he had not checked.

He returned to the room and knocked again. The bearded man answered, widened his eyes and ordered Viktor to leave. The top bunk was now empty.

"I'm sorry, sir. Another room requested more towels, but I've forgotten which . . . "

Viktor left and tried to convince himself that it was nothing. But he remembered the cabin number and vowed to return when he had finished.

Wolfgang moved through the casino, his gaze meeting as many passengers as he could, not that there were many at this hour in the morning. Most folks had gone directly to their rooms and to bed, but a few, the more adventurous tourists, wanted to see the ferry before heading off to sleep. He counted about twenty in this area.

Were Wolfgang not studying faces, he might not have noticed the man following him, a tall, clean-shaven, dark-skinned fellow with a dark brow. He wore an expensive wool coat and had a cell phone to his ear, his gold pinky ring flashing. He could easily be mistaken for a businessman, but Wolfgang knew better. He'd spotted the guy back at the bar and then at the disco. He was Middle Eastern, no doubt . . .

And Wolfgang didn't know why, knew it was foolish, but he swung around, brought his pair of brass balls toward the man, who looked up and frowned.

"Let's go for a little walk."

"No need, Mr. Wolfgang. I know exactly who you are. I've just been looking for the right time to make contact, making sure you haven't been followed."

The man had a British accent that sounded just like Bibby's. "So who the fuck are you? And why are you at this party?"

"The name's not important."

"Yeah, it is. Should I just call you fuckhead? Or do you prefer Mr. Fuckhead?"

"You're very crude. I'd prefer Isaac, if you must. Can you tell me where I might find Mr. Bibby?"

Wolfgang almost grinned. "If you had asked me that a few days ago, I would've said it was the million dollar question. Really the forty million dollar question. Or maybe I would've said I don't know who you're talking about. But somehow you know my name. So I gotta ask, why you looking for him? You want to kill him, like everyone else?"

"No, Bibby's been coordinating with us. And I've been sent to help."

"No, shit. Who you with?"

"Not important. Finding Bibby is."

"I'll make a call." He dialed Bibby, who told him to take Isaac back to their cabin and wait.

Bibby had his cap pulled tightly over his head in an effort to conceal himself from the colonel, should their paths unfortunately cross. Mad Dog likewise donned his cap, and the two of them had gone down to the lower deck, choosing a path on the port side, along the hull and end row of cars and trucks. Bibby carried two paper bags that could presumably contain food but in fact contained pistols.

No pizza, anchovies or otherwise, for the two Russkies guarding the nukes.

Albert and Patrice back in London had been generous enough to loan Bibby one of their agents, a man named Isaac, and Bibby was glad the man finally made contact. They could use all the help they could get.

He felt reassured as they crossed along the stern, intending to come up on the two Russians from behind. Wolfgang had last reported that both men were in the cab, but as they approached, Bibby only spotted one man there. *Shit.*

Their little food delivery diversion would have worked, had both men been in one place.

Bibby damned that plan to hell, ducked behind a car and grabbed his silenced pistol. He handed the other to Mad Dog, who gave him the signal: Bibby would take out the man in the cab, while Mad Dog crossed behind the truck, searching for the other guy. Damned sloppy to do it this way, but they had no other choice.

Bibby closed in on the truck, got down on his haunches near the back wheel.

His pulse mounted.

Time for the kill.

But then he spotted a pair of boots on the other side of the truck. He signaled to Mad Dog, who noted them as well, and now they had them.

Mad Dog nodded.

And off they went. Bibby reached the truck, seized the door handle. Locked. *Shit*. The guy faced him.

Thump! Glass shattered. The bullet penetrated the guy's head.

Bibby hung on to the door, just breathing for a second.

Another thump, then Bibby hustled around the truck to see the other Russian lying on the deck—

But Mad Dog was hunched over, clutching his chest.

Hannah was at that point between sleep and consciousness, the one her favorite poet Keats had written about, like the moment before a kiss, when an epiphany took hold.

Well, it wasn't quite an epiphany; it was a fact that she'd tried to overlook because her father had come for her, tried to prove he loved her, risked his life, his career, everything for her.

And so she had concluded that he did, indeed, love her, but that beast inside that drove him on to the next mission would never leave.

He would never change.

But maybe, just maybe, Sergei would. He was still young, had his whole life ahead of him. And though she feared him, she still wanted him, needed him, couldn't abandon hope.

Abruptly, she rose and went to his cabin, having overhead the number when her father was speaking to his American friend Hertzog.

The hallway was empty. She banged on the door repeatedly but he wouldn't answer. She called his name, then reached into her purse, dialed his cell phone, heard it ringing inside.

And then a hand slapped on her shoulder and she whirled around.

"What are you doing?" Wolfgang asked.

She glared at him, glanced at the man with him, a tall Middle Eastern guy. "Nothing."

"You need to get back to your room. Let's go. I'm heading over there myself."

"Hannah?" asked the Middle Eastern guy.

"Yeah? How do you know my name?"

The man smiled, reached into his coat and produced a pistol with a long barrel. He brought it around toward her chest just as Wolfgang cried, "Fuck!"

Kat had been charged with guarding Papa Svetlanov while Bibby and Mad Dog took out the men guarding the warheads.

If Papa had more men on board, well, they'd have to deal with that, but Kat sensed that the old Russkie wasn't lying. He wasn't some maniacal killer, some maniac bent on power; he was an unadulterated opportunist whose loyalty to his family was unfaltering but whose loyalty to anyone or anything else swayed according to who had the money. Pure and simple. An easy guy to read.

And now he seemed resigned to his fate, even jovial. "It's too bad you're not a prostitute. I would have paid a lot."

"Yes, too bad."

"My wife is frigid. But you know, there are worse things in this life."

"Yeah, like your son losing twenty million in diamonds, and you losing the warheads. This was the biggest deal of your criminal career, I assume."

He nodded.

"I'm shocked at how well you're taking all of this."

"How you say? Easy come, easy go? I have many other deals, and there will be many more."

The pain radiating through Mad Dog's chest was not un-familiar. Whether he was having an actual heart attack or not, he wasn't sure, but it was the same pain he'd felt when he first heard Bibby had ripped him off.

"Yes," he told Bibby. "I'm all right. Not shot."

"Did he hit you?"

"No, just . . . " He caught his breath, stood upright. "There it is."

"Michael, tell me."

"Well, it's not my colon cancer. Come on. Fuck me and my chest pain. No time for this shit. We'll stuff these guys in another car."

"All right. Then we'll get back and you'll meet Isaac, an old friend. We could use an extra pair of hands."

Wolfgang had a point-blank shot, and the only thing that might have saved Hannah's life was his hand, which knocked into Isaac's the moment he pulled the trigger.

The gun went off and she fell back toward the door, which suddenly opened.

But Wolfgang wasn't paying attention to that as he got one hand on the gun while Isaac fired again, the shot thumping into the overhead. Wolfgang forced him around, back through the open cabin door and into the room, where the young Svetlanov had fallen onto the floor.

They crashed into a chair, slammed into the lower bunk, and Wolfgang tugged even harder, trying to free the gun. He had both hands on it as Isaac used his free hand to pry him off. Then Wolfgang tripped, his hands came free—

And he fell back, staring up at Isaac, who shook his

head. "I don't want you. I just want her." He turned his pistol toward the doorway, where Hannah had crumpled, clutching her shoulder.

But then the drunken Svetlanov threw himself toward Hannah, and Isaac fired, hitting him in the back—

As Wolfgang drew his own pistol from his waistband and—

Thump! Thump!

—fired two silenced rounds into Isaac's back, dropping him fast to the floor.

Wolfgang rushed to the man, rolled him over. "Why are you here? Why'd you want to kill her?"

"They wanted the wife dead. They wanted her dead."

"Who? MI6?"

"No."

"Who?"

Isaac's head fell limp, his eyes vague.

Wolfgang went to Svetlanov, dragged him away from the door. He was still alive, moaning, reaching for his back. The gunshot wound was high, might've missed his major organs.

Then Wolfgang hunkered down next to Hannah, swung her arm around his shoulder, gingerly helped her into the cabin and quickly shut the door.

The call from Wolfgang would have sent waves of anger through Mad Dog had he not been wincing over the pain still radiating in his chest. He and Bibby were almost to their cabin when he turned around, answering the Brit's quizzical look with one word: "Trouble."

They reached Svetlanov's cabin, knocked, then Wolfgang answered.

"Jesus Fucking Christ!" cried Mad Dog.

"Hannah!" Bibby echoed, practically diving toward his daughter.

Wolfgang was talking a mile a minute, but Mad Dog wasn't hearing a goddamned word. Svetlanov was shot in the back and bleeding, some other fuck lay dead on the floor, and Hannah had been shot in the shoulder.

Mad Dog's phone rang: Moody. "I'm in Svetlanov's cabin. Get your ass over. We got a fucking problem."

"Yeah, yeah . . . "

"Wolfgang, go find us some bandages, morphine, whatever they got."

"On it."

"Where the hell's Viktor?"

"Still looking for the colonel, but he hasn't checked in for a while."

"Call him while you get that doc, but let him keep looking."

"Roger that, boss."

"Bibby, who is this fucking guy?"

The Brit was at a loss. He'd been talking to Hannah, who must've told him the same thing Wolfgang was yapping about: The guy had said he was Bibby's friend, here to help, then he shot her, but he wasn't working for MI6.

"He was an old friend. Somebody got to him, paid him off, and I can't believe he'd turn like this."

"Well, trust me on that one. I know what that feels like."

Moody arrived, entered breathless and said, "I told you boys those pistols are not toys."

"Shut the fuck up."

"Listen, asshole, all I need is twelve hours of you staying out of fucking trouble. Can you do that? What do we got now? Another fucking body? Who the hell is this? Don't answer that. Answer a more important question: Do we control the nukes?"

"Well, there's no one guarding them . . . "

*   *   *

Hirbod had gone back to his cabin to get some sleep. His phone rang, and he rolled over and answered it. The man he'd posted in the hold, Azad, called to say that two men had come, killed the guards in the truck and left them there. Azad had not engaged them, only observed. He had not been seen.

"Good," Hirbod told him. "Remain there. Do not take your eyes off that truck."

When they heard knocking at their cabin door a third time, Colonel Boris Sinitsyna went into the bathroom, as he had the second time. He'd instructed the engineers to invite the crew member into their cabin and had told them to shut the door.

Once the boy was inside, the colonel sprang from the room and pointed his gun at the young man's head.

"Hello, are you looking for me?"

The kid's eyes burned. "Yes."

The colonel frowned. "Who are you?"

"My name is Viktor. You should remember the name of the man who is going to kill you."

"You are young. And hopeful. And obviously blind." The colonel took a step forward, the gun trained on the kid's head.

"You hired some men to attack Hertzog in Khabarovsk."

"Yes, I did."

"They killed my father."

"And who was your father?"

"Obviously no one important to you."

"Obviously." The colonel grinned. "Before you kill me, let's sit down and talk some more."

Chapter 17

....

During the past eleven hours, Mad Dog had been struggling to hide his chest pains. He had assured Bibby that he was all right, but the pain continued to return. No, he didn't think he was having a heart attack—the radiating pain had vanished, but there was a significant burning in his chest now, like reflux. Maybe he was having a goddamned panic attack in the middle of it all.

There was enough to be concerned about: Hannah had been shot, along with her scumbag boyfriend; old Papa Svetlanov was still tied up in his room; and Bibby had been trying to figure out exactly why an old friend from MI6 allowed himself to be bought and turned into an assassin.

Add to the fact that Viktor was still missing, the colonel had still not been found, and you had a few good reasons to pass out from stress, on top of being a forty-something cancer survivor with the mileage of a seventy-year-old.

It wasn't all bad, though. Wolfgang had found a nurse practitioner whose equipment they needed more than her. They treated Hannah, whose wound wasn't serious, clean entry and exit, and she'd be okay. Her boyfriend, on the other hand, should have died within an hour but had hung on. Hannah sat with him in the room, stroking his face, whispering in his ear, while Bibby shook his head and cursed. He eventually gave up after seven hours.

"I hope it hurt," Bibby had said to the corpse.

They'd left the kid's father gagged and tied in his room, along with the nurse practitioner and the bodies of Papa's dead men. Wolfgang had gone off to find Viktor, but he only had until 1940 hours. After that he had another job to do, and Mad Dog was trusting him with their entire plan.

At the moment, Moody was in their cabin, glued to his computer, along with Hannah, who was sleeping. Mad Dog, Kat, and Bibby were down in the hold, staring out across the rows of cars and trucks.

"We need to clear a path," said Bibby, glancing from the heavy equipment elevator to the truck in the distance.

"Mr. Fucking CIA didn't plan that," snapped Mad Dog.

"I need at least three car lengths of working space behind that truck," said Kat, who was seated in the idling forklift they had procured from the main deck at gunpoint. The crewman on duty up there went for a long swim to Japan.

Mad Dog and Bibby jogged aft to the stern, found the ramp control box located on the starboard side next to the ramp assembly itself. While Bibby figured out how to lower the ramp, Mad Dog busted in the windshield of the last car in the truck's row, threw it out of gear, and waited until Bibby got the ramp fully extended. Once it was down, Mad Dog shoved the little Peugeot off the stern, less than ten feet away.

With Bibby's help, the next two cars in line joined the Peugeot. For the next few minutes Mad Dog and Bibby, sometimes using the forklift, if Kat had maneuvering room, piled the remaining cars back at the newly emptied space. It wasn't pretty—more like a seven-car pile-up on L.A.'s 405—but the forklift now had enough space behind the truck.

Azad was sitting inside a small sedan near the port side of the hold. He had already called his boss to say that the men down there were rolling cars into the ocean.

He asked his boss if he could stop them.

"Not yet." Hirbod sounded confused, but ordered him to continue observing them.

Using a small pair of night vision goggles, Azad leaned out of the car window, zooming in on the men as they dropped the next vehicle overboard.

He never saw the woman approach, only heard her voice when it was already too late: "What the fuck are you doing?"

And suddenly she had his head in her hands.

Wolfgang checked his watch as he moved quickly down each passageway. He wanted to open every door, the same way Viktor had, but there wasn't time, and he was beginning to panic. The kid hadn't left any word, and he wasn't answering his phone.

He had found the colonel, all right. And Wolfgang shuddered at the thought.

After another glance at the time, he moved on, heading to the crowded restaurant for another look there.

His phone rang: Kat. "What's up?"

"I just nabbed a guy down here. Don't know if he's working for the colonel or not, but we're out of time. Get up to the bridge right now."

"Roger that."

Wolfgang sighed. "Aw, Viktor. Sorry, buddy."

Viktor glanced up through teary eyes at the two bearded men who had been watching him for the last eleven hours. The old man had bound him to a desk chair and beaten him until he talked. He just couldn't take the pain anymore. He'd told the old man about the mercenaries, about Bibby, about the tall ugly man who met them on the ferry. But that's all he knew, and he wondered when the old man would return, and if he would live or die.

He prayed.

And he listened to the words of his father, who seemed to speak to him from the afterlife. *Be strong, my son. Be strong.*

I'm sorry.

No, you did your best, Viktor.

Then the door opened and in walked the old man, who raised his silenced pistol to Viktor's head.

"Why do you have to kill me?" Viktor asked.

"I don't," said the old man.

He lowered his pistol, then raised it again and fired.

Viktor felt the sharp pain in his head, heard the old man say, "I need help, you bastards! Some passengers spotted cars floating in the water behind us! They're trying to steal the warheads!"

And that was all.

Kat guided the forklift toward the back of the truck, where Bibby and Mad Dog were waiting. She had a hard time concentrating. Breaking a guy's neck five minutes ago had something to do with that.

And she felt her own neck grow hot as she repeatedly glanced over her shoulder.

The two crated warheads sat on a wooden pallet, and she lowered the fork and slid it between the slats, then drove the lift forward, engaged the fork, and raised the warheads.

Hydraulics groaned against the weight, and she made several adjustments, tipping the load toward her.

She saw Moody then, running down the cleared path, shouting, "It's going to hell in like five minutes!"

"Shit, what now?" asked Mad Dog.

"There's a crowd gathering up on the deck. They see some cars floating. Apparently, those pieces of shit are taking too long to sink!"

The hatch leading into the bridge would be locked, Wolfgang assumed, but as he neared it, some Russkie wearing a pretty officer's suit came busting out, took one look at him, and began screaming at him, although the man kept on hustling down the staircase.

Wolfgang wrenched open the hatch, moved through a short hall, then found the captain and two other officers at the ship's controls. He waved his pistol, ordering them in broken Russian—Kat had taught him what to say, but he'd already forgotten half the words—to move into the chart room. They frowned at him but complied, and he locked them inside.

Most commercial merchant vessels had the equivalent of an autopilot called "Iron Mike." Once the ships were clear of the sea buoy, their crews would switch over to Iron Mike and rely on a lone radar operator located somewhere else on the ship to warn them of danger.

Wolfgang knew enough about ship operations to use good old Iron Mike to his advantage. Moody had instructed him to set the ferry's course at 160 degrees, speed five knots. With the bridge crew locked in the chart room, he locked in that fixed speed and course, then went out on the bridge wing to begin the next phase of their plan.

Kat was just driving the forklift into the heavy equipment elevator when shots began pinging off the lift—

And thumping into the crates containing the warheads.

Mad Dog, Bibby, and Moody, who'd been staying close to the lift, ducked for cover and returned fire, the shot originating from the other end of the hold.

"Kat, don't stop!" cried Mad Dog.

"I'm not," she shouted, then drove into the elevator.

"Moody, go with her!" Mad Dog ordered.

"You get the gunfire, I get the girl. No argument here."

"You're an ass," Kat hollered as he came running into the elevator and threw the switch.

Large twin doors slowly lowered and chinked into place. The elevator rumbled and rose with a creak.

Wolfgang was on the starboard side of the ship, working the winch controls on one of the lifeboat davits. He'd already swung the boat over the side, and was now lowering it quickly into the water. The gig hit the waves with a considerable splash, and he released the boat from the shackles.

Someone slapped a hand on his shoulder, wrenched him around. It was one of the officers, his eyes wide. He screamed something in Russian, probably, "What the fuck are you doing?"

Seizing the man by the neck, Wolfgang drove him back against the bulkhead, slammed him hard into the metal, then swung him back around—

And flung him over the side, into the ocean.

Two seconds later came the welcome drone of Kat's forklift. Wolfgang raised the cables, then got to work, spreading out the heavy cargo net.

Bibby came up behind the bearded man and put a bullet in the back of his head before he turned around.

Then he shifted around another small car, where he spotted the second man, crouching near the wall, and moved toward him. Mad Dog was somewhere behind, pursuing the third of their attackers.

Despite the dim light, Mad Dog glimpsed a man on the other side of a small truck. He came around the back of the truck and threw himself at the guy, knocking him hard to the deck.

A slight turn of the man's head revealed his identity: Colonel Boris Sinitsyna.

Mad Dog gritted his teeth as, with one hand, he choked the colonel, and with the other hand he dropped his own pistol and grabbed the colonel's wrist, slamming it hard against the deck until he lost his grip on his gun.

Then Mad Dog used both hands to choke the man. The colonel tried to pry off his grip, but he'd die before that happened.

"Wait . . . " the man gasped.

"You don't want it quick?" Mad Dog asked, his voice burred with exertion. "Just like back in your kitchen?"

"There are more warheads."

Mad Dog loosened his grip, but just a little.

"Zakarova only brought down two. There are three more, hidden in the mountains. I'm the only one alive who knows where they are."

"What if you're lying?"

"What if he's not?" asked Bibby, who had moved up behind them.

"Doesn't matter. He dies, no one finds them."

"Keep me alive, and we can do a deal. Sell the location back to my country. You make a quick two million during the plane ride home and pay me a ten percent finder's fee. I'll set you up with right people to make the deal."

"Can you prove the warheads are there?" asked Bibby.

"Yes."

"How?"

"Zakarova shouldn't have trusted me. I have satellite photos taken during the transfer of the first two."

"Then someone else knows where they are."

The colonel grinned darkly. "No, I took care of that."

Mad Dog looked at both of them as though they were insane. "Do you have any idea what this fucker has done? Killed my friend." He glowered at the colonel. "Did you send people to Cebu?"

"What do you think?"

"Then fuck you." Mad Dog tightened his grip.

"Mr. Hertzog. He's worth more as our prisoner. Even he knows that. And remember, he can fetch us the necklace from his safe deposit box without having to use Wolfgang to blow it. We don't have time for this."

Mad Dog thought a moment, then climbed off the man, snatched both weapons, ordered the colonel to stand. "Okay, let's go get my necklace, then we'll talk about these other warheads . . ."

Hirbod reached the main deck, along with his two remaining men. They jogged along the port side, then came around the stern and saw the forklift lowering the two crates to the deck.

"It's too late," he muttered to himself, then ordered his men to wait.

"Why don't we attack?" asked one of the men.

"It's too late! The weapons are exposed. The crew will spot them any minute. It's over. We've already failed our mission . . . but then again, maybe we can make sure that no one gets them."

Hirbod watched as the two mercenaries pried open the crates and struggled to roll the two warheads into the center of a cargo net.

Then he ordered his men to take up positions above the boat davit, along the railing above the bridge, while he kept low and in the shadows below them.

Wolfgang spotted the Virginia-class nuclear submarine coming up alongside the ferry like a metallic shark about to nudge a fat whale aside. Suspicions confirmed. Low-life Moody had friends in deep places. "Our ride's here!" he cried.

"Where the hell are they?" Kat asked, referring to Mad Dog and Bibby.

"Call them!" he said.

"I did! No answer."

"They got two minutes to get here," said Moody. "Two fucking minutes!"

He finished the sentence—

Just as a shot rang out, and he dropped hard to the deck.

"Fuck!" shouted Wolfgang as he ducked and shots pinged off his winch control.

Mad Dog followed the colonel directly to the purser's office, where Bibby put a gun to the purser's head and ordered him to open up the colonel's safe deposit box.

"That is and will forever be my daughter's necklace," said the colonel.

"I'll take good care of it for her," Mad Dog quipped as

he opened the case, then removed the necklace, and shoved it into his pants pocket.

"You hear that?" asked Bibby.

"What? Sarcasm?" Mad Dog asked.

"No! Listen!"

The faint sound of gunfire sent Mad Dog's pulse racing. "What the fuck? The crew is armed?"

"Maybe you should've answered that call from Kat," said Bibby as they raced through the casino, turning the heads of passengers there.

"How many men did you have?" Mad Dog asked the colonel.

"Two," he answered, sounding dumbfounded. "Just two."

Bibby had his phone to his ear. "Hannah? We're ready for you now! You go just where I told you. Come on!"

Seeing that Moody had been shot, Kat dove for him, dragged him closer to one of the empty crates. Then she reached into her waistband, drew her weapon and returned fire at the man crouching near the railing.

Her phone began to ring, but she ignored it, ducked back behind the warhead crate. Moody rolled over, gripping his shoulder. "At least I ain't dead," he said.

"It ain't over yet." Kat sprang up, aimed for the man at the railing, who shifted to the right, and—

Bang! She caught him squarely in the chest.

Meanwhile, just above them, Wolfgang was trading fire with another guy at the opposite corner of the railing, rounds ricocheting and sparking like fireflies.

The wind and frigid air had kept most of the passengers belowdecks, preventing even more carnage.

"Got one," she told Moody, ducking beside him.

"We have to move. He can't keep that sub alongside us for very long!"

*   *   *

Wolfgang was annoyed. He was ready to tear the asshole's head off. He had a job to do, and this scumbag was pissing him off. He raced away from the davit's controls, found the stairs and raced up, reaching the top—

Just as the man was coming toward him.

Their arms rose almost in unison, point-blank, but before Wolfgang could fire, the man dropped to the deck, a shot echoing from the main deck below.

"Come on!" hollered Bibby, lowering his pistol.

"Whoa." Wolfgang blinked and nodded. "Nice fucking shot!"

Hirbod, who had positioned himself at a corner near the lifeboats, realized he was the only man left of his team. He had spotted two shooters already, then noted three more men jogging toward the crates, two of them armed. He raised his binoculars and saw that one of the men was Sinitsyna. The old fool had allowed himself to be captured.

Now what? He knew if he attacked, he would draw all of their fire and become pinned down, while the others escaped.

But to where? Was there another boat waiting? Hirbod slipped out from the corner, jogged to the railing, and saw the gray-black silhouette of a submarine cruising beside the ferry.

He would wait until the right moment. If he couldn't stop them now, he could at least make sure that no one took possession of the warheads . . .

Mad Dog gave Wolfgang the signal, and the four ends of the cargo net began to rise around them.

He, Kat, Moody, Bibby, Hannah, and the colonel were all huddled over the warheads, which now poked their noses through the webbing at the bottom of the net—ready to be lowered overboard for their thirty-foot descent to the submarine below.

"I'm starting to bleed pretty bad," said Moody.

"They'll patch you up good down there," Mad Dog assured him. "Unless they don't like CIA guys, which could very well be the case."

"All right!" cried Wolfgang. "Here we go!"

Thirty feet below, Commander Jordan David Spencer saw the boat davit extend out, and then the cargo net began to swing wildly away from the ferry's side.

"Sid, rig in the bow planes," he ordered.

There was no way to avoid damage to the sub's anechoic coating and possibly to the sensitive acoustic surfaces embedded in the hull, so he'd damn well better have two Russkie nuclear warheads to show for it.

Back at the after hatch, the Chief of the Boat called off, "Distance to go," and finally, "Mark."

Spencer picked out a long rust stain between two portholes on the ferry's hull. He'd use minute throttle changes to stay lined up with that mark.

He worked the sub in closer to the ferry and cringed when the two hulls made contact. He spoke into his headset, "The clock's ticking, COB."

Old "Crank," the Chief of the Boat, watched the cargo net jerk to a stop in the dark sky above him. The net was headed right for the junction where the two hulls were grinding against each other. He needed a guide rope to pull the net out over the sub's deck, and he needed it now! He was about to order a man in a life jacket and a life line out on the sub's slippery, curving hull to do just that—when the shooting started.

* * *

Wolfgang glanced back in the direction of the incoming fire. Christ, there was one meathead left, and he was firing at everyone inside the net as they swung over the side. If he could lower them fast enough, they'd be out of the guy's line of fire, so he worked the winch a little quicker—

And not more than a handful of seconds later one of the four cables holding the cargo net, the warheads, and the team, suddenly snapped.

"What the fuck?" he cried as everyone inside the net lurched in the direction of the snapped cable, the warheads' noses prying deeper into the webbing as the entire net turned like a pendulum gone haywire.

It wasn't the weight that had snapped the cable, Wolfgang knew. It was a lucky shot from that fucker back there.

"Get us down!" shouted Mad Dog.

"Wait, wait!" cried Bibby. "We're too close to the hull. We have to get out farther over the sub."

Another few rounds of gunfire struck the net, glanced off a warhead, and Hannah screamed.

"Just lower the goddamned net!" shouted Kat.

"Skipper, I got small arms fire between the ferry and folks inside that cargo net, and there are stray slugs pinging off the deck," the COB yelled into his headset. "Tell me this ain't a bunch of fucks in one cluster?"

"Deal with it, COB! You got nine minutes," Spencer reminded him.

"That was a status report, sir. Not a complaint. Seagate, bring up my shotgun, a full coffee can, and break out that hundred footer I stow in the goat locker."

"Eight minutes, COB," said Spencer. "Now what the hell are you up to?"

"I'm unraveling the cluster fuck, sir. And did I mention that the cargo net's also unraveling?"

The net dropped another ten feet, then stopped, just as Petty Officer Seagate returned and held the coffee can at arms length while the COB aimed what resembled a single barrel shotgun, actually a line-throwing gun, at the net.

A heavy knot called a "monkey fist" impaled by a steel rod flew from the gun barrel, propelled by the discharge force of a modified shotgun shell.

Mad Dog whirled around as the line pierced the cargo net just above his head. He grabbed the line, pulled it through the net, and hauled it in until he got a working thickness to tie to the net, even as the others clung for dear life and the warheads rolled a little closer toward the abyss.

As he finished securing the line, Kat tugged on his shoulder, grimacing. She raised her head at Bibby, who had collapsed atop a warhead.

"Daddy!" screamed Hannah. "Daddy!"

Chapter 18

....

After observing that the sub crew had launched a rope to the net, Wolfgang bolted back to the winch and set it to automatically lower the team the rest of the way down. Then he left the controls.

"Wolfgang!" Mad Dog shouted. "Come on!"

He was supposed to climb onto the davit, then slide down one of the main cables to join them.

But that lone gunman was still up there, somewhere, and Wolfgang wouldn't risk a bullet in the back of his head.

So he tore off, thundered down the deck, turned a corner and bounded up the stairs, determined to find that asshole.

And take him out.

"Oh, God," muttered Kat, pulling up Bibby's shirt to reveal his blood-covered torso. Her hand went to his neck. "He's still got a good pulse. Jesus, he's bleeding out pretty bad!"

"So am I!" hollered Moody, who was still clutching his own gunshot wound.

Mad Dog glanced up at the cables, then back at the sub and the man he assumed was the Chief of the Boat. They hit the deck with a considerable thump.

Mad Dog's nerves finally found his mouth. "Let's go! Let's go!"

With the net firmly on deck and slack growing in the lines, he began releasing the davit cables, which swung back and clanged against the ferry's hull.

The COB shouted orders to his men, but all sounds seemed lost in the grinding of the sub's hull against the ferry's and the heavy slapping of the sea.

"We need help with these two!" Mad Dog cried as three figures in Hazmat gear came on deck, ready to check the warheads for radiation leakage.

"Don't worry, buddy, I'm on it," barked the COB.

By the time Wolfgang reached the deck overlooking the boat davits, he realized that their last shooter had climbed down and was heading for the railing. That asshole was prepared to open fire on the sub's deck.

He knew if he would have remained where he was, he would've have had more time to intercept him.

So he leapt over the rail and dropped the two and a half meters to the deck, his feet stinging as made contact, rolled, and got up, the pain still reverberating up his legs.

He raised his pistol, pulled the trigger.

The goddamned clip was empty.

And the shooter, a man about his age, with dark features, shouted something to the men below.

He fired a round.

Wolfgang threw himself at the man, knocking him across the railing and onto the deck.

Now it was all about getting the man's pistol, but the

fucking guy was like a worm, squirming out of his grip, and, in a flash of movement, the guy sat up, brought the pistol around—

And in another flash Wolfgang knocked his arm as he fired, the round nicking Wolfgang in the shoulder instead of burrowing into his chest.

But even so, the pain was sharp, and Wolfgang let loose his war cry as he rolled his hand around and seized the man's wrist. At the same time, he leaned forward and delivered a roundhouse to the guy's cheek, his head lurching back.

And then it was time for the real beating, payback Wolfgang style.

Now he choked the man with one hand, held his gun hand at bay and forced him onto his back, screaming, "What did you do with Viktor? Where the fuck is Viktor?"

The man grunted something in Arabic, which would have been unintelligible to Wolfgang even if he hadn't been choking him.

Faint screams came from the submarine below, and Wolfgang knew they'd leave him behind if he didn't get down there soon.

He released his hand from the man's throat, used both hands to wrestle the gun free as the guy kicked him in the shin, in the groin, struggled for any leverage he could get.

But Wolfgang came up with the weapon, turned and hurled it over the side.

Then he glanced fire-eyed at the man, panting, salivating, as the wind tore across his face. "You're next!"

Gritting his teeth, he hauled the asshole to his feet, drove him toward the railing.

Just as Mad Dog was going below, the last of the group to do so, something caught his eye, a shadow wiping across the stars—

Then he realized that shadow was a man plunging toward the sub's deck.

He struck the dark hull, his appendages flailing, then lay there, inert.

Seeing this, the COB hollered, "Seagate? Get that garbage off my boat!"

"COB, I got one more man up there!" Mad Dog cried.

"Sorry, buddy, we're about to pull away!"

Wolfgang glanced over the railing, saw that the davit cables would get him down near the sub, but it was already moving away from the ferry. If he got down there, he wasn't sure if they'd throw him a line.

His cell phone rang. Dumbfounded, he answered, "Boss?"

"What the fuck are you waiting for?"

"Will you throw me a line?"

"Shit, yeah, now you gotta jump, motherfucker! *Go!*"

Wolfgang was about to tuck the phone safe and sound into his pocket, where he kept his portion of the diamonds, but it dawned on him what he was about to do. He smiled bitterly and tossed the phone into the waves.

He looked down. Hell, it didn't seem too bad, so he swung one leg over the railing, then the other—

And that was that. He gave himself no time to back out. As old Yoda, the Jedi master, would say, airborne he was.

Now, with the wind rushing up at him and the waves growing fast, he had some serious regrets.

Jesus Christ, it was a long way down. He held his nose and had his elbows locked at his chest. He thought he already saw two men in the water, SEALs probably, and was reminded of Billy Pope, their resident SEAL back home, who hadn't had the extreme pleasure of coming to Russia and enjoying the ultimate pleasure of jumping off a ferry.

Seriously, Pope would've loved this, Wolfgang thought as he smacked into the water like a turd ejected from a cannon.

The water was not cold at all. It was a steaming hot shower! Who the hell was he kidding? He kicked up for the surface, and when his head broke water, a word exploded from his lips: "Ahhh!"

It was the coldest, thickest, saltiest water he had ever felt or tasted.

The divers reached him, lines shot out, and he found himself being hauled up the deck and toward the hatch. He spat seawater, coughed, shuddered, and thought, Billy? Even you wouldn't have liked this shit.

USS *Seatiger* SSN-804
Leaving Point Romeo
1145 Hours Local Time

After pausing at communication depth long enough to transmit "Mission accomplished," the sub continued down to nine hundred feet. Then, as Commander Spencer had informed them, it set course for the Honshu/Hokkaido gap.

Mad Dog was relieved and grateful that the doctor and chief hospital corpsman on board the submarine were able to remove the bullets from both Moody and Bibby, stop the bleeding, and stabilize them. Wolfgang was still being warmed up and demanding to confront the colonel regarding Viktor's whereabouts. Mad Dog kept them apart to avoid bloodshed. Meanwhile, the docs treated Hannah once more, noting that Mad Dog and his motley crew had done a decent if not professional job of bandaging her wound.

At the moment, Mad Dog and Kat were seated in the wardroom, staring across a table at Commander Spencer and his executive officer, Lieutenant Commander Evans.

"I don't know where to begin," said Spencer. "I'm just a little curious how you people got your hands on a couple of nuclear warheads. I can only assume it involves the Russian you claim is your informant."

"Well, we started off on eBay," Kat began, "but we kept getting outbid."

Spencer smiled. "Probably not far from the truth these days. So . . . I trust yours is a very long story." He regarded Mad Dog. "Mr. Moody tells me you were a gyrene."

"That's right. Force Recon, sir. My last tour was in A'stan. Once a Marine, sir . . . "

"Well, we don't care much for gyrenes around here, especially those turned mercenary."

Mad Dog wasn't sure how to take that: Was he joking? Or just being asshole?

"But seeing how my dad was a Marine—Force Recon, too, by the way—I'll let you stay awhile, so long as you and your people do not stink up my boat."

"No, sir."

"Well, you're not obligated to tell us anything, and I'm sure your friend with the Central Intelligence Agency will work it all out for you."

"I wouldn't call him a friend."

"Then you're smarter than I thought."

"Thank you, sir. And actually, if you'd like to hear some of the story, I'd be happy to share it. I don't think you'll believe half of it anyway."

Spencer chuckled. "No, I probably wouldn't, and by the way, Hertzog, you seem to have phenomenal luck. We usually don't carry a doctor on board, but for this cruise the squadron medical officer decided to ride with us, and the doc and my chief corpsman didn't get left behind when we scrambled out of Sasebo. You know, the Chinese culture venerates jade, believe it brings them great luck. You guys aren't packing a bunch of jade are you?"

Mad Dog tried to hide his guilty expression as he shrugged.

Someone must have seen him removing the necklace from his soaked pants when he'd been changing, and that someone had informed the skipper.

"Hannah, don't worry, your father's going to be okay," Wolfgang said. He was seated next to her in the hospital, and still trying to shiver the ice from his blood.

She lifted her head to him, her eyes bloodshot, her nose cherry red. "I love him. And I hate him."

"Me, too."

She almost smiled. "It's funny, one minute I don't think he cares, the next I realize he'd die for me."

"Life's too short for this petty bullshit. He's your dad. He's all you got."

"That's what he says."

"And I was thinking, if you want to keep him on his toes, not take you for granted, you and I should get together—because that would drive him nuts."

She frowned at him.

"I'm just kidding."

She tucked her head into his shoulder. "I'm not."

Hawaiian Airline Flight H-12
Honolulu to San Francisco
One Week Later
1340 Hours Local Time

Mad Dog and Kat sat in first class, despite her protests to save a few bucks and ride in coach. He'd called her insane. She'd called herself thrifty.

They'd already had a few cocktails, and he was feeling pretty loose.

"Got a question for you," she asked. "Define a rare disease."

"Easy. One that's cured by a cheap pill."

"So why did Bibby use that password question?"

"One day I let him come with me to chemo. And we got to talking about the high cost of health care, and you know Bibby's droll British humor. He said a rare disease is one that's cured by a cheap pill."

"But why did he think you'd remember that?"

"Because when that conversation was over, I thanked him for being a good friend. I told him how much it meant to me to have him come along."

They kept quiet for another half hour and two more cocktails. He thought about his plan to take her down to the beach in Cebu and ask her to marry him, and then he opened his big, drunken mouth and told her just that.

"Oh, yeah?" she said. "Why do you have to make such a big event out of it? Is that for your ego?"

He went on the defensive. "No, I just thought it'd be a good memory, going to place like that."

"A *good* memory? You assume a lot, G.I. Joe."

"I'm going to have one of those diamonds made into a ring that'll blow you away."

"You see, Michael. That's just it. You're not supposed to tell me about any of this. You just do it. Now I won't be blown away."

"Aw, hell. There must be a boot camp for this."

She leaned over and placed her hand on his cheek. "There is. And you're about to kiss your drill sergeant."

He crinkled his nose. "Oh, gross."

Arlington National Cemetery
Arlington, Virginia
Three Weeks Later
0945 Hours Local Time

They were all there: Mad Dog, Kat, Bibby, Wolfgang, and Pope, the remnants of IPG. The funeral was over and had included standard honors with a casket team, a firing party, and a bugler. The Arlington Lady had presented the card of condolences to Mad Dog.

Everyone took turns saying a few words about old Dan, and when it came time for Mad Dog to speak, he just couldn't say anything, couldn't do anything but salute.

The streets of Heaven were, indeed, guarded by United States Marines, and Old Dan was back on patrol.

The Dog Pound
Talisay City
Cebu, the Philippines
2230 Hours Local Time

Mad Dog sat up in bed, his notebook computer balanced on his lap. Kat was downstairs, making them some hot chocolate. He'd spent most of the day in the guest house, removing Dan's clothes and shoes and boxing up his massive book collection, which Mad Dog was donating to Operation Shoebox, a nonprofit organization that sent food, snacks, toiletries, games, CDs, and a billion other things to troops serving outside the United States. During his time in A'stan, he had received quite a few packages from the "shoeboxers," and Old Dan would be proud to know his books would be put to good use by his brothers in arms. Mad Dog planned to save Dan's military clothing and boots, but he'd donate the other stuff to local charities.

At lunchtime the phone rang, and James Moody was cackling on the other end, telling him to shove his job offer straight up his ass, that they could never work together but that they should use each other like a couple of prostitutes trading tips on johns. Nice comparison, asshole.

But there was something in Moody's tone that said, *I admire you. I wish I could do what you do but I'm scared because I've been married to the goddamned establishment for way too long.* Maybe he was hearing things, Mad Dog thought, but he knew they hadn't heard the last from Mr. James Moody, CIA.

In his laptop, Mad Dog continued logging into his journal under the heading, ACCOUNT #A013, CODE NAME: MAD DOGS AND ENGLISHMEN, which was the code phrase for a runaway freight train through Hell, bad puns, metaphors, analogies, and all that shit intended:

So we made the deal with that fucking Russian, Sinitsyna, even though I wasn't too happy about it. He wanted us to believe the "buyers" of the information were official members of the Russian government, but I had my doubts. Bibby was more comfortable about the whole thing, but if those goddamned warheads turn up again on the black market, I'll know who to blame. We're up $1.8 million on the deal, plus the $20 million in diamonds, which is an incredible gain. I've more than doubled IPG's assets since that night we stole all that gold and cash from that cave in Afghanistan.

And speaking of dear Mr. Bibby—he quit. No big surprise. And I was actually happy for him. He's accepted a political appointment to the British Foreign Office, enabling him to "dabble" in sensitive foreign issues of interest to the Prime Minister—at least that's the way he put it. I think he's back to working for MI6, but that's just me. Either way, he'll get to spend more time with his daughter, and that's what really counts.

Just ask Wolfgang, who is, in fact, spending more time with Bibby's daughter. They're sneaking around, and I warned him about it, but Wolfgang's always been one to play with fire, which is why I keep him around.

Went and had my chest pains checked out. Turns out they were chest pains. Took a half-dozen doctors and two stress tests to conclude that. At least I'm still cancer free. Just can't let myself get too bent out of shape. News flash: I'm getting old. Shit.

Kat and I still aren't married. She keeps giving me that look, and I keep telling her I got plans but I don't want to ruin them by telling her.

Truth is, I haven't come up with anything better than just taking her down to the beach and asking her to marry me, which is what I'll do when I finish typing this crap. The ring looks great.

I'm thinking now that this journal is getting more personal and less official. I thought I'd be sticking to the facts so this would be a record of lessons learned. Seems like these entries are more about life, about taking some time to redefine.

But there are some things that will never change.

A day doesn't go by when I don't think about all the good men I've lost, both with the Marines and with this company.

Dan has joined their ranks, joined all of us, the living and the dead, as we raise our fists at the midday sun and cry, "Hoorah!"

*   *   *

Kat entered the room with their mugs of hot chocolate, and Mad Dog closed the lid on his computer. "After this, you feel like taking a little ride?"

"Really? It's late. Where we going?"

He yawned. "Just a little drive."

"All right. We can talk, too. I got a call from Waffa's wife, Melissa. The Israelis would like to meet us."

"No shit. They owe us big-time."

"They might have a job as a way to say thank you. I don't know the details, but I'm thinking we'll have to regroup like we've been talking about."

"So we'll need to get married," he said in a deadpan voice.

"Exactly," she said in her own deadpan.

"I got a ring."

"Good."

"You want it?"

"I'll take it."

"I'll give it to you later. Now that we got that out the way, let's have some hot chocolate."

She looked at him, grabbed her pillow and shoved it in his face. "You bastard."

He pushed the pillow away, took her up in his arms and said, "That wasn't my proposal. That was only practice."

"I hope so."

"Hey . . . *Ya lublu tebya*."

She beamed. "You finally learned your Russian. And I love you, too."

Their business is war—and they're the best there is

P.W. STORM's

»»» THE MERCENARIES «««

THE MERCENARIES:
BLOOD DIAMONDS

978-0-06-085739-4

After assembling his own "private security" force made up of the able and disenchanted from the U.S. military and British Secret Intelligence Agency, warrior Michael "Mad Dog" Hertzog and his team are off to Angola to recover a missing cache of gemstones.

THE MERCENARIES:
THUNDERKILL

978-0-06-085797-4

The assignment for Mad Dog and his men is Uzbekistan, where an American-hating warlord plans to assassinate the country's newly elected, U.S.-supported president. But the mercenaries don't know they're flying straight into a state-sponsored double-cross.

THE MERCENARIES:
MAD DOGS AND ENGLISHMEN

978-0-06-085809-4

Hertzog's right-hand man has vanished. . .along with $30 million of Mad Dog's money. The evidence says a trusted British merc has gone rogue, but there may be a different, more virulent form of treachery here, as time ticks rapidly away on a terrifying plot to bathe the Middle East in nuclear fire.